THE MASQUE OF
A MURDERER

THE
MASQUE
— OF A —
MURDERER

Susanna Calkins

MINOTAUR BOOKS ❧ NEW YORK

THE MASQUE OF A MURDERER. Copyright © 2015 by Susanna Calkins. All rights reserved. Printed in the United States of America. For information, address St. Martin's Press, 175 Fifth Avenue, New York, N.Y. 10010.

www.minotaurbooks.com

The Library of Congress Cataloging-in-Publication Data is available upon request.

ISBN 978-1-250-05736-5 (hardcover)
ISBN 978-1-4668-6112-1 (e-book)

Minotaur books may be purchased for educational, business, or promotional use. For information on bulk purchases, please contact the Macmillan Corporate and Premium Sales Department at 1-800-221-7945, extension 5442, or write to specialmarkets@macmillan.com.

First Edition: April 2015

10 9 8 7 6 5 4 3 2 1

To Matt, Quentin, and Alex

ACKNOWLEDGMENTS

There are many people I wish to thank for their invaluable support in helping me create this novel. To Lindsay Yoelin, speech teacher extraordinaire, I appreciate the time you took to figure out what kinds of sounds a person without a tongue can actually make. To Gretchen Beetner, thank you for allowing your namesake to be killed off in the plague. To my beta readers, Maggie Dalrymple, Margaret Light, and Mary Schuller, thank you, thank you! My characters would have been doing all kinds of weird things if you hadn't questioned their actions and speech. Your comments inspired me to improve. To my amazing editor, Kelley Ragland, and all the other wonderful people at Minotaur, thank you for taking such care of Lucy. Your thoughtfulness and dedication are truly impressive. To my readers who ask me all sorts of interesting questions, I thank you for helping me think through my subplots. To my family and my children, Alex and Quentin, thanks for being awesome. I love you! And last, to my husband, Matt Kelley, who humbly said I didn't need to dedicate another book to him, I thank you for everything you do. You are on every page, and it is to you I dedicate this novel.

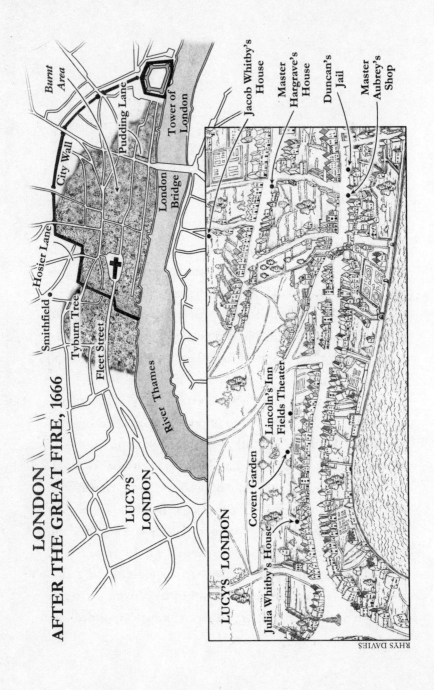

LONDON
AFTER THE GREAT FIRE, 1666

Burnt Area

City Wall

Pudding Lane

Tower of London

London Bridge

Hosier Lane

Smithfield

Tyburn Tree

Fleet Street

River Thames

LUCY'S LONDON

Jacob Whitby's House

Master Hargrave's House

Duncan's Jail

Master Aubrey's Shop

LUCY'S LONDON

Covent Garden

Lincoln's Inn Fields Theater

Julia Whitby's House

RHYS DAVIES

LONDON

—◆—

March 1667

· I ·

Let me tell you!" Lucy Campion shouted, trying to make her voice heard against the rising wind. She scrambled onto the overturned barrel outside of Master Aubrey's printer's shop. "Of a murder most absurd!"

A few passersby on Fleet Street stopped at her words, eager for a story, despite the bitter chill that had marked the long winter months. Huddled together, they looked up at her, waiting. Taking advantage of the gathering crowd, another woman took down a heavy earthenware pot that she'd been balancing on her head and began to sell hot cooked pears to the freezing people around her.

"Go on, lass! Haven't got all day!" a man called to Lucy, shifting a dead chicken from one gloved hand to the other.

Over her head Lucy waved a ballad that Master Aubrey had recently printed. Taking a deep breath, she began to half sing, half chant the song as the printer had taught her. "A cheese-monger, tired of his cuckolding wife, did end her life with his sharpest knife!"

Lucy looked about. Good. A few more people were moving toward them. Ever since the Great Fire had beset them some six months before, Londoners had sought out any entertainment they could find, hoping to dispel the dark mood that had descended upon them during the long gray winter.

She continued, adding a flourish here, a flourish there, using the little tricks she had learned to keep her listeners enthralled to the very end of the tale. With any luck, the people would throw a coin or two into the small woven basket resting against the barrel, or better yet, buy a penny piece to take back with them to share with their family or neighbors.

Reaching the end of the ballad, Lucy delivered the last jest with a chuckle. "Had he been more cheese than whey, she'd not have cozened him that day."

Satisfied, the crowd guffawed and pressed in toward her, coins in hand. She and Lach, Master Aubrey's other apprentice, scrambled about, selling their ballads. She sold a few recipe books as well—they had found the story of the murderous cheese-monger always left people longing for delicious fresh cheese.

As the small crowd dispersed, someone stepped forward, quietly murmuring her name.

Lucy stood stock-still, squinting at the young woman standing before her. Clad in a Quaker's gray gown and cloak, the woman was pale and drawn, her brown hair pulled back severely under a white cap. Looking straight into the woman's blue eyes, Lucy stiffened in shocked recognition. "Sarah!" she croaked, a flood of emotion filling her.

It was Sarah Hargrave, the daughter of the magistrate, Lucy's former employer. For several years Lucy had worked as a chambermaid in Master Hargrave's household, emptying pots, scouring bowls, and making beds. There, she'd also learned to read and write, as the magistrate did not approve of dull-witted servants. She and Sarah Hargrave, while not friends exactly, had been companions of sorts. Later, after several tragedies befell the Hargrave family, their bond had been further solidified.

Staring at Sarah now, Lucy could scarcely recognize the girl she had once known. Dressed completely in gray, unrelieved by a single ribbon or flash of color, Sarah Hargrave was nothing like the merry girl Lucy remembered. This young woman looked drawn and serious, more like a wren than a blue jay. Nearly two years had passed since she'd last seen Sarah, during those terrible days before the plague had cast its vengeance upon London. The magistrate had sent his only daughter far out of harm's way, only to discover too late that he'd sent her to live among Quakers and that she had taken up their convictions.

They'd all been a bit shocked, saddened truly, by Sarah's decision to join the Quakers. She'd always seemed a bit silly, more interested in silks and laces than in pursuing a path to God. Master Hargrave, in particular, seemed to have been devastated by his daughter's decision, rarely speaking her name. As a magistrate, he had prosecuted a number of Quakers and others who violated the Conventicle Acts, a fact that must have added to his deep disappointment in his daughter's choices. Her family

knew very little about what she'd been doing. From the few letters they had received from her, they learned that she'd been
traveling through Barbados and the colonies, seeking to share
what she called her Inner Light with others. Beyond that, they
knew little else.

Now, as they regarded each other uncertainly, Lucy did not
know whether she should curtsy or embrace her. Although she
was no longer Master Hargrave's servant, Lucy's years of training won out. "Miss Sarah," she said, doing a little bob. "I am
truly glad to see that you are well."

"Lucy, my dear. Thou dost not need to bow to me." Sarah
spoke in the odd manner of the Quakers, all thees and thous.
The plain speech, they called it. From some Quakers she had
once known, Lucy knew that the Friends, as they called themselves, used the more familiar form of speech because they did
not recognize one man as having authority over another.

Despite her funny Quaker speech, the smile Sarah gave to
Lucy was kind and loving. Extending her arms, Lucy found
herself caught in a warm embrace. As they hugged, Lucy could
feel Sarah's slight frame beneath her wraps.

"When did you return?" Lucy asked, stepping back to study
Sarah more carefully. Clearly, Sarah had lost weight, but there
was a sturdiness to her demeanor that kept her from seeming
frail.

"I have only just returned to London," Sarah replied. "My
companions and I arrived in Bristol ten days ago, and it has taken
us that long to walk from there to here."

Lucy's knowledge of geography was scant, but she knew
Bristol was a good distance away. Her amazement must have

shown on her face, for Sarah laughed slightly. "Yes, it was about one hundred miles we walked. I am well used to traveling such distances. 'Tis the Quaker way." She hesitated. "My father, thou mayst know, wrote to me bidding me to return home." She shivered as a gust of wind blew against them.

"Pray, let us go inside," Lucy said, opening the door to Master Aubrey's shop. As they stepped inside, she asked, "Is that why you have returned?"

Following her in, Sarah shook her head. "No, 'twas the letter that thou sent me that compelled me to return. I cannot describe the joy I felt when I received it, although I was quite pained by thy news."

Lucy nodded, understanding. Last November, Sarah's brother, Adam, had been hurt, and Lucy had taken it on herself to inform his sister of the strange events that had led to his injury.

"I would have returned when I first received thy letter," Sarah said. "Few ships will traverse the ocean during wintertime, though. So I was not able to book passage for several months." She paused. "Home is different now. Everything is different."

Lucy nodded. The Hargraves had moved shortly after the Great Fire. "That is to be expected," she replied. "Your father—Master Hargrave—must be so pleased that you have returned home."

"I suppose," Sarah said, craning her head this way and that as she took in the details of Master Aubrey's shop. Lucy tried to see the printer's shop through Sarah's eyes. Two printing presses in the middle of the room. A few tables and shelves, all holding the boxes and trays containing different fonts and types of letters and woodcuts. Tied leather bags stacked side by side under the benches, containing older pamphlets and tracts. All manner of strange tools hanging from pegs on the walls. A great stack of common-grade paper that Master Aubrey used for the cheaper pieces. The finer paper used for the occasional special printing.

"I can scarcely believe that thou art a printer's apprentice now," Sarah said. "My father's letters have been few. However, he did inform me of thy grand new occupation. A printer! Father is so very proud of thee." A funny look crossed her face then. Hurt? Confusion? Lucy couldn't tell.

Nevertheless, Lucy patted her hand. "I am but a simple apprentice. Truth be told, not even that."

"Well, now, the lass speaks the truth," Lach interrupted, moving his stool over to the long wooden table. "'Tis not likely you will ever be recognized by the guild."

Lucy frowned at the gangly redheaded youth. Lach's dig reminded her again of the tenuous nature of her current employment. She scrambled to explain her odd position to Sarah. "I started working for Master Aubrey shortly after the Great Fire. The printer was looking for something special to print, and, well, I provided it to him. A story that had emerged from the ashes—I promised it to him and he agreed to take me on." She paused. The tale that had come from that discovery had been very strange indeed. "I could not pay the full apprentice fee, you see. So I agreed to take on many of the household duties, though a washer-woman does the heavy work. In exchange, Master Aubrey has been teaching me the trade. I have learned much about printing books, and selling them, too."

It was also true, as Lach had said, that Master Aubrey had not introduced her to the Worshipful Company of Stationers, nor, she suspected now, did he intend to. Lucy guessed the printer was not sure how the guild would respond if he put forward a female apprentice, although Lord knew that since the plague and the Fire, there'd been few enough able-bodied men interested in joining the trade. "Thus my brother, Will, and I have leased rooms above the shop," Lucy concluded, pointing at the stairs that led to their chambers, "and Master Aubrey pays me a smallish wage." *For now,* she thought. She smiled at Sarah, hiding the tingle of worry that flickered over her every time she wondered how long the printer would keep her on.

"Still, it is wonderful that thou hast found such an occupation," Sarah said. "I can see that it agrees with thee well."

Again Lucy caught that same note of longing. "I should very much like to hear more of your travels," she said. "Alas, now I must return to work. Master Aubrey is not one to beat us, but I should not like to anger him by larking about." She began to take the type letters out of the press and return them to their appropriate cases, since Master Aubrey wanted them to be ready to set and print *The Lady's Lament* in two days' time.

"Oh, but that's why I'm here. Father said I might invite thee to dine with us. Cook has the most delicious meal planned."

Lucy smiled at Sarah doubtfully but did not speak. The magistrate had always been gentle and courteous to her, and would on occasion take a meal with his servants. Nevertheless, it was very unlikely that even a man of Master Hargrave's sort would formally extend an invitation to dine with his former chambermaid. She gently said as much to Sarah.

"Oh, pfft," she replied, tossing her hair in her old way. Or she would have, had the stern cap not kept her hair in place. "We

Quakers do not recognize such divisions among us. We are all equal in the eyes of the Lord."

Her eyes shining, Sarah looked almost as Lucy remembered. Then a new expression passed into her eyes, taking on a distant forlorn quality that made Lucy's heart ache. "Please, Lucy. I know Father respects thee. And truly, I have no other friends now, at least none who would feel welcome in a magistrate's home." She lowered her voice so that Lach would not hear her. "Ever since I returned home, Father has seemed so angry and disappointed in me for not coming home sooner. For traveling to the New World. For being a Quaker." Her eyes were pleading. "I would feel more comfortable if thou wert beside me. Even just for a few hours."

"Even if that were so, I cannot just leave the shop," Lucy protested. She continued to put the letters back in their cases. "I should not like to rile Master Aubrey in such a way."

Lach looked up then. "So you're a Quacker now, hey?" he said to Sarah, apparently having heard everything. He put his hands to his armpits and began to flap his arms like wings. "Quack! Quack! Quack!"

"Lach!" Lucy exclaimed, embarrassed by his antics. "Sarah is a Quaker, not Quacker. Do not call her that ridiculous name."

"So you quake, then?" Lach asked, ignoring Lucy's retort. "You do not quack?"

For the first time, a slight smile tugged at Sarah's lips. Lucy was glad to see that Sarah seemed more amused than anything at Lach's jests. "I don't think I have ever quacked," she said.

Thankfully, they were spared any more of Lach's nonsense when Master Aubrey appeared in the doorway of the shop.

Despite the cold weather, the rotund printer was sweating from the exertion of his walk.

Taking off his hat, the master printer greeted Sarah warily. "Miss Hargrave," he said, throwing Lucy a warning glance. "I am glad that the good Lord has seen fit to bring you safely back from your long voyages. I hope that you will extend my best wishes to your father as well." He held open the door and beckoned outside. "However, I should like Lucy to resume her work now, and it is time for you to return home."

"Ah!" Sarah said brightly. "Lucy's work is why I am here." She pulled out a pocket from underneath her skirts. "My father gave me this purse. It is full of coins. Even though I told him I need little in the way of worldly goods."

"Ah, yes," Master Aubrey said, clearly perplexed by the idea of not needing worldly goods. Still, he nodded his head. "I see."

From the corner, Lach bugged out his eyes, pretending to be a madman, before mouthing the word "Quacker." Fortunately, Sarah did not see the gesture.

"So I thought," Sarah continued, "that even if I need nothing, I might purchase a few recipes for Cook—I know that she already has Culpeper's *Herbal*. Perhaps another of the same sort?"

"Yes, yes," Master Aubrey said, rubbing his hands, his earlier surliness gone. "We have a number of recipes. Lach, you imp!" he shouted, boxing Lach lightly on his ear. "Go bring up the bag of herbals and recipes from the cellar."

Murmuring under his breath, Lach slunk off.

Sarah was not done. "I had thought perhaps to get Father a copy of"—she consulted a piece of paper—"William Dugdale's

Origines Juridiciales. My brother told me that most copies were burnt in the Fire, but that perhaps thou wouldst know where one might be found."

"Most, but not all. I happen to have a few in my possession. Leather bound. Very rare! I shall go get the Dugdale from my private collection. Nothing but the very best for your father, naturally!"

At that point, Sarah produced a letter sealed in red wax, which she handed to Master Aubrey along with the coins for the book and tracts. "From Father," she said.

Coins in hand, Master Aubrey had grown jovial. Scanning the note, he chuckled. "Lass," he said to Lucy, "Master Hargrave has asked you to dine with his daughter. I suppose he has paid enough for you to take a few hours off."

"Thank you, sir!" Lucy cried, grabbing her cloak from the hook by the wall. As Sarah pulled her from the shop, Lucy could not refrain from sticking her tongue out at Lach, who, as always, made a disgusting face at her in return.

· 2 ·

A few steps along the street, their giddiness passed, and once again Sarah took on her somber demeanor. "'Tis a strange thing," she said, stepping aside to let an old woman pass them by. The woman moved slowly, nearly doubled over by the great pack on her back. "To see London. When I lived here before, I did not see what I see now."

Lucy cocked her head, trying to see what Sarah saw. The Great Fire had not reached these streets where they were currently walking. On that fateful day last September, the winds had shifted, and the blaze had turned back upon itself, saving the areas to the west and north of the old city walls.

"The Great Fire stopped before it reached these parts," Lucy said, puzzled. "It was more to the east." She pointed in that direction. Where once all the great church pinnacles had illuminated the skyline, now there was an unusual expanse of gray sky.

Sarah nodded. "I know. I walked a bit through the ruins today, including where St. Paul's had once stood. How fearful I once was, sitting in those pews, reminded every day of my weak and foolish spirit." She looked at an old man holding out a tin cup, his eyes rheumy from sickness and the cold. She took out a penny and pressed it into the man's hands as she passed. "What I mean is that now I see the despair and filth and dirt, in a way I never did before the Inner Spirit moved me."

Pausing, she turned toward Lucy. "Do you know, I was still in the Massachusetts Bay Colony when we heard tell of the Great Fire. Of course, by that time, it was all over. God's plan it was, for the Fire to burn away the sinners of London."

Lucy nodded. The Lord's will had been done, to be sure. Still, tensions about what had caused the Fire had not dissipated, and she'd seen fisticuffs brought about by a single word on the topic. She'd heard many people speak about the causes of the Great Fire. Some people blamed the French, while many more blamed the Catholics. "Those dirty papists!" she'd oft heard the cry. Many had blamed the confused watchmaker Robert Hubert, who had indeed been hanged for the crime. Lucy thought it was just as likely to have been the Fariners, who might well have failed to bank the coals of their bakery.

"So many have lost so much," Lucy said. "I hope that they will all one day find justice. I know that is what Adam believes the new Fire Court will accomplish. To help restore order and to ensure that landlords receive their just due when the streets of London are plotted and built." For a moment she felt so proud of Adam that she did not even realize she was smiling until she saw Sarah glance at her curiously.

"That is the first time I have ever heard thee address my brother in such a familiar way, Lucy," Sarah said.

A painful flush flooded Lucy's cheeks. "I meant, Master Adam. Er, Mr. Hargrave. I beg your pardon for the familiarity."

Sarah waved away Lucy's consternation. "Hearing thee speak of my brother in such a fashion, I should almost imagine that thou hast *feelings* for him." Her tone was sympathetic, not judgmental.

Lucy had heard such sympathy before. Sometimes, as with Sarah, it was heartfelt and well intentioned, although at other times, it rang false and was mocking in nature. Either way, the message was clear. Falling in love with the master's son—even if she no longer worked for the magistrate—was a pitiful plight for a servant.

Without replying, Lucy simply turned her face so that the bitter wind would cool her cheeks. She could guess what so many people assumed—that Adam had bedded her when she was serving in his father's household. That she foolishly believed he would marry her. How many ballads had been set to this same tune? Surely, Master Aubrey made many a coin on this very tale. The handsome gentleman wooing the comely maid. Depending on who wrote it, the story became a bawdy joke or the recipe for a young woman's ruin.

The truth was far different, although Lucy had never told anyone. *I am not the besotted fool they all think me to be,* Lucy thought. Certainly Adam had never forced himself upon her; such a dishonorable act would have been vile to him. However, during the Fire, when passion and emotion had overcome them both, Adam had declared his love for her and pledged his troth. For a short while, Lucy had lived and dreamed in a happy haze, thinking that all would be well.

Yet even as the shock and aftermath of the Fire continued to numb and overwhelm the people of London, for Lucy the smoke in her eyes had gradually cleared. The old world that she once knew—where servants marry servants and gentry marry gentry—had begun to right itself.

Now, when Adam spoke of marriage, Lucy put him off as new worries and doubts began to surface. What would such a marriage look like? Certainly, he was handsome and good—her breath still caught when she thought of the lengths to which he had gone to right some terrible wrongs. What former servant could ever even hope to wed a man like him? Most women in her position would have dragged him to the church the moment his declaration of love had been made, being assured income, property, and a good name for their children. But for Lucy, therein lay one of the greatest problems.

Would Adam come to be embarrassed by her humble upbringing? Could he overcome the fact that she had been a chambermaid, cleaning up his own family's slops? His mother had served Queen Henrietta, as a young lady-in-waiting in the court of King Charles I. Her parents had been poor tenant farmers, and before that, in service. Adam claimed he did not care about such differences, but it was hard to believe that one day he would not wake up and resent her for her low station. His father, the magistrate, had even given his blessing, but surely that, too, could change when everyone's senses were restored.

And what of Lucy's newfound occupation? Adam had said

that he would not want her to give up her training as a printer and bookseller, but surely she would have to, once a babe or two came along. Indeed, many servants and tradesmen she knew waited to get married and have children until their midtwenties, for precisely this reason. At twenty-one, Lucy had hoped to wait a few more years before getting wed, so that she could build her dowry and develop her livelihood. Of course, the gentry married earlier, and Adam was a few years older than she was already. He was eager to marry and get their lives in order.

That was the worst part about it. If Lucy was to be completely honest, she was not even sure whether it was Adam she wished to marry. Certainly Lucy had adored him almost from the moment they met, and indeed their love had flourished during a time of terrible stress. Yet as she had come to realize, Adam was also one of the only young men she had ever spoken with at length, and she had had no opportunity to meet other potential suitors.

That had changed, however, when Lucy left the magistrate's household and became better acquainted with Constable Duncan, a man who also seemed to respect and admire her. Though she had not seen him recently, the constable occupied her thoughts in a way that both pleased and distressed her.

Sarah continued on, unaware of Lucy's musings, speaking now about the Fire Court. "For my part, I do not put much stock in earthly courts, or the men that use the law to better their own ends." She looked at Lucy. "How I have shocked thee. Thou art thinking that I have impugned the vocation of my father and my brother." Her laugh was more sorrowful than bitter. "Perhaps

I have. They will never understand the suffering that the law of this earthly realm has caused my spiritual brothers and sisters."

Her words disturbed Lucy, causing an unexpected lump to form in her throat, as she thought of how the magistrate and his son revered the law and the pursuit of justice. Sarah's words seemed to tarnish what they cherished. She did not know what to reply, and so remained silent for the remainder of the walk.

A short while later, Lucy took a deep bite into a piece of meat pie, savoring the well-seasoned meat, leeks, and potatoes. Indeed, the warmth of Master Hargrave's kitchen embraced her, and she looked about in pleasure. Cook and her husband, John, the master's all-around Jack, had worked for the magistrate for nearly twenty years. Cook's niece, little skinny Annie, had come to them only a year and a half before, after Lucy had found her half starved, begging on the streets. In time, she had taken on Lucy's old duties as chambermaid. Right now, Cook and Annie bustled about while John sat in the corner, sharpening knives. For an instant, Lucy felt as if she had never left Master Hargrave's employment. Sarah seemed to be enjoying herself as well, her earlier discontent forgotten.

As Lucy had expected, the magistrate did not join the servants for their meal, but given what Sarah had said about their strained relationship, perhaps that was for the best.

Annie was now plying Sarah with questions about her travels. She had pulled out a pamphlet that Lucy had given her called *A True Narrative of the Splendors of the New World.*

"How terribly exciting this must have been for you!" Annie said.

Sarah looked at the piece, her expression unreadable. "Exciting? Yes, I suppose thou couldst say that." A shadow passed over her face. "Crossing the Atlantic was no easy feat. On many occasions, I thought for certain that I would die. Indeed, some of my dear companions did not survive the ordeal. My spirit was much nourished by the grace of the Lord, and I thanked him mightily for sparing my life."

Lucy and the others murmured a quick prayer as well.

"I did meet some true Indians, though," Sarah said, then fell silent when her father, the magistrate, entered the kitchen.

Master Hargrave was not a tall man, nor was he heavyset, but his stately presence seemed to fill the small room. Under one arm, he carried a well-thumbed book with a blue-and-gold-checked binding.

With a slight thrill of anticipation, Lucy wondered whether he was planning to read a passage or two to them. Master Hargrave had always honored his duty as head of the household to instruct his servants in the Bible. In addition, he had sometimes passed the long hours at home reading passages of other works aloud to his servants. Lucy remembered those moments fondly, thinking of how she had hung on every word, even when she did not understand all that he said. The first time she had asked him a question, she did not know who had been more stunned, but he had answered it regardless. From then on, he would ask her questions about what he read, regarding her with approval as she puzzled through an idea. Indeed, Lucy suspected that it was from those moments that she had developed some of her own peculiar notions. Right now, the magistrate's stern face relaxed when he saw her.

Lucy stood up hastily, wiping her mouth on a cloth. "Sir," she said, giving him a quick bob.

"Good afternoon, Lucy," the magistrate said, nodding at her. "I'm glad my old friend Horace Aubrey was able to give you some time off today, to celebrate my daughter's return. She was quite intent to have you join us." He gave his daughter a stern glance. "Next time, daughter, I expect that you will have Annie or John accompany you. There are many wretched sorts about who might prey on a young girl alone."

It was one thing to let a female servant—or, for that matter, a bookseller—travel alone. It was quite another matter for the daughter of a magistrate to do the same. Lucy could see that this restriction did not sit well with Sarah—after all, hadn't she traveled halfway around the world with few companions?

Seeing an angry retort rising to Sarah's lips, Lucy jumped in hastily. "Thank you, sir. I do so appreciate being able to see Miss Sarah. I am quite looking forward to hearing more about her travels in the New World—"

"That's fine, Lucy," Master Hargrave said. His voice, though kind, had the effect of stopping her little speech. "It is good to have my daughter home again," he said to Lucy. He turned back to Sarah. "I daresay I should like to get used to seeing you at my table again."

Sarah's lips tightened. "I will not be staying long, Father. I came back only to ensure the well-being of my brother, and of yourself, of course." As she spoke, Lucy noticed that she no longer used her adopted Quaker thees and thous. "As I am now assured of both, that you are in good health and good spirits, I must soon continue to follow the path the Lord has set for me."

The magistrate frowned. "Daughter, I cannot in good faith allow you to continue this traipsing about the earth, putting yourself in heaven knows what predicaments and travails." He stopped short, seeming to recall that he was in the presence of his servants.

Cook and John had busied themselves with other things, and after a bewildered look around, Annie did the same.

Lucy bent her head. Oh, why had Sarah not given her father the gift? Perhaps if she had, these terrible tensions might not have flared so fiercely.

"I am sorry for having spoken of this subject in such a way," the magistrate said to his servants. He seated himself at the end of the table. To his daughter he added, "This conversation is not over."

Sarah, however, did not seem to care that the servants were all in attendance. "Father," she said, tears in her voice. Once again she resumed her Quaker speech. "I love thee, but I obey only the will of God."

The magistrate was about to say more, but thankfully they were interrupted by an insistent knocking at the door. As he was closest, John pulled the door open, revealing a man dressed in somber clothes.

"I am here for Sarah Hargrave," the man said, without offering any greeting.

Lucy caught Cook's eye. She could tell by her scandalized expression that Cook was as taken aback as she. How odd that someone of Sarah's acquaintance would call at the servants' and tradesmen's entrance.

With silent decorum, John stepped aside, allowing the man to step into the room. In the brightness, Lucy could see the man was panting heavily, as though he'd just been running. He was perhaps in his thirties; his face was long and drawn, and his cheeks slumped a bit, as if he did not smile very often. At a middling height, his frame was lean. His clothes were worn and heavily mended. Another Quaker.

Lucy looked at the magistrate nervously. She could tell by the tightening of her former master's jaw that he had reached the same conclusion.

The Quaker's eyes immediately fell upon Sarah. "I must speak to thee," he said, without offering any greeting.

"Sam?" Sarah asked. "Why ever hast thou come to *my father's home?*" She emphasized the last three words, nodding in the direction of her father. The magistrate was sternly regarding the man as if he were a criminal awaiting his judgment.

Sam's eyes widened when he saw Master Hargrave, and Lucy could tell that the man had come to the servants' entrance with the hopes of avoiding the magistrate.

Apparently catching Sarah's intonation, Sam moved his hand to his head, as if to remove his hat. His hand hovered near the brim before he let it drop back to his side, his hat still squarely on his head. 'Twas the Quaker way, Lucy knew, to show no deference to earthly authority. Still, that deliberate breach of etiquette had not come easily to him. Though he kept his eyes steadily on Sarah, Lucy could see that he had flushed deeply and that his hand was trembling.

Nor had the slight gone unnoticed by the magistrate. Lucy could see that his jaw had tightened as he rose from his bench. "Pray tell us, *sir*," he said, coldly emphasizing the word "sir." "Who are you, and why have you come to see my daughter?" Though he was civil, Lucy could hear the taut anger beneath his words.

"I am Sam Leighton," the man said, regaining his sense of purpose. Again, Lucy could tell, he very nearly added "sir" at the end, but caught himself in time. "'Tis Jacob Whitby," he said softly, looking again toward Sarah. "Last night he was struck by a great ailment, and I fear he has little time left on this earth."

Sarah drew her breath in sharply. "No!" she exclaimed. All color drained from her already pale face. "Not Jacob!"

Lucy dimly recalled Jacob Whitby. A friend of Adam's from Cambridge, Mr. Whitby had been one of the several handsome young men who had on occasion dined at the magistrate's table. Other than this vague recollection, she could not remember any details of the man's countenance or character, having not seen him in several years. She did remember, though, that the Whitbys were people of means. Not the sort one would expect to become a Quaker. Still, one could say the same of Sarah.

Sam Leighton continued. "I'm afraid 'tis true. He said he knew thy daughter. Thy son, too."

The magistrate looked sorrowful. "Jacob Whitby. His is a name I've not heard for some time." Sighing, he added, "This is a tragedy indeed. I thank you for letting us know. I will inform my son when next I see him." He moved toward the man, as if to escort him out.

To their surprise, Sam did not move. "His wife, Esther Whitby, I fear, is in great need of womanly solace and a spiritual outpouring of strength and love. Jacob asked for our Sister Sarah to attend to her."

The magistrate stiffened. "Absolutely not," he said. "I will not permit my daughter to attend a sickbed."

On this, Lucy heartily agreed with the magistrate. She did not want Sarah venturing into a house of sickness. They'd both seen firsthand the horrible effects of the plague. Lucy had some knowledge of the physick and the healing, having read several of Nicholas Culpeper's household remedies.

Although it was not her place to speak, Lucy did anyway. "What is wrong with Mr. Whitby?" she asked. "From what ailment does he suffer?"

The man smiled down at her in a grave, kindly way. "No need to be a-frightened," he said. "Brother Jacob was run over by a cart. The two horses did stomp upon him greatly. I am aggrieved to say that his injuries are within his internal organs. The physician was called in, but assured us that there is too much damage, too much bleeding inside his body. There is nothing more that can be done for his physical body. Soon he will be in heaven, flooded with the love and light of God."

"Sarah!" the magistrate said sharply. "What are you doing?"

His daughter had retrieved a heavy, nondescript gray cloak from a hook by the door. "'Tis the Quaker way, Father. To give solace to those in need."

"How well do you even know this man?" her father asked, in his quiet dignified way. Because Lucy knew the magistrate so well, she could hear the deep anger—or was it fear?—in his voice as well. "I cannot allow you to accompany a man with whom

I have no previous acquaintance to visit the deathbed of another."

"Please, Father," Sarah said. She then repeated what she had said before, with more urgency this time. "'Tis the Quaker way!"

Seeing that her father had not relented, Sarah turned to Lucy, her eyes pleading and serious. "Lucy could accompany me, could she not? Wouldst thou, Lucy?" In an instant, Lucy was thrown back three years, when Sarah pleaded with her father to see the wondrous sites at Bartholomew Fair. This time she had none of her wheedling ways.

Lucy glanced at the magistrate but remained silent. She had no wish to step in between father and daughter.

The magistrate studied his daughter's now-resolute face. "All right," he consented. "So long as Lucy does not mind."

"Indeed, sir, I do not," Lucy said, despite her mouth watering for the last few bites she had left on her plate. Tugging her cloak into place, she followed Sam and Sarah into the unpleasant winter sleet.

· 3 ·

The walk to the Whitby home did not take long. As they followed Sam Leighton's brisk stride through the chilly, foggy streets, Sarah clutched Lucy's upper arm.

"I've not seen Jacob Whitby in three years. Since before either of us found our Inner Light," Sarah whispered. "To think that he is asking for me now—" She choked back a sob. "I wish I could have seen him before this. If only the Bull and Mouth had not been destroyed in the Great Fire, I might have met him then. As it is, I have scarcely met any Friends since my return to London."

Lucy nodded. She had heard of the Bull and Mouth, that Quaker stronghold. She had never been inside, of course, but she knew that the meetinghouse had been located near Newgate prison and that the Quakers had long been assembling there, since the earliest days of Cromwell's reign. She knew, too, that many Quakers had been hauled off to jail from that very place, under the terms of the Conventicle Act, which barred nonconformists from meeting in secret. Sarah's own father had sentenced some of these men and women himself. Thankfully, the persecution of the Quakers had lessened in recent years.

Voicing none of her thoughts, Lucy turned her attention back to Sarah, who had continued speaking. "They had announced Jacob's donation to the widow's fund." Her voice trailed off.

"Widow's fund?" Lucy asked, stepping carefully around a puddle of sludge and muck that had pooled along the street.

Pulling herself from her reverie, Sarah explained. "We have a fund to ease the existence of those wrongly imprisoned in the jails or to help their wives and children. We call it the widow's fund." Her voice grew tense. "How wronged so many of us have been, by men like my father!"

Sarah jutted out her chin, as if daring Lucy to reproach her for her defiant words. When Lucy stayed silent, she continued more calmly. "A sizable sum it was, too. When I heard them say the donor's name, I could scarcely believe it. Jacob Whitby! I had not even known that he had become a Quaker." She smiled slightly. "He was hardly a man that one would have believed to seek out the Inner Light. Perhaps, though, he would say the same about me."

Sarah paused again, still lost in thought. "I looked for Jacob after the meeting, but he was away, petitioning King Charles to repeal those unlawful acts against the Quakers. His wife was there, though. I met her briefly." Even in the overcast light, Lucy could see Sarah frown. "I hadn't known he was married. But

why wouldn't he have married? He was always so charming."
She choked a bit on the last words.

Lucy pressed Sarah's arm, hoping to offer her a bit of comfort.

To her surprise, Jacob Whitby lived less than a mile from
the magistrate, on Whitcomb Street in the expanse northwest
of the burnt-out area of London. His was one of the few homes
in the area that was not connected to other homes or shops on
either side. Seeing this home confirmed Lucy's recollection that
Jacob Whitby came from a family of some means.

At Sam's knock, a woman dressed in a drab gray dress and
white apron opened the door. If not for the Quaker's customary
white collar about her neck, Lucy would have taken her for a
washer-woman, for her hands were more ruddy than her cheeks.
Her face was wide and flat, and her eyes were as faded as her
dress. Lucy guessed she was probably in her early thirties, about
ten years older than herself, but life had clearly exacted a great
toll from her.

"Theodora," Sam said to the woman, "I have brought Sarah,
as Jacob bid me to do. This is Sarah's companion, Lucy."

Hearing Sam Leighton refer to the women by their first names
quite jarred Lucy, but neither woman seemed affronted or even
surprised. Lucy supposed such leveling was also part of the
Quaker way.

"Theodora is Sam's wife," Sarah added, which helped explain
some of the disconcerting familiarity. "She and Sam are among
the few Quakers I have met in London."

Theodora Leighton nodded curtly. "Thou art both welcome

here, though it be a tragic time indeed. Pray come inside, and I will fetch our sister Esther."

As Theodora walked away, Lucy noticed that she had a significant limp and moved stiffly, as though she'd sustained an injury. Perhaps she'd been flogged, Lucy thought, recalling the times she'd seen Quakers held in stocks, or worse.

Sam led them inside Jacob Whitby's home, gesturing toward three wooden chairs that awaited them in what was intended to be a great hall. Sarah seated herself and waved her hand for Lucy to do the same. Lucy, however, could not bring herself to sit as a visitor would and remained standing. Sam did not sit either. Instead, he moved across the room, where he tapped his fingers against his leg as if eager to be off.

Perched uncomfortably next to Sarah, Lucy looked around. This was the first Quaker home she'd ever been inside. The decor was far more spare than even Master Hargrave's, and the magistrate was certainly not a man who squandered much on luxury. The white walls were bare, and the wood floors were covered with only the simplest of straw matting to help keep the house warm. Except for the size of the rooms, which were fairly large, the home could have been owned by the meanest of the poor.

Watching her glance around, Sarah smiled. "We are urged to give up our worldly comforts," she whispered. "When we feel the pull of Christ, we bring only what we can carry ourselves. We learn how little we truly need to express our Inner Light. It is clear that Jacob has given most of his fortune away, to the widow's fund that I mentioned, and to fund our travels on behalf of the Lord."

Lucy eyed the bare tables and empty walls. Having grown up with very few possessions, she could not imagine giving up the little luxuries she'd managed to accrue during her time in service.

Sarah's eyes, however, were shining as she took in the bare walls. "He has truly given himself to the Lord," Lucy heard her murmur.

Lucy shifted uncomfortably from one foot to the other. Although earlier there had been glimpses of the gay young woman Lucy remembered, this soulful version of Sarah was difficult to understand. Thankfully, Lucy was spared having to reply when a woman in her late twenties entered the room.

Upon seeing her, Lucy drew in a deep breath. Like other Quakers Lucy had seen, Esther Whitby was dressed simply. Yet simplicity, while drab and colorless on the others, somehow seemed to enhance the woman's considerable natural beauty. Slim and elegant, she could easily have been a grand lady. Though she wore her blond hair tucked neatly under a white cap, the style emphasized her high cheekbones and slender neck to great effect. Despite being rimmed red with tears, her eyes were a startling shade of violet, compelling and alive.

Esther Whitby held out her hands in greeting. "Sister Sarah, I bid thee welcome, and thy companion, too. I thank thee, Brother Sam, for bringing these most welcome guests to my door. Perhaps thou wouldst like some victuals or to sit a spell by the fire."

"No, no, Sister Esther," Sarah said hastily. "Pray, do not trouble thyself with our comforts. Bring us to Brother Jacob, so that we may say our farewells."

They followed Esther Whitby to a flight of stairs at the end of the great room. As they mounted the steps Sarah said to her, "I must thank thee for summoning me, Esther. I have not seen Jacob in many years. I should not have thought he would remember me."

Esther turned back to her. "He insisted upon it. When I told him that we had met, he seemed overjoyed at the idea of reacquainting with you and your brother."

Jacob's wife continued to lead them until they stopped before a closed door, from beyond which they could hear a great murmuring. Esther laid a hand on the door's handle. Before opening the door, she turned to the two women. "Prepare yourself. My husband's wounds are extensive and"—she hesitated— "difficult to view." Tears filled her eyes. "And his words are difficult to hear. He is scarcely himself. At first, the good Lord saw fit to guard his tongue so that he did not dishonor us, but now . . ." She wiped away a tear. "I fear the words of the Lord are already flowing through him, as he finds his path to heaven."

Sarah nodded. "We are ready," she said. But she did reach her right hand backward to clasp Lucy's hand in her own.

Slowly, the two women and Sam followed Esther through the doorway. The shutters were latched, so little of the afternoon light could stream into the airless room. Lucy could barely keep from gagging as the smells assaulted them. Piss. Blood. Pus. Sweat. Lavender. The stench of approaching death.

"Oh," Sarah said, stopping so abruptly that Lucy almost bumped into her.

There were already several people present, all huddled around a large bed that seemed to take up most of the available space. Theodora, Lucy saw, was one of the mourners seated in the carved wooden chairs. Clearly, the other sternly dressed figures were Quakers. Their glances were curious but not unwelcoming.

Sarah still had not moved, transfixed by the heavily bandaged figure lying motionless on the bed. Had Jacob already succumbed to his injuries? Lucy felt a pang that Sarah had not been able to tell her old friend farewell before he passed on.

As if he heard her unspoken thoughts, however, the man drew in a great breath, a long tortured inhalation of air. *His ribs are likely broken,* Lucy thought, *or at least horribly bruised.* She could only imagine how twisted his insides must be, given the unnatural position he was currently in. Still, that wretched exhalation proved he was alive, and she murmured a small prayer of thanks. Mercifully the man's eyes were closed, so perhaps he was more asleep than awake.

Lucy squeezed Sarah's hand. "He still lives," she murmured. Sarah squeezed her hand in return, too overcome to speak.

Seeing this, one of the Quaker women arose and moved toward Sarah. A stout woman, clad in gray and brown, she was much older than the others, but Lucy could not say her age for certain. Surely she'd witnessed much in her life, at least fifty years' worth, if not more. Her face was careworn, but her brown eyes were lively, and her movements were quick and spry. Gently, she took Sarah's hands in her own.

"My dear child," the woman murmured. Her voice was raspy, although her tone and touch were kind. "How I have missed thee these last few days. 'Tis a terrible thing that has reunited us." Her voice grew stronger, more resolute. "Now we must seek solace in the Lord and be strong for our much-suffering brother."

Sarah turned to Lucy then. "This is Joan, my dearest

companion, my spiritual mother. She and I journeyed together through the New World, and if it had not been for Joan, I would have been lost many times over."

Joan pressed Lucy's hand before returning to her seat next to Theodora. The two women appeared to be mending old garments stored in a great straw basket between them.

Sam moved past them, seating himself on a low wooden bench at the foot of the bed. When he picked up a sheaf of papers that had been resting on the bench, Lucy caught the unmistakable smell of fresh ink. Someone had been writing recently in the bedchamber.

Spying another long low bench in a shadowy corner of the room, Lucy began to pull Sarah toward it, so that they would not be in the way of the other mourners. She'd been to vigils before, but never for a Quaker, and she didn't want to draw any more attention to herself or Sarah.

Except Esther seemed to have other plans. She had been silent while Sarah had been speaking with Joan, but now she spoke up. "Sister Sarah has come to see thee, dear heart," she said loudly to her husband. "Sit here," she said to Sarah, patting the chair closest to the bed.

With its embroidered back and seat, the chair was clearly the finest item in the room, perhaps the entire house. Sarah hesitated, but sat down as she'd been bidden, and Esther took the other wooden chair alongside her.

At the sound of his wife's voice, the man on the bed jerked slightly, emitting a small moan. When he opened his eyes, Lucy could see they were glazed over in pain. She wished he had not been awakened.

How he must be suffering, she thought.

"I am ever so grateful to be surrounded by such true friends," Esther said to Sarah, gesturing widely to all the mourners. "That is our dear brother Gervase," she added, pointing to a man with blond hair, quietly whittling near the great wardrobe.

Hearing his name, Gervase looked up. Catching Lucy's eye, he nodded at her, smiling slightly in greeting. His demeanor was calm, if somber. For such a large, hearty-looking man, he seemed surprisingly comfortable in the small, enclosed space. "Jacob and I have been like brothers," he said, pressing his hand to his chest. His speech was quite cultured, perhaps even more than Adam's, and Lucy wondered if he had attended university with Jacob. Lucy could hear the emotion in his deep voice. "It is with a heavy heart I sit vigil here."

"Thank you, Gervase. I am sure my husband feels the same toward you," Esther said. She extended her hand gracefully to the young woman perched atop a wood stool close to the small fire in the chamber hearth. "And this dear one is Deborah. The niece of Ahivah, one of our greatest conveyers of Truth."

"Right now my aunt is a great conveyer of sleep," Deborah said pertly. Seeing Esther's lip curl slightly and the others frown at her little jest, the young Quaker murmured a little apology. "I just meant she has been asleep for much of the day. My deep sorrow over Jacob has cost me some control over my tongue, it seems." She smiled slightly at Lucy and shrugged.

Lucy could not help but notice that Deborah did not look pinched and gray, like most of the other Quakeresses. Instead, her cheeks were rosy and smooth. Her hair, too, was different from that of the other women in the room. While she wore the same cap as the other women, light brown tendrils curled gently against her neck and temple. The overall effect was less severe. Indeed, she looked more like a fellow servant than a handmaiden of the Lord.

"These people are all my brothers and sisters in Christ," Esther continued, as if Deborah had not spoken. Her voice was starting to choke up. "Indeed, we were together at Sam Leighton's house when a neighbor's boy came bearing the terrible news of my husband's accident. If only dearest Jacob had come with us to the meeting," she cried, "this terrible accident might never have occurred."

Great tears began to roll down Esther's cheeks. Seeing this, Joan handed her a handkerchief, which she accepted from the old woman with a grateful smile.

Sarah had scarcely taken her eyes off Jacob as his wife was speaking. Now, as Lucy watched, she gently took one of his bandaged hands in her own, a tear slipping down her cheek. "Oh, dear Jacob," Sarah said. "I'm so heartfelt sorry to see thee in such distress."

The man opened his eyes again, trying to focus. "Dearest Sarah," he murmured, sounding pleased. "Thou hast come back to me."

Positioned as she was, Lucy could look straight at Sarah's face as she leaned toward Jacob. There was a softness there that reminded her of the girl Sarah had once been.

"Oh, Jacob," Sarah replied, keeping her voice steady. "I'm here." Her eyes flicked toward Esther Whitby, who had rested her head against one of the women. "I was pleased that thou asked for me."

"I only just learned that thou hadst become a Friend. I heard it mentioned at the meeting that thou hadst returned from thy great travels through Barbados and Massachusetts. I was hoping to see thee at the next meeting, but I was unable to attend." His grimace held a semblance of smile. "I'm afraid my petition to our king was for naught."

Sarah smiled. "I only heard about thee as well," she said gently. "How generous thou hast been to our brethren."

He attempted another grin. "So hard to believe. I remember thee imploring me to take thee to Bartholomew's Fair. For more ribbons and creams."

Sarah wiped his brow with a piece of bleached linen. "What a fool I was for ribbons and fripperies then. I begged thee to win me a prize."

Jacob smiled slightly. "I remember." He paused. "Thou looked lovely."

Hearing Theodora cough, Sarah spoke. "Certainly this was before I knew the power of God's love, during a time when I still gave in to earthly temptations."

Seeing Sarah's chagrin, Joan reached across Jacob to pat her gently on the arm. "We do not seek to judge thee, child," she said. "So long as thou understand now that such ribbons were the devil's hand at play."

Sarah turned back to Jacob. "Like thee, I have been transformed by the Inner Light." They gazed into each other's eyes. Lucy shifted in her chair. Such intimacy, even with one on his deathbed, transgressed propriety.

Sarah seemed to realize the same thing, recalling herself with a start. "I've had the pleasure of meeting thy wife already, and we've just now renewed our acquaintance."

Here Jacob nodded, frowning slightly. "I would rather thou hadst done so under different circumstances. There is much thou and she have in common, and I should have liked to see thy friendship flourish."

His wife leaned over then, placing her left hand over Sarah's hand, which was still holding Jacob's. "We shall become bosom companions, dear husband, as I know this would please thee."

"My dear wife will need thy strength, Sarah," he said, his voice trembling in emotion.

"She shall have it," Sarah replied. The hands of all three remained clasped together, almost as if a pledge between them had been made.

Lucy shivered. A deathbed pledge was not one to take lightly, and she prayed that Sarah would be able to see it through. The moment passed when Jacob began to cough, and Sarah eased him forward so that he could breathe a bit more easily. A bit of spittle dripped from his mouth, which Sarah wiped with her sleeve.

Swallowing hard, Jacob faced Sarah again. "Did thy brother accompany thee? I was rather hoping he would."

"Adam?" Sarah said. "I've scarcely seen my brother myself. He has been so busy with the Fire Court."

"Do not fret, my dear," Jacob said to Sarah, his lips stretching into what Lucy supposed he intended as a smile. "I should have liked to see my old friend Adam Hargrave one last time, but I think it will be in heaven when I do." His voice trailed off, and his face contorted in pain. Again he looked like he might drift away.

"Have thy parents come to see thee?" Sarah asked. "Jacob?"

He opened his eyes again. "My parents have cast me off."

"What?" Sarah gasped. "Oh, no."

"I'm afraid it's true." He gulped.

Cast off. How horrible, Lucy could not help but think. Master Hargrave would never cast off his only daughter. Or would he? Clearly he was unhappy with his daughter's choices. She noticed that Sarah was avoiding her gaze, and a flush had risen in her cheeks. Perhaps she was thinking the same thing.

Jacob groaned again, recalling their attention. "None of it matters now. For the Lord will take me soon."

From the foot of the bed, Sam repeated some of Jacob's words. " 'The Lord will take me soon.' "

Lucy glanced at him in surprise, noting for the first time that he was holding a small square board in his lap, upon which he had a piece of paper. In his right hand, he held a quill, with which he had begun to write sure strokes. Catching her look, he explained, "I am recording Brother Jacob's last utterances, so that others may be inspired by his goodness and courage."

Lucy nodded. This was a common enough practice, and not just among the Quakers. Many sects sought to publish the final testimonies of their members, particularly those more scandalous pieces that described how a sinner regained grace after a great fall. Usually such pieces had titles such as *Last Dying Words* or *The Sinner's Journey.*

"Master Aubrey sells such speeches at our shop," she said to Sarah, without thinking about how her words would sound to others in the room. "Indeed, they sell very well."

Everyone turned and looked at her. "Forgive me," Lucy whispered, flushing over her crass words. "I fear I have spoken out of turn."

"Whatever dost thou mean, child?" Joan said, not unkindly.

Lucy squirmed under the collective scrutiny of the room. "I work for the printer Master Aubrey, as his apprentice. We sometimes sell pieces like what you are writing now."

"Oh, is that so?" Theodora said, exchanging a quick look with her husband. "Perhaps the good Lord has brought thee to us."

"Oh, no," Lucy said hurriedly. "I am not a Quaker."

"What words didst thou just say?" Jacob called weakly from the bed. "Thou art not a Quaker?" His eyes were fervent, searching. "Who art thou?"

"My name is Lucy. I am—was—Miss Sarah's servant. I accompanied her here, at her father's request." She looked at Sarah a bit helplessly. "Shall I leave? I did promise your father that I would stay with you, but perhaps it would be better if I left since I am not a Quaker. I do not wish to interfere. Perhaps I should not be here?"

"No, no, certainly thou must not leave," Joan said reassuringly before Sarah could speak. "We have no quarrel with others who are not of our conviction, and I can see that thou hast been a loyal companion to one of our own. Thou art very welcome, as a friend of Sarah's." She glanced at Sam. "Indeed, we should like to share dear Jacob's last words with others. We've had so few opportunities since the Great Fire to print our pieces. Perhaps thou art the answer to our prayers."

"Isn't there a Quaker printer?" Lucy asked. She knew that Master Aubrey had published Quaker tracts in the past, but he'd warned her and Lach to take care where they sold such pieces. Although King Charles had been more tolerant of Quakers of late, they could still run the risk of being arrested and even imprisoned for supporting seditious acts, which included the publishing or selling of Quaker tracts.

"Robert Wilson, but he's still getting his family resettled after the Fire," Theodora replied. "Hasn't returned much to printing. He's no Quaker, though."

Jacob spoke again, in that painful halting speech. "I should very much like," he said slowly, "for Lucy, Sarah's companion, to write my piece. Have her printer sell it. Perhaps we can spread my words to others besides Quakers."

During the exchange, Esther had sat silently, her lips pursed. When she spoke, Lucy could sense her reluctance. "Thy master would print a Quaker piece? Take on that danger?" she asked, voicing Lucy's own concerns.

"He has printed such pieces before," Lucy said honestly. "But truth be told, I do not know what he will say." Particularly since Master Aubrey had already experienced some problems at the hands of Roger L'Estrange, the Licenser of the Press. But she thought it prudent to keep that last point to herself.

"There must be a fee," Esther said. Again her reluctance was clear. "More than I can afford."

"Yes, I'm afraid the cost might be dear. I will have to ask Master Aubrey, of course, but I imagine that he would charge at least several pounds to print," Lucy replied. "I know he takes into account how many copies you would like, how long it will take us to set and print the piece, and how many pages it will be."

"Do not fret, dearest Esther," Joan said, patting Jacob's wife on the arm. "So many others will receive solace from his words. I believe it to be our duty to share with others how Brother

Jacob found his Inner Light. We will able to spread his words further if we print them." Seeing Esther opening her mouth to protest, she added, "We will pay for it, from our widow's fund." She held up her hand. "Now not another word. 'Tis decided."

Sam and his wife stood up. "Dearest Esther," Sam said, "now that Sister Sarah and her companion have joined thee in thy vigil, Theodora and I shall leave for a short while, to attend to some duties of our own. We will return in a few hours." He looked down at Lucy. "I will leave more paper and the quill, should Jacob be moved again to speak. Perhaps thou wouldst be so good as to record his testimony, should he revive again?"

Lucy took the pages and the ink that he had extended to her. "Oh, yes, of course."

Gervase stood up as well. "I've some things to attend to as well. I shall return soon."

After the Leightons and Gervase left, as if on cue, Jacob began to groan again. Hearing the sound, Joan began to tremble and sway. "Oh, sweet soothing of the Lord," she cried. "Let us pray that this man be nourished in the Light of God, and that he is cleansed of the sins of his youth."

Jacob moaned. With great difficulty, he continued to speak. "Indeed, I was a madcap youth, a young man of folly and indiscretions."

Dipping the quill in the ink, Lucy obediently wrote down his words. This seemed to be the kind of phrase the Quakers like to say, and no doubt what readers expected when they purchased a tract like this one. Sin and repentance, two very old themes indeed.

But then Jacob went on, speaking more fervently, passion

rising in his voice. "I was unwilling to wait for what I truly wanted." Did he glance at Sarah here? Lucy was not sure. He went on. "I spent many a coin on sinful doings, and for this I am heartily ashamed." Here he seemed to glance at his wife.

"There, there, sweetheart." Esther came over and soothed him. "That was all before we met. I have long forgiven thee thy youthful follies." She looked at Lucy. "You may note that he has repented," she said.

Lucy nodded. "And thus, Jacob Whitby repented his youthful follies," she said out loud as she wrote his words.

"Repented his youthful follies? This I did!" Jacob exclaimed. "Why then the cart? Why then should the wild beasts strike me down?" He rolled awkwardly on his side, to look at his wife. "Have I not been a good man?"

"Oh, yes!" Joan interjected, seeing that Esther was swallowing, unable to form words. The old Quaker looked across the room at Sarah. "Why, just last week he gave the last of all his wealth, everything he inherited from his family before he was cast off, to help the widowed and the sick." Joan nodded in satisfaction. "Every penny and shilling. Indeed he did."

Esther leaned down and smoothed her husband's forehead. "Such a loving and godly man, so he shall be nourished by the light of God."

"Why hast God forsaken me, then? Does he mock me?" Jacob asked. "Was I not a good husband?"

"The very best, dear husband." Her eyes teared up again. Lucy saw her hands ball into fists. "Curse the driver of that ill-fated cart!" She began to sway and would have fallen if Sarah and Joan had not both leapt to support her.

"Please, Esther, lie down for a spell. It does my heart ill to see thee in such distress," Jacob whispered.

Joan put her arm around her. "There, there, Sister Esther, thou must rest. Even Jacob says so." Joan turned to Sarah, who still was holding Esther up. "Her chamber is just this way. Sarah, wilt thou help me? She must rest. Deborah, be a dear. Please make a restorative for our sister Esther."

Deborah smiled again. "Of course," she said, practically bouncing out. Lucy saw her face as she departed—she looked pleased and relieved to escape the sickroom.

Esther still looked uncertain. "I should not leave my husband's side."

"Thou must," Joan said firmly. "Everyone knows thou art a most devoted wife. But thou must be refreshed in thy body as well as being nourished in the Lord."

"Joan, thou art so very kind. My own true spiritual mother," Esther murmured, allowing the two women to steer her out of the room.

"Wilt thou tend Brother Jacob while we tend to Esther?" Joan asked Lucy. "Perhaps he will take some restorative soup, although I fear he may be in too much pain for that. One of us will be back shortly."

When they left, Lucy sat in the chair that Sarah had vacated. "I am so sorry this happened to you," Lucy whispered to the man lying on the bed. "Though I am not a Quaker, I do believe God will forgive you for your sins. If you are in pain, perhaps you must let go."

To her surprise, Jacob opened his eyes again and looked straight at her, no hint of the great anger she had just witnessed.

Speaking carefully, he said, "I must tell thee. There was a reason that I summoned Sarah and Adam to my side."

"They were your dear friends," Lucy said, trying to sound reassuring.

"Yes, that is so. And I have my regrets, especially for a falling-out that we had several years ago. Youthful indiscretions." He made a rueful sound. "I had hoped to speak to Adam, but perhaps thou canst help me." He clutched at her hand frantically.

Seeing this, Lucy grew alarmed. Perhaps his time was closing in. "Shh," she tried to soothe the man. Whatever potion he had been taking seemed to be wearing off. She looked about. A small vial lay on the table next to his bed; she picked it up and worked the tight cork out. Passing it under her nose, she breathed in the deep pungent aroma of the restorative. She poured a few drops onto a spoon. "This would taste better in some soup."

The man shuddered in pain again. "No soup," he said faintly. "Just that."

Lucy held the spoon to his lips and dribbled a few drops into his mouth. "Maybe I should call your wife back? So that she can be with you when—" She did not finish the thought.

"Listen to me," he repeated, swallowing with difficulty. He seemed to be trying to sit up, to get closer to her. His voice began to drop, forcing Lucy to put her head down so that his mouth was against her ear. "I must tell thee something, and there may not be much time. I do not know whom to trust. I wanted to talk to Adam. Oh, why didn't Adam come? And Sarah, I hardly know her now."

"You are getting very excited. Perhaps you should lie still—"

"Listen to me. Thou must tell Adam. He will know what to do. Dost thou understand?"

Fearful of the man's intensity, Lucy managed to nod.

"I was pushed in front of that cart," Jacob whispered. "Deliberately. Someone wanted me to die."

Lucy froze. Had she heard him correctly? Surely the man's wits were addled. "No, sir. That couldn't be. It was dark, foggy. Maybe someone bumped into you and—"

"No," Jacob interrupted. His speech was labored and was growing more difficult to understand. "I was pushed. I did not trip. I was not jostled. Someone put two hands on my back and pushed me straight into those horses." His face contorted as he remembered the horrors of the accident.

Against her better judgment Lucy felt moved to believe him, even though what he was saying terrified her. "Who would do such a dreadful thing?" she whispered. "Did you see who pushed you?"

"No, I could barely see anything in that wretched fog. But I have an idea." Another paroxysm of pain passed over his body.

"Who was it? Someone you know?"

"Yes, I believe so. I had received a letter from my sister, Julia." He stopped to cough a bit. Lucy winced as a bit of bloody spittle trickled from his mouth. "We'd still managed to exchange letters, even though my father had cast me from the house."

"Yes? What did she tell you?" She wiped his chin.

Another deep pain ran over the man. "She said she had received information that one of the Quakers in our group is an impostor." He paused, licking his dry lips. "Water."

Lucy held a cup up to his mouth. "Who? Who was she talking about?"

He took a tortured sip and continued. "She didn't want to write more in the letter. She bid me to come see her. That was where I was going when I was pushed."

Lucy sat back, her hand to her lips. "You believe that a Quaker, a Friend, a lover of peace, would have pushed you in front of a cart?"

"I can see thou dost not believe me. I understand, what I am saying seems preposterous." His voice dropped further, and Lucy leaned in even closer to hear him. "I'm afraid now that the person who came after me might threaten my wife. I tried to tell her, but she did not believe me. The Quakers have been such friends to her, I could not bear to break her heart."

He grabbed her arm. "Please, tell Adam to talk to my sister. Have my murderer brought to justice. I must protect my wife from harm. She has no one else, and I'm afraid she will turn to the wrong person. Promise me that thou wilt tell Adam what I told thee, but no one else!"

Hardly knowing what she was saying, Lucy nodded her head. "I promise, Mr. Whitby," she whispered. "I promise."

Jacob began to cough then, and could speak no more. Lucy brought the cup to his lips, but he could not swallow. "My time has come!" he said, his voice raspy. "Oh Lord! My time has come. I feel no pain. I have seen his glory and tasted of his most precious Truth, and it is sweet unto my taste. Judge me, Lord. Judge me." His voiced faded away.

"Mrs. Whitby! Miss Sarah!" Lucy went to the door and called out in fear, then returned to his bedside.

The women burst back into the room. Esther threw herself on her husband's form. "Oh, dear husband," she called to him, weeping. Lucy backed up against the wall, still shocked from what she had just learned.

Sarah backed off. Lucy slipped her hand in hers. Together they all watched Jacob take his last dying breath.

"Did he say anything else?" Esther demanded, turning back to Lucy. Her purple eyes glowed with tears. "Any other message?"

"No." Lucy gulped. "Just that his last thoughts were of you and that"—she could not keep her voice from breaking—"he felt his time had been called too soon."

Even as she spoke, Lucy could hear the man's last whispered words over and over in her mind, as though he were still there to utter them. Their significance began to settle more deeply upon her. Mr. Whitby had been murdered, and no one knew it but her.

· 4 ·

The next two hours passed in a strange blur of tears, shrieks, and general confusion. Never in her life, not even when she saw neighbors and friends felled by the plague, had Lucy witnessed such wild, unchecked distress.

Esther Whitby had begun to tremble and shake in the most alarming way—"Quaking in the presence of the Lord," she said. Joan had begun to shriek outright, half praying, half crying, proclaiming her gratitude to the Lord for relieving Jacob of his suffering. Deborah had begun speaking in what seemed like another tongue; Joan, regaining her own lucidity, called her name sharply, and the young Quaker continued her lament in English.

At some point Theodora and Sam returned. Theodora took one glance into the room and began to wail much as Joan had done. Sam let out one sad gulp and sat back on a bench, preferring to remain in the shadows with his sorrow.

Amid it all, Sarah sat silently, staring at Jacob's corpse, tears slipping down her pale cheeks.

Since the Whitbys had no servants, Lucy began to do what she knew best, more to calm her own tumultuous thoughts than anything else. Creeping down to the kitchen, she prepared a soothing brew of chamomile, lemon peel, and nutmeg. She wished for a bit of wormwood, but she could see none in the Whitbys' bare stores. Instead she took the last drops of Jacob's restorative and added them to the concoction, then began to pass it out among the Quakers, pressing a mug into Sarah's cold hands first.

Jacob's last words weighed heavily on Lucy. As she walked into Esther's bedchamber with two steaming mugs, she looked at the Quaker lying facedown on her pillow. Esther had taken off her dress and was now wearing a sleeping gown. Joan was sitting beside her, humming a tune and stroking her long blond hair, which had been released from its bun. Theodora was sitting on the other side, silent now, but rocking back and forth, a great pain evident in her face.

Hearing Lucy's soft step on the floor, Esther rolled over, looking for a moment more like a forlorn child than a woman who had just lost her husband. She even managed a tremulous smile as she reached up to accept one of the mugs from Lucy. Joan leaned over and pushed some wayward hairs off Esther's flushed forehead and cheek. The gesture was loving, compassionate. Esther just couldn't be in danger, Lucy thought. Jacob had to have been mistaken. It was difficult making sense of anything, with

Sarah so distraught. After a while, not having anything to do, she just sat beside Sarah, and neither one spoke.

When Lucy heard a knock at the servants' entrance, she was ever so grateful to see John standing there, having been bidden by the magistrate to bring them home.

"How does Mr. Whitby fare?" he asked, shuffling back and forth, trying to warm his feet.

"Oh, John," she said, sinking down onto the kitchen bench. "Jacob Whitby is dead." She sat there for a moment before heading off to tell Sarah that John had arrived to escort them home.

Sarah followed her back to the kitchen, and Lucy picked up their cloaks, prepared to leave. "Please leave my cloak, Lucy," she said. Turning to John, Sarah said, "Thou must tell Father that I am needed here. Pray, escort Lucy back to Master Aubrey's. My place is here. I will return to my father's home in the morning."

From behind Sarah's shoulder, Lucy met John's eyes in mutual comprehension. This was the old willful Sarah speaking, chaffing at her father's bidding, and such blatant rebellion would never do.

Besides, Lucy was uncomfortable leaving Sarah at the Whitby home. Could one of these mourners have murdered Jacob? Her duty was first and foremost to the Hargraves, even if she was no longer employed by the magistrate. She could not, in good conscience, leave his daughter in such a place.

Lucy touched Sarah's arm gently, hoping to work on her

more tender sensibilities. "Miss Sarah, please. I beseech you. Return to your father's home tonight. Do not force John to explain his failure to do as the magistrate asked."

Sarah looked from Lucy to John and sighed. "I should not like John to bear the burden of my liberty." She passed her hand to her forehead. Lucy tensed, anxious that she would swoon. But instead she smiled wanly. "I admit, too, that I should like to lie down. I will return home with thee. I do not promise, though, how long I will stay."

It did not take long to bid their farewells and head out the door. As they started down the street, Sarah began to shiver violently, so much so that she could barely walk. The shock of Jacob's death had begun to overcome her at last. Without speaking, Lucy took one of Sarah's arms while John took the other, supporting her so that she would not stumble on the icy streets.

Over and over again, as they drew closer to the magistrate's house, Lucy could hear Jacob's whispers in her mind, raising disturbing questions. Had he truly been pushed as he claimed? Could someone he knew have done such a thing? Or had he imagined the hands on his back? And what of Jacob's sister— what had she known? She glanced at Sarah's downcast face. *I must tell her,* Lucy thought, *but how?*

Before she could speak, Sarah broke the silence. "Jacob was such a charming man. A gadabout, to be sure, cavorting and gaming. Yet there was a goodness to him, despite that. Quick with a jest. Of course, I was different then, too." She sighed. "Jacob and I—we had gotten on very well. I do not know if he would have asked for me, but I cannot imagine Father having approved our match. I know that Adam did not approve." Her lips twisted. "Then I found the Quakers. Put him from my mind, as a figment from my youth. When I learned that he had found the Quakers, too—" She broke off with a choked sob.

Lucy waited helplessly, tightening her cloak about her to ward off the chill. So she had not been wrong when she'd seen the anguished love in Sarah's eyes earlier. Regaining her composure, Sarah continued. "I know I should say that I am grateful that Jacob is now cradled in the arms of the Lord," she said, her voice low and full of emotion. "But I am angry. Angry that such a terrible accident should have befallen a man as good as he. He was too young to die."

Hearing those words strengthened Lucy's resolve. "Miss Sarah," she said, "there is something I must tell you."

Sarah gently squeezed her arm. "Thou mayst simply call me Sarah now, dearest Lucy. We Quakers do not recognize such earthly markers of status. All men are equal in the eyes of the Lord, and women, too."

Lucy put that thought away to ponder later. "Sarah," she started again, a little awkwardly, then stopped. How could she explain what Jacob Whitby had told her? Perhaps it was better to say nothing, she thought again, miserably.

"I have cut thee off," Sarah said. "Pray, Lucy, share thy thoughts with me." Her eyes were kind and encouraging.

That was all Lucy needed. "Mr. Whitby said it wasn't an accident," she said in a rush. "He told me he'd been pushed in front of that cart."

"What?" Sarah exclaimed, pulling herself free, her mouth agape. Behind her, John wore a similarly shocked expression.

"It's true," Lucy said. "Jacob Whitby told me he had been

pushed." She almost added *And his sister may know who did it,* but something kept her tongue still. *Let her recover from the first blow first,* she thought.

"Why ever would you say such a terrible thing?" Sarah demanded, angry tears slipping down her cheeks. Dimly, Lucy noted that she had dropped her Quaker speech again. "Surely you could see his torments! You must have misunderstood his words!"

Sarah's pain was difficult to bear, and Lucy hastened to explain, in heavy, halting words, what Jacob had whispered before he died. "Mr. Whitby was afraid that the person who had hurt him would try to hurt his wife, too."

Even to her own ears, the story spoken aloud sounded fantastic and unbelievable. Still, she went on. "Mr. Whitby was afraid to tell anyone there, out of fear that he would confide in the wrong person, and put her in danger. He told me he did not know who to trust."

This was the wrong thing to say, which Lucy realized when Sarah's face darkened in anger. "So he would trust thee? A stranger?"

Lucy sighed. The burden of Jacob's words was already flattening her under its great weight. Reluctantly, she explained the rest. "Mr. Whitby said he had reason to believe that his killer was someone he knew, although he didn't know who. Maybe even a Quaker. I think that's why he told me, since I am not part of your sect. He tried to warn his wife, he said, but she did not believe him. He was very anxious, being worried that she will confide in the wrong person. I know it sounds far-fetched," she added, her voice fading away.

"Far-fetched! I should think so!" Sarah exclaimed. "Why, that would mean—"

"That he'd been murdered," Lucy concluded. She straightened up, no longer wishing to mince words. "Yes, I daresay that's exactly what he meant."

Behind Sarah, John was shaking his head at her. Lucy tried to ignore him, but they'd worked together long enough for her to know exactly what he was thinking, and she felt a flash of shame. *Why would you say such a preposterous thing to our young mistress, particularly when she's grieving so?*

However, he did not voice his thoughts. "I will fetch a lantern," he said to Lucy. "Master Hargrave would want me to see you back to Aubrey's."

As John walked away, Lucy caught Sarah by the arm before she could go inside. "Mr. Whitby wanted me to tell Adam what had befallen him. He believed that Adam would have his murderer brought to justice," Lucy said, sounding more determined than she felt. "We should tell your father, too."

Sarah stamped her foot. "Lucy Campion! Thou shalt do no such thing," she cried. In a more strangled voice, she added, "Promise me thou wilt not. We Quakers are already stifled under the Conventicle Act. News of a murder would bring suspicion down upon us all."

Lucy sighed. Truth be told, she knew the magistrate could do nothing. The man bore no obvious marks of murder; it was clear his injuries had been sustained in being trampled by the horse and cart. Without a witness, it would be nearly impossible to prove. "Fine. I'll say nothing to your father. For now."

"Or to Adam either!" Sarah said hotly. "I know thou dost think this will give thee a reason to see my brother—"

Lucy held up her hand in warning, much as the magistrate would do, to keep someone from speaking. She did not know what Sarah knew or assumed about her relationship with Adam, but she could not let such aspersions be stated aloud.

To her surprise, Sarah stopped in midsentence, looking a bit ashamed. "I am sorry, Lucy. I did not mean what I uttered just now. Jacob's death has upset me more than thou canst know." She stifled a sob.

"Please, Miss Sarah," Lucy said, knocking on the front door. She put her ear near the wood, listening intently for movement within. "Go inside and get warm."

When Annie opened up the door, Lucy spoke quickly. "Miss Sarah is unwell. Have Cook prepare her a tisane. After that, please help her to bed."

Annie nodded and put her arm around Sarah's waist, supporting her. Before they went inside, Sarah looked at Lucy over her shoulder. "Please, Lucy," she said. "Promise me that thou wilt forget what Jacob said. He was under great distress when he passed. Promise that thou wilt not speak of his words to anyone else."

"What if Mrs. Whitby is in danger?" Lucy pleaded. "I cannot go against a man's dying words. Pray, do not request this of me," she said, feeling a bit sick. "I will not tell your father, but please, I must tell Adam. Please let me make good on the promise I made to Mr. Whitby."

Sarah frowned, but did not speak again as Annie helped her inside before shutting the door behind them. For a moment,

Lucy stared at the wooden door. Although she did not like to anger Sarah, she knew it was important that she learn about Jacob Whitby's life. That meant she needed to return to his home on the morrow.

The next day, the Sunday morning service at St. Dunstan's finally concluded after three long painful hours. The sermon had been very dull indeed, although the minister had spoken passionately enough about Original Sin and the evils that women continued to bring upon their menfolk.

Standing alongside Master Aubrey, Lach, and her brother, Will, Lucy smoothed her best Sunday dress, trying to relieve some of the numbness and pain in her legs and haunches. Like most of the congregation, she tried not to fidget very much, lest she draw the ire of the minister, which would in turn draw the anger of Master Aubrey, who did not enjoy, as he would say, "being on the outs with the Lord."

Her mind had wandered, though, as she kept thinking about what she needed to do. She'd spent much of the night tossing and turning, worrying about what the dying man had whispered before he slipped away. Was it true? Or was it as Sarah supposed, the confused thoughts of a pain-riddled man?

When the service concluded, Will pecked her cheek and bid her farewell. Off to see one of his ladyloves, Lucy thought, eying him as he ambled away. As always, he had dressed on the fine side, looking more like gentry every day, and less like a smithy. A journeyman now, he no longer had to report to a master as he had when he was an apprentice. This meant he could set his own hours and work at his own pace, a fact of his life that Lucy very much admired.

On their way back to the printer's shop, Master Aubrey half-heartedly asked them questions about the minister's sermon. As head of the household, his duty was to make sure that all members of his family—in this case, his servants—were leading good and virtuous lives. That he was looking forward to his ale and a bit of stew was clear, however, because he accepted any answer they dutifully shared. When Lach solemnly informed him, with a mischievous glance at Lucy, that the most important thing he'd learned was that women should never be trusted, Master Aubrey did not even bat an eye. "Yes, yes, very good," the printer had muttered, much to Lucy's chagrin and Lach's obvious delight.

Ladling out the stew, one of the few dishes she made truly well, Lucy told Master Aubrey about Jacob Whitby and the Quakers' request that they publish the man's last dying words. Naturally she didn't say anything about his final wild accusation.

"I know that it can be dangerous to publish or sell Quaker tracts," she added, watching the printer's face. "I shouldn't like to get us in trouble."

"You shouldn't like to get us in trouble," Master Aubrey repeated, looking heavenward. "I suppose I should be grateful that my apprentices don't *want* to get me in trouble."

"No, sir," Lucy said, still trying to gauge what the printer was thinking.

From across the table, Lach grinned. Playfully, he made a sign of a knife across her throat. *You are in for it now,* he mimed.

Master Aubrey took a bit of his bread. "How'd you haggle?"

Lucy smiled. Though his tone was even, she could tell he was interested now. Her years dickering over prices with merchants at market had finally come in handy. She and Sam had had a quick conversation while the other women were still consoling Esther Whitby. She named the sum, a goodly amount. "They want thirty copies to distribute among themselves. The rest we could sell."

"Just so, just so," Master Aubrey said, trying to keep his mouth from twitching.

Lach mouthed a word at her when the master wasn't looking. She just grinned.

"I was thinking, sir," she said to Master Aubrey as she ladled more stew into his bowl and added a touch more salt, just the way he liked it. "Perhaps I could get a little more for the story. Find out more about Jacob Whitby's early life, talk to his widow. Add a little flesh to the bones, as it were. If I called on her today, it should not keep me from any work I need to do tomorrow."

Lucy held her breath. Truly, she was not supposed to be doing work on the Lord's Day, but she also knew from the yawns that the printer kept attempting to hide that he would far rather take a nap than continue to read the Bible aloud, as he really ought. She was not too surprised when he waved her off with his approval, much to the avid disappointment of Lach.

·5·

Standing now at Esther Whitby's front door, Lucy hesitated. Normally she would use the servants' entrance, except on the few occasions she was accompanying a member of the Hargrave family somewhere. But the Quakers seemed to eschew such formality. With a quick decisive knock, she rapped on the door, holding forth a small jar of stew intended for Jacob's widow, which she had ladled out under Lach's annoyed gaze.

From within she could hear some muffled comments before the door was cracked open. Theodora peered out cautiously. Seeing Lucy, she frowned. "Yes?"

Lucy held up her heavy basket with a slight smile. "I've brought a good warming stew for Mrs. Whitby," she said. "I thought she might be in need of some nourishment." When Theodora did not say anything, Lucy faltered even further. "I thought it would be all right to come here, but perhaps—?"

To her relief, the Quaker opened the door wider, although she did look furtively up and down the street before she moved aside. "Come in," she said.

After Lucy had stepped inside, Theodora shut the door firmly behind her. The house was warmer than it had been the day before, a fact for which Lucy was grateful. The long walk in the slush had made her toes painfully numb, although she would never admit as much to anyone. Her brother had given her new shoes for her birthday, back in October, and with all the walking she'd done, the timber heels were starting to wear down. Still, they looked nice, and they were among the finer things she owned. She smiled gratefully at Theodora.

Theodora did not return her smile, and instead appraised Lucy from head to toe. "There are few who would venture to a Quaker household alone," she said, taking the basket from her and pulling out the jar of stew. Lucy wanted to protest but instead just watched as Theodora opened the lid and took a deep sniff.

"Might have brought some for the rest of us," Theodora commented, refastening the lid. Still holding the jar of stew in her hands, she handed the basket back to Lucy and opened the door. "Good day to thee." And somewhat more reluctantly, "God bless."

Her response was more abrupt than Lucy had expected. "Perhaps I may pay my respects to Mrs. Whitby myself?" she asked, not wishing to leave the house without speaking to Jacob's widow. "Master Aubrey would like to print this piece about Jacob Whitby, but he said it would sell better with more details about his early life. Before he became a Quaker. Sinner turned saint, and all that."

Theodora's features hardened noticeably. "I should not like to bother Esther right now." She took a step forward, forcing Lucy backward so that she was on the threshold and practically back onto the front walk. With her hand on the knob, she clearly was about to shut the door in Lucy's face. "I will extend thy respects to her."

As Theodora swung the door shut, Lucy put her foot out to stop it, still smiling in what she hoped was a calm and friendly way. "I spoke to your husband about this yesterday."

Theodora frowned at her more fiercely. Lucy did not know what the Quaker would have done if Sam Leighton had not appeared then behind his wife. Clearly he had heard their exchange.

"Theodora," Sam said, "Sister Joan and I believe that it was Divine Providence that Sarah brought Lucy along yesterday. I believe the Spirit is moving through her, to bring Jacob's last words to light. It is God's Will that this lass print his testimony."

Theodora sighed as she deferred to her husband. "I will alert Esther to thy presence. Come with me."

Lucy followed Theodora just as she had done the day before. As she moved through the great hall, she could see no evidence of mourning or death. No crepe silk hanging in the shuttered windows, no black cloth draped over mirrors. Although, Lucy supposed, Jacob and Esther had possessed no lavish decorations that needed to be subdued in honor of the dead.

As they moved toward the steps leading to the bedchambers

above, Theodora shut a door leading off to the drawing room, but not before Lucy caught a glimpse inside. Four or five people were all quietly assembled around the table.

Seeing this, Lucy felt her stomach lurch uncomfortably. Was this one of the Quakers' secret conventicles? What would Master Hargrave say if he knew what was going on here? Whatever would he say should the authorities break into the house and arrest them all under the Conventicle Act?

Sam and Theodora both glanced at her. Sam's eyes held a question, while Theodora's held a clear warning. The presence of these people might explain Theodora's earlier reluctance to let Lucy enter the house.

Lucy pretended she had not noticed the meeting, which she was sure was illicit. To calm her escorts a bit, she asked, "Is Mrs. Whitby upstairs, then?"

"Esther is still sleeping. We will bring you to the others," Theodora replied, her voice still tense as they mounted the stairs. After bringing them to the door of Jacob's bedchamber, she continued down the hall toward Esther's chamber.

All thoughts of the conventicle flew out of Lucy's mind as she and Sam entered Jacob's bedchamber. An eerie sense of repetition washed over her as she looked about. As on the day before, Jacob's still form occupied the great bed in the middle of the room, again with several mourners seated around him. The room was more crowded, though, with four mourners she recognized and three others she did not know.

Gervase was there, in the same chair he'd occupied the day before, and Deborah was again perched on the wood stool by the fire. Sarah was there, too, sitting on a chair next to Joan, across from where she'd sat yesterday. She had looked up with a sorrowful and perhaps resigned expression when Lucy entered the room. She did not seem angry, though, which was good.

Lucy nodded at Sarah, trying to convey that she would not share what Jacob had told her. To her disappointment, Sarah looked away, and Lucy felt a strange sense of isolation.

This sense only heightened when Sam edged out of the room, disappearing down the same stairs they had just mounted. For a moment, Lucy just stood there, wishing Sam had done more to explain her presence, particularly when one of the women whom she did not recognize eyed her garb suspiciously. Lucy began to feel very conscious of the blue ribbon attached to her cap, the bright scarf around her neck, and the brooch that secured her cloak together. Fortunately, they could not see her fine Sunday dress, and she twisted her feet inward so that they would not notice her nice shoes.

Spying the same bench she had occupied yesterday, Lucy crossed the room and sat down in silence. Looking around, she felt shut out of a circle she could not see. The mourning had created an intimacy among them that she could not enter. Indeed, by thrusting her way into their presence, Lucy felt she had violated that closeness.

Trying to avoid the gaze of the others, Lucy could not keep her eyes from flickering to Jacob's corpse. Since she had last seen him, someone had crossed Jacob's arms and shut his tortured eyes. Lucy could see that his clothes had been changed, too, but they did not look particularly fine; indeed, the clothes he wore looked homespun and a bit cheap. A far cry from the burying suit that even poorer families could usually muster, and unrecognizable to a family of Jacob Whitby's ilk. What had happened to his fine clothes? Apparently not even a single scrap of cloth remained from his former gentry life.

This meant there would be no Sunday burial for him, of that Lucy was certain. Most likely, his corpse would remain in the bed for several days, until his neighbors and friends had finished paying their respects. At that point, Lucy suspected, the Quakers would have the corpse carted off to Bunhill Fields, just north of London. There, it would be buried alongside other deceased nonconformists in the unofficial and unsanctified graveyard known commonly as Tindall's Burying Ground.

Lucy sighed. So far, she knew a great deal about Jacob's death, but next to nothing about his life. As quietly as she could, she pulled out a jar of ink and a slightly crumpled sheet of paper from her small sack. Expectantly she waited, quill in hand, for someone to speak of Jacob's life.

Except no one did. For the next twenty minutes, the mourners only made utterances when the Spirit moved them, lamenting in strange bursts of tears and incomprehensible murmurings. At one point, Deborah sang a snatch of song and Gervase laughed deeply, as though someone had spoken an uproarious jest. Nothing occurred, though, as wild or as exultant as the day before, for which Lucy was secretly grateful.

However, the longer Lucy sat, the more uncomfortable she felt. What if no one ever spoke about Jacob's life? What if no one ever said anything useful? Could she ask a question? She did not want to anger the Quakers by interrupting their mourning, but she was rather afraid of returning to Master Aubrey without anything to show for her afternoon away.

She was about to speak when at last she caught Sarah's eye. To her surprise, Sarah seemed to understand her dilemma and unexpectedly decided to help her out.

"I have been moved by the Lord to speak," Sarah said loudly. A few people looked up, startled by the break in the stillness. Others continued to keep their heads bowed in prayer. "I am moved to give testimony about the life of Jacob Whitby. Let us speak, so that our friend here, Lucy Campion, might record our words, and be faithful to how his life is rendered in print. It was Jacob's own dying request that his words be recorded that has brought Lucy here today."

The heads turned toward Lucy, and she gestured weakly with her quill. Her presence finally explained, she seemed to be accepted by the other Quakers.

Sarah then went on to speak about how she had met Jacob, and their early friendship, Lucy scratching furiously the whole time. Truth be told, she could not write all that easily, as a quill had come to her hand long after she was a child, but she hoped her memory would help fill in any gaps later.

After about five minutes, Sarah looked around the room. "I bid thee, Friends, to speak thy pieces as well. I should like to know how my friend became instilled with the love and life of the Lord. How he moved from being a young man of raucous pleasures to a man with a most devoted and serious spirit. The answers to these questions, I beseech thee."

She looked at the middle-aged woman sitting on the bench at the foot of Jacob's bed. "Sister Katherine?"

The woman nodded. She was the one who had regarded Lucy with suspicion when she first walked in. "Yes, I will speak. My name is Katherine Barnes, and this is my husband, Devin." She pointed at the middle-aged man who was standing by the wardrobe. Like Gervase and Sam, he had not removed his hat. "I can share the story of how Jacob converted, which he told Devin and me when we first met, some fifteen months ago." Katherine then proceeded to relate much of the same tale Jacob had told Lucy before he died.

"Had he already been married then?" Lucy asked, looking over what she had just scrawled.

"No, he and Esther were married just last year. They met after the great sickness, he told me. Her family had passed, I expect. A good man he was," Katherine explained. "He even set aside funds for us to travel. Some of us went to Malta and even Turkey a few months back, and he believed enough in our convictions to help us on our journeys.

"That was before his family cut him off," Gervase explained. "He told me once that when he was a youth, full of folly, he was vain and capricious. Yet he was accepted as their natural son, a reflection of his father's worth." His jaw tightened. "Once he had been warmed in the Light of Christ, he was treated most unnaturally by his parents, forsaken and forgotten. Ah, 'tis the most cruel irony."

Katherine's husband spoke up. "As sure as my name is Devin Barnes, I can tell thee that Jacob Whitby did right by me. That is why my wife and I are here to honor his life today. I know that he had been selling off all his possessions to raise money for the rest of us. He would have given them all away, otherwise." He gulped. "Jacob Whitby was a good man."

Theodora and Esther entered the room then. Devin looked at Jacob's widow. "He had wanted to raise money for all of us who'd been in cast into jail. That's what he did. Raise money for widows and orphans. His generosity kept my wife, and the babe she held in her arms, with food on our table."

"I thank thee for thy wondrous testimony concerning my dear husband," Esther said to Devin. Her smile was both sad and grateful. She looked at Lucy. "Sister Theodora told me that thou hadst returned."

"Your husband seems to have been a very generous man," Lucy said, indicating her hastily written script. "Devoted to helping others."

"Oh, how the Light of God flowed through him!" Joan said. "He did petition the king and Parliament, in our name. We must not forget how the Spirit moved him, and we must continue as the Lord wishes."

The woman in white began to sway and croon softly again, and Lucy could make no sense of her words.

"She is Ahivah," Deborah whispered. "My aunt. She likens herself to the Old Testament prophet, the one who warned Jeroboam that his lost kingdom would soon be restored. She foretold the return of King Charles seven years ago. The king called her his 'Woman in White.' That is why she still wears white today. Hoping he will recall her and her 'strange prophecy.'"

Was there a hint of scorn in Deborah's voice? Lucy noticed the other Quakers were starting to frown, although Ahivah paid her no attention.

"Hush, child," Joan said, a warning in her voice.

"Sister Joan, I assure *thee*," Deborah said, a slight emphasis on the plain-speech address, "I am being moved by the Lord to speak."

From the corner, Sarah spoke, trying to change the direction of the conversation. "Sister Esther, Lucy was just asking how thou met Jacob. I'm afraid I had lost touch with Jacob before the plague struck, and had only just heard that he had become a Friend at a recent meeting. How did thou and he meet? I should very much like to know, so long as it does not distress thee overly much."

"Very well," Esther said, settling down in the embroidered chair closest to her husband's corpse. "I was working with a tailor when the great plague struck. He and the rest of the family died. I can tell thee, 'twas a terrible time that I do not care to recall."

Around the room there were small murmurs. Everyone had lost someone during the plague. Lucy glanced at Sarah. Sarah's own mother had succumbed to the great sickness during that dreadful time, as had many of their neighbors.

Esther continued, "The tailor had left me the shop in his will, being that he saw all his other kin around him pass into the embrace of the Lord."

"Was that the Beetners?" Deborah asked. "I think I remember Jacob saying so."

Drawing a great breath, Esther put her hand to her heart. "Yes, the Beetners," she said. "A Dutch family, they were. Good people. I was with them for several years. Went into service with them when I was a lass. My mother, a seamstress, had done piecework, so I'd learned at her knee. My father worked for a mill, delivering the pieces, bringing the wool to women like my mother."

"They left you their livelihood?" Lucy asked. "You must have been a good and loyal servant." She was thinking of Master Hargrave, how he had given her so much when she left his service. He'd even offered her his wife's clothes, which surely would have set her up nicely had she taken them.

Esther lowered her eyes. "Yes, I was fond of them, and I believe they returned the sentiment. I managed on my own for a while, but few were buying woven cloths, so the business dried up. I sold what I could, and it was then that I met Jacob. I was but the daughter of a miller's man, but my dear husband never held my lower birth against me," Esther said, blowing her nose into a linen square.

"Oh, what a good man he was," Deborah said, starting to weep, too. She pulled out an embroidered handkerchief, dabbing at her eyes before spreading the cloth across her skirts to dry.

Lucy could not help but notice the handkerchief, thinking it was rather ornate for a Quaker. It was adorned by an intricate pattern of leaves and flowers along the border. Within the bower she could see a lengthy phrase worked in a delicate script.

"How lovely," Lucy said, pointing at the handkerchief, hoping to distract the woman from her sorrow. "Did you embroider it yourself?"

An odd, almost smug look crossed Deborah's features. "A remnant from before I became a Quaker," she said, holding out the linen for Lucy to examine. "I know that such frippery is not the Quaker way."

"She clasped a little posy, a posy full of grace," Lucy read. "Oh, I remember that tune." Under her breath, she hummed the first few notes as the song from her childhood came to her mind. Beside her Theodora coughed, and Lucy stopped abruptly, feeling a bit embarrassed.

"Thou shouldst burn that cloth," Esther said, all but wagging her finger at Deborah. In a more gentle tone she added, "Best embrace the Lord and leave your worldly goods behind, as he would wish." The other women nodded.

"I keep it for the memory of my earlier days," Deborah explained, dabbing her eyes again. "My mother crafted this cloth for me when I was still a child. Before she died of the galloping sickness."

"In time, you will learn, my child," Joan said, with a kind smile. "Such frippery simply does not matter to those who follow the Light of God. But for now, I think no one minds that thou dost hold something so dear, kept close to thy heart."

Sarah turned back to Esther, seeming impatient at the interruption. "Thou wert just about to tell us how thou met thy husband."

Esther smiled sadly. "When Jacob met me, he said there was no other woman in the world he could love more than me."

Lucy noticed Sarah stiffen. "Had you already become a Quaker then?" Lucy asked hastily so no one would notice Sarah's expression.

"No, my dear Jacob had already been called. He was so very glad when my conscience brought me to the cause of the Friends as well."

"Is that when you met everyone here?" Lucy asked. *Or are some of these people strangers to you?* she wanted to add.

"This piece isn't about me, is it?" the widow asked. "'Tis about my dear husband, is it not?"

"Oh yes, of course." Lucy looked around the room. The other Quakers were also looking at her a bit distrustfully. "I'm just interested in how Quakers became Quakers," she stammered, "when they decided to, er, leave the church." She thought her answer sounded lame to her own ears, but to her surprise, the Quakers now looked approving.

"Is it thy wish to know more about the Friends?" Joan asked kindly. "About our calling?"

Sarah jumped in then. "Alas, Lucy must return to her work now. Perhaps another time."

As they stood up to go, Esther looked straight at Lucy with her shining violet eyes. "My dear Jacob. He had already become a Quaker, and it was he who convinced me of my wayward ways, of the path that I needed to take. Not so long after, we got married in the Quaker way. He announced our intent to wed in every public spot. I felt he was very pleased indeed to marry me." She smiled at the memory.

As Lucy wrote down the words, she wondered what a Quaker wedding would be like. No trappings, no finery, that was for sure.

"Oh, thou art confused," she said to Lucy, correctly reading her thoughts. "Naturally, we Quakers do not post banns. Instead we openly declare our love and fidelity where the public may hear of our betrothal—in the markets, by the shops, and even before a church, though we do not share their conviction. Jacob took my hands and said, 'This, my Friend Esther, until death.'" She began to weep, and the women in the room rushed to attend to her.

After a short spell, Esther wiped her eyes. "I was ever so grateful to be welcomed into thy loving fold," she said, fluttering her hand to include the women gathered around her.

Joan looked up at Lucy. "Thou art welcome here anytime, child. Perhaps thou wilt find what thou art seeking with us." For a second she paused and looked at Theodora, who puckered her lips. "If thou art able to join us, we will be meeting at our Devonshire house in two days' time, near Bunhill Fields. If thy conscience so bids, thou art very welcome. Our vigil here will be done, and we will bury our brother Jacob. At nine o'clock in the morning."

"Th-thank you," Lucy stammered, startled by the invitation. Before she could say more, Sarah bundled her out of the room.

Only when they reached the street did Sarah speak. "The Quakers do like to proselytize, Lucy. A little longer, and they'd have converted thee. I could not have that on my conscience."

"I thought Quakers expect people to follow their own conscience," Lucy replied carefully. "So it could not be on your conscience, should I choose to follow mine."

Sarah looked at her in surprise. "Lucy, I always forget how intelligent thou art. I suppose all that time listening to my tutors from behind the curtains—yes, I knew thou wert there—helped thee develop thy intellect. What I meant was that I do believe it would verily kill my father should thou join the Friends, too. And Adam would be none too happy either, I should think."

"Miss Sarah, I mean, just Sarah," she said, letting the comment about Adam pass. She never knew how to speak of the delicate subject. "There is one other thing about what Mr. Whitby told me, before he died of his affliction."

Sarah looked at her suspiciously. "Lucy, I cannot bear to hear those wild accusations again. Pray do not tell me more."

"No, no, it's not that," Lucy said hastily. "It's just that Mr. Whitby told me that he wanted his sister to know he'd been thinking of her when he died. He'd been on his way to see her, you know, when he was struck by the cart. I think he had hoped to make amends to his family."

"Oh, I didn't know that!" Sarah said, looking stricken. "How awful! I wonder now if anyone even told them he died?"

"I'm sure they were informed, by a constable or some other official," Lucy said reassuringly. "Perhaps, though, they'd like to see you. As a gesture of your family friendship."

Sarah shook her head sadly. "I do not think the Whitbys would want to see me. I will ask Adam to go, on our family's behalf. He said he would like to have his midday meal with me. We've scarcely spoken since I arrived home." She sighed. "I won't lie. I dread spending time with Father and Adam. I've spent enough time around judges and courts. I was even brought to trial myself."

"Sarah!" Lucy exclaimed. "Were *you* tried? In the New World?"

Sarah grimaced. "You must not tell Father. But yes, I was tried in court. In the Massachusetts Bay Colony."

"What happened?" Lucy asked, her mouth agape, trying to imagine it all to no avail.

"Joan and I were both hauled to court for speaking the Truth.

Found guilty. I was put in stocks and pelted with rotten food for thirty minutes. Then they released me. Joan was whipped first and left there for four hours, since that was her second offense."

"How dreadful!" Lucy gasped.

Sarah's laugh, a hollow mirthless sound, made Lucy wince. "It could have been worse. I could have been tarred and feathered. Or even branded with a hot iron. All in the name of order and justice. Whatever would Father have said? Maybe I should tell him. He will no doubt think I received the punishment I deserve."

There it was again. That bitterness toward her father.

"I think," Lucy said carefully, "your father would have been unhappy if he knew you'd been punished in such a way. Not just because you are his daughter. I've seen him speak out against such punishments for Quakers."

Sarah's eyes welled with tears, which she angrily brushed away. "Perhaps," she said.

Seeing that Sarah had no more inclination to talk, Lucy bid her farewell and headed back to Fleet Street and Master Aubrey's shop.

·6·

"Which woodcut shall I use?" Lucy muttered to herself as she looked at each of the wooden blocks in turn. Master Aubrey and Lach were both out selling, and she had been left to finish composing a single-sheet ballad about a monstrous birth in Leicester. As was common, they would use the same images over and over, so long as there was some tenuous connection to the tale at hand.

As she was trying to decide, Adam unexpectedly strode into the printer's shop, his dark blue eyes crinkling when he saw her. "Good afternoon, Lucy."

"Oh, Adam, I am so glad you are here," Lucy said, returning his smile. She held out two woodcuts for him to inspect. "Do you think we should use this woodcut of a witch giving birth to a monster? Or this one, of the devil singing to a baby?"

Adam took them both, taking his charge importantly. "Oh, the devil, to be sure!"

"What brings you here today?" she asked.

His manner turned serious. Setting the woodcuts back on the table, Adam grasped Lucy's hands gently in his own. She noted that the hand he had injured last November seemed to be completely healed. As on his face, though, there was still a scar from the shrapnel that had struck him when a gun had exploded unexpectedly. She knew that sometimes his injuries still ached a bit, but today he seemed to be without pain. Still, his face was sorrowful.

"Sarah told me that Jacob Whitby has passed," he said. "That you'd been with him at the last." From his tone she could tell that Sarah had not shared Jacob's wild accusation with him. Perhaps that was better, for now.

"I am so sorry, Adam. I know Mr. Whitby's passing must be difficult for you."

"Yes. Certainly. His death is a great loss," Adam said, shifting uncomfortably. Reluctantly, he dropped Lucy's hands. "He was a young man. Newly married. Not yet a father. He died before his time, that's the truth."

"He said to me, as he was dying, that—" She hesitated, trying to decide how much to say. "That he was your friend, though he had not spoken to you in a long time. Was it because he . . . ?" She did not finish her thought, but Adam seemed to understand.

"Because he had become a Quaker? No. To be honest, from what Sarah told me, he became a better man." He looked uncomfortable.

"He said that he regretted a disagreement that the two of you had?"

Now there was definitely something odd about Adam's demeanor. He looked guilty, almost.

"What is it?" She searched his face, noting how tired he looked. Working at the Fire Court, taking the testimony of witnesses, was surely taking its toll.

He ran his hand through his dark hair. "I do not wish to discuss it. Not right now." He changed the subject. "Sarah also said that Jacob had a message for his sister. To be conveyed by you." He looked at her questioningly.

"It's a simple enough message," she said. "You could easily deliver it on my behalf. Wait, why are you smiling?" Adam was grinning at her fondly again. "Oh, I see. A chambermaid ought not to be bidding her former master to deliver her messages." There was a time she would have flushed at the seeming impropriety of such a thing, but now she just grinned back impudently.

"I can only think of how changed you are," he said before a shadow returned to his eyes. "I should like you to accompany me to the Whitbys' home. Deliver the message yourself. Besides, Sarah said Master Aubrey has asked you to add to Jacob's story. What better way than to speak to his family?"

Lucy hesitated, feeling conflicted. Sarah had pleaded with her to say nothing about Jacob's dying accusation. But Jacob had made her promise that she would bring Adam to see his sister.

Remembering the man's tortured face and horribly twisted body, Lucy nodded. "I will speak to Master Aubrey. I think he will allow me to leave at half past four, since we will have little enough daylight left. So long as the typesetting is done and I've set a pot on the stove for supper, I think he will be pleased that I have finished this *Monstrous Birth*."

Indeed, just past four o'clock, as the shadows lengthened around them, Lucy and Adam walked to the home of Jacob Whitby's sister. As she had imagined, Master Aubrey had consented to her request, although he had mopped the sweat from his ruddy head a few times while he listened to her, a slightly confused expression on his face. After all, he'd already given her leave to see Jacob Whitby's wife yesterday, after church. She could almost guess his thinking, having thumbed through *The Apprentice's Duty to His Master.* Where in that lengthy pamphlet did it say that an apprentice could be given such freedoms twice in as many days? Nowhere, that was certain. Only when she said that she was going at the special request of the Hargraves did he finally just wave his hand at her. "Go!" he'd said, half exasperated, half befuddled. That's when it came in handy that she was not a full-fledged apprentice.

Now Adam gave her a sidelong glance. "I noticed that you are not wearing the bracelet I gave you for your birthday," he said. Lucy could hear the note of disappointment in his voice. "Did it not fit? Or—" He paused, searching her eyes. "Do you not still like it?"

Her hand flew guiltily to her wrist, for she knew full well that the bracelet was in a lovely wooden box on a shelf in her bedchamber. "Oh, Adam! It is a beautiful bracelet," she said hurriedly. "I . . . I treasure it, I do."

"Why then do you not wear it?" he asked. "It looked beautiful on you. It pleases me when you wear it."

"Oh!" She swallowed. He could be so gallant. "I just worry that it will catch in the press when we are pressing the paper across the type, or that I will lose it when I am tending the porridge, or that it will catch the eye of a filcher when I am out selling or—" She broke off, then repeated what she had said before. "It is not because I do not treasure it."

Or you, she almost added. How could she explain how often she had fallen asleep, holding the bracelet in her hand or pressed against her heart? But, truth be told, he could not have given her a less practical gift. "I would wear it on my day off, except . . ."

Again she trailed off. Unlike women of Adam's circle, who seemed to live more leisurely lives, her time away from the printer's shop consisted of attending church, or visiting Annie and Cook at the Hargraves, or on occasion walking to Lambeth, where her mother lived. In the past, she'd even used her rare mornings or afternoons off to investigate something curious, a trait that both baffled and amused him. There were no elegant dances or masques or even fancy dinners for her to attend that would require her to don a more luxurious style of dress. That he did not, could not, truly understand that a silver bracelet did not belong in her everyday life endeared him to her, even though it also tore at her heart.

Lucy's attention was diverted, though, when they turned the corner onto Chancery Street. A simple glance told her straightaway where Jacob Whitby's family lived. Rush matting had been laid in the street in front of the house, to dull the sound of the horses clip-clopping as they passed the house. There was no doubt that a family member had recently died.

Nervously, Lucy stood beside Adam as he knocked on the front door. A young servant with red-rimmed eyes opened it. "Yes, sir?" she said to Adam with a quick bob, having correctly identified him as a member of the gentry.

"We are here to see Miss Julia Whitby, if you would," Adam replied. Lucy smiled inwardly at his courteous manner with the young girl.

The maid opened her mouth and then shut it again soundlessly, looking rather like a fish. Adam and Lucy exchanged a glance. It was a bit surprising that the Whitbys had employed such a dull-witted servant, especially one who would be charged with answering the front door. They might have been calling a little later than was common, but surely the family was not yet sitting down for supper.

"Is something wrong?" Lucy asked the girl kindly. "I know the family has recently suffered a loss. That is why we are here. We should very much like to pay our respects to Miss Julia Whitby and her parents."

"Miss Whitby's not here," the servant said, her eyes darting about wildly. "And no one knows where she is! Been missing since Saturday, she has!"

"Oh, dear!" Lucy cried. "Has the constable been summoned?"

"Indeed he has," called a familiar Yorkshire voice from within the drawing room. "He is here!"

"Constable Duncan!" Lucy said, unable to keep from smiling when she saw the red-coated soldier come stand behind the maid. Like Adam, Jeb Duncan was just a few years older than herself, having been made a constable at a fairly young age. She had first met the constable three years ago, when he had brought news of a terrible murder to the magistrate's household, when she was still employed as a chambermaid. After Duncan arrested someone she loved for the crime, her feelings toward him had been far less friendly than they were now. However, their paths had crossed once again, just after the Great Fire, and she helped him right a terrible injustice. Since then, something subtle and unspoken had changed between them. Comments he had made here and there, looks he had given her, had made her heart beat a little faster, even though she tried to put them out of her mind, being unsure of her own feelings toward him.

Right now, the constable wore a quizzical look on his face. She felt, rather than saw, Adam stiffen beside her. He did not appreciate the constable's interest in Lucy, which had become more apparent in recent months.

"The question, of course, is what are *you* doing here, Lucy?" Duncan asked. His eyes flicked toward Adam, nodding slightly. "Mr. Hargrave."

Adam nodded in return. "Constable."

Lucy glanced at Adam. "We're here to pay our respects to Miss Julia Whitby. Her brother, Jacob, was just killed in a terrible accident."

"Yes, I heard about his death. Rotten luck." The constable was still looking at Lucy, clearly trying to make sense of her presence in the household. "Is Miss Julia Whitby an acquaintance of yours, Lucy?"

At his tone, Lucy flushed slightly. Although he sounded

more surprised than disrespectful, the insinuation was clear. *Why are you* here, *Lucy? Former servants do not call on the friends of their employers, and certainly do not make condolence calls with members of the gentry.*

Adam spoke then. "Lucy was with Jacob Whitby when he died. He asked her to bring a message for Jacob's sister."

"What? I just knew it," the constable muttered, putting his hand to his head. He gestured to the maid to leave. The girl scurried out without another glance. "Pray tell me, Lucy. Under what possible circumstances were you with that man when he died?"

"He had asked for Miss Sarah, Adam's sister. The magistrate asked me to accompany her, as he was not comfortable letting his daughter attend a sickbed alone," Lucy said. She thought about saying more but decided against it. It still did not seem to be the right time to say anything about Jacob Whitby's claim that he had been deliberately pushed in front of the cart. "Please, what happened to Julia Whitby?" she asked. "The maid said she was missing."

Constable Duncan rubbed his eyes in a tired way. "'Tis the damndest thing," he said quietly so that his voice would not carry. "She seems to have taken off just after she was informed of her brother's death. The maid said she fell into a great state, throwing clothes into a satchel, running this way and that. She left this note, before heading off to hire a hackney."

He held the letter open for them to read. Unlike most servants, Lucy had learned to read fairly well, a skill that now helped her at the printer's. *"Mother, Father,"* she read out loud, squinting a bit. "Her writing is very ill indeed. She must have been writing very hastily. *Pray do not worry*," she continued. "*I am going to stay with Elizabeth Wiggins, to help her through her confinement. I will mourn my brother there. I will send you a note when I have arrived safely. Your loving daughter, Julia.*"

"That seems straightforward enough," Adam said. Lucy nodded, equally puzzled.

"Except that her parents sent a note around to Mrs. Wiggins. She'd not seen Julia Whitby, nor had she asked her to visit," the constable replied. "Now she is missing."

"Perhaps she's run off? Eloped?" Adam asked.

The constable shook his head. "There was no indication of a romance, although I can't rule that out completely. It is the timing that strikes me as strange. That she would run off so soon after the news of her brother's death. Could a daughter be so heartless as to leave her mother when she needs her most?"

"It is strange," Lucy said slowly. "She must have been very afraid, to leave so suddenly."

Both men looked at her. "Afraid?" Adam asked. He took a step closer to Lucy. "Afraid of what? Do you know something more than what you've already said?"

"Jacob told me something before he died," Lucy whispered. "I am sorry I did not tell you."

"What did he tell you? Something about his sister?" Constable Duncan asked, his gaze sharpening. Adam was frowning slightly.

"Yes. No. Not exactly." Lucy replied reluctantly. She looked at the constable. "Mr. Whitby claimed that his pending death was no accident. He said he'd been pushed deliberately in front of that horse. Someone wanted him dead."

They both stared at her. "Did he know who pushed him?" Adam asked.

Lucy shook his head. "He wasn't sure. He had received an urgent letter from his sister, Julia, though, bidding him to come see her. That's where he was going when he was struck by the cart. He said that I needed to speak with her. He said she might know something more about who had pushed him, and why."

She stopped at that point. To protect Sarah, she just could not bring herself to share the other thing Jacob had said—that the impostor might be among the Quakers.

They didn't seem to have noticed the abrupt end to her explanation. The constable clicked his tongue. "Assuming it was no accident, and that he had been targeted, it is likely that he knew his killer. A business acquaintance, perhaps? An enemy of some sort? His wife? He was married, you say?"

"Yes, he was," Lucy said. She thought about how distraught Jacob Whitby had been, thinking that the killer might be in their community. "He was very concerned about his wife. He told me that he was worried she might be in danger, too."

Adam mused, "I could look into his will. Perhaps the bequests will shed light on who may have wanted him dead."

Lucy thought about the sparseness of Jacob Whitby's house, feeling doubtful. "Jacob seemed to have given most of their possessions away," she said. "Do you think that we might be able to speak to his parents for a spell?"

Constable Duncan frowned. "They have not been very forthcoming, at least not with me, I'm afraid. Mrs. Whitby, Julia's mother, had just sent for me before her husband came home. She is convinced that her daughter has been abducted, so I came here to look into the matter. Now her husband claims the girl ran off of her own volition, and he wants nothing more to do with her. I was about to leave when you came." He frowned. "Now, of course, I have to wonder, given what you've just told me." He jerked his head at Adam. "I suppose with him at your side they'll talk to you."

Adam looked angry, but Lucy put her hand on his arm. "Well, Adam is an old friend of Jacob Whitby's. I should think they would." She beckoned to the maid, who had just stepped back into the room. "Pray, take us to your mistress. Tell her that Mr. Adam Hargrave wishes to pay his respects."

Lucy and Adam were ushered into a luxurious drawing room. As was the custom when someone died, the great mirror hanging above a long side table had been draped with a black cloth. The silver candlesticks on the mantel, as well as the silver platter on the table, had been similarly draped. Lucy's mother had done the same thing when her father died. "Keep the evil spirits away," her mother had insisted. "They come to us when we mourn the dead, and use the mirrors to reflect their way into our homes." Master Hargrave had never put stock in such notions, of course, so they had not upheld such traditions when his wife and other members of the household had died.

Adam and Lucy waited in a tense silence. He and the constable always rubbed each other the wrong way, she had noticed. Neither seemed like himself when around the other. Adam grew stiffer and more clipped, making him seem arrogant, which did nothing to endear him to the constable. For his part, Duncan became resentful, although he remained outwardly respectful in his words and tone. To make matters worse, she knew that neither man trusted the other's intentions toward her.

Lucy could not worry about that now, though. Looking around at the elegant furniture, she wondered if she should sit. Seeing that Adam had remained standing, she did the same. She gazed at the large family portrait above the hearth. A father staring sternly down at them, with his wife beside him. A young woman stood behind him, and a younger boy, maybe around twelve, stared in admiration at his father, a sword at his side. Lucy looked closer. The boy looked like a younger version of Jacob. Lucy wondered if the girl might be his sister, Julia.

The maid reopened the door, ushering in an older woman and man, whom Lucy took to be the Whitbys. The woman wore a full mourning dress and clearly had been weeping. The man looked somber, but his wool suit was gray rather than black.

As Adam stepped forward, the woman gracefully extended both her hands in greeting. "Adam," she murmured. "We're so pleased to see you."

Adam bowed his head. "And I you, Mrs. Whitby."

Mr. Whitby clasped his hand. "How ever is your father faring? We've not seen the magistrate in a long time. Not since before the Fire, that is certain. Perhaps even since the plague."

"He is well," Adam paused. "We wish to convey our deepest sorrow for your loss. I considered Jacob a friend, and he shall be missed."

Tears sprang to Mrs. Whitby's eyes, and she gave Adam a grateful smile. Mr. Whitby coughed. "Yes," he spoke gruffly. "Thank you."

Lucy shifted her feet, the movement drawing her to the attention of the Whitbys. They both studied her curiously, scrutinizing her clothes, clearly trying to determine her station.

"This is Lucy Campion," Adam said. "She is"—he hesitated—"a friend of our family."

"Indeed?" Both the Whitbys looked at her more closely. Lucy straightened under their gaze, hoping neither would notice the spots of ink that had splattered on her dress or the mud crusted along the bottom hem.

"She is also here to pay her respects," Adam continued. "Lucy was with your son when he passed and—"

Mr. Whitby's face grew purple. "Did you bring a wretched godless Quaker into my house?" he asked Adam through clenched teeth.

"No, sir, no, sir!" Lucy exclaimed. "I'm not a Quaker but—" She broke off, looking helplessly at Adam.

"My sister, Sarah, is a member of their community," he said. "She received word that Jacob was dying, and Lucy was kind enough to accompany her. They were both at his side when he died."

The Whitbys stared at Adam. "You have not cast off your sister?" Mr. Whitby exclaimed. "You allow her to be with this godless sort? To travel about with them? She is no more than a fallen woman!"

Seeing that Adam had been shocked into silence by Mr. Whitby's base accusation, Lucy stood up. "Your son, Jacob, was a loving man who was devoted to God." She steadied her voice, which had become shaky with indignant tears. "As he died, the last words he spoke were about the love he had for you and your daughter, his sister. That is why we came here today. To tell you that."

Mrs. Whitby began to weep a bit. "Oh, my dear Jacob. He was always a good son."

"He begged me, in his last dying breath, to tell his sister what I have just told you." Lucy took a deep breath so she would not lose her courage. "Do you know where your daughter may have gone?"

"Probably ran off to those damned Quakers!" her father said angrily. "I have now cast her off, as I have done my son. Let God judge them as he will." With that, he angrily whipped the black wool off the platter and threw it on the floor before stalking out, slamming the door behind him.

Adam and Lucy looked at each other and then back at the woman, who was now weeping uncontrollably into her hands. "Do not judge us! I did not forsake my son. I always made sure his tithes to the church were paid! I did all I could to keep him from jail, even though he told me not to do so. And now he's dead! Never to return! Who is God judging? Us or him?" She sank into a chair, visibly trying to control herself. Without looking up, she whispered, "Forgive me, I must lie down."

Crossing the room, Lucy opened the door. As she had hoped, the young servant was in the corridor. Whether she was eavesdropping, Lucy could not say for sure, but she could see the girl's cheeks had turned a bit pink.

"Ho there," Lucy called to her. "Your mistress needs assistance. Come here."

"Yes, miss," the servant said, walking over.

Lucy had to suppress a little smile. Who would have thought that she, a former chambermaid, would ever be giving orders in such a fancy household. "What is your name?"

The servant gave her a little bob. "Evie, miss."

"Evie, I will help you take your mistress to her chamber. Quietly," she added. "No need to alarm the master. It's clear that she's exhausted and unwell. A spot of sleep is just what she needs."

Evie looked at her mistress nervously. Jacob Whitby's mother was now shaking and rocking back and forth. She was clearly distressed. "Right, miss."

"I'll be back straightaway," Lucy said to Adam, giving him a meaningful glance "I will just help settle Mrs. Whitby down a bit."

He raised an eyebrow. "Take your time," he answered. "I'll be right here. If Mr. Whitby leaves his study, I'll do my best to forestall him." The message was clear. *I will keep him busy so you can do whatever you need to do upstairs.*

"Thank you," Lucy said, tucking her hand firmly under Mrs. Whitby's arm. "Let me help you, mistress."

Obediently, Mrs. Whitby stood up, leaning heavily on Lucy.

"This way," Evie said.

Slowly, Lucy and Mrs. Whitby followed Evie up the stairs to the floor above. As they walked down the corridor, Lucy noticed three other closed doors. Evie opened the one on the end.

"This is the mistress's bedchamber," she said. The two women helped Mrs. Whitby lie back on the bed, and then Evie took off her shoes while Lucy loosened her hair from its bun.

After pulling a blanket over the shaking woman, Lucy knelt

down beside her. A sharp memory overcame her, remembering how she had taken care of her own mistress, before the black sickness had taken her to an early grave.

Gently, she touched Mrs. Whitby's forehead, smoothing the long black and gray hairs from her face. How terrible it must have been for her, to have her daughter disappear on the same day her son was in a fatal accident.

"Mrs. Whitby," Lucy whispered, "I do not think your daughter has joined the Quakers."

Mrs. Whitby looked up at her, her listless eyes showing some hope. "You do not?"

"No," Lucy said, then hurriedly continued, before the woman would think to ask her more questions. "Is there someone else, another friend, who your daughter would have run to, should she have felt afraid? Perhaps she just said she was going to see Mrs. Wiggins but then changed her mind." She paused, trying to think of a way to ask the next question delicately. "Perhaps there was someone else . . . ?"

Mrs. Whitby looked around the room. "Evie," she said in a weak voice, "I should like to take the sleeping draught that the physician made for me." She pointed to a corked vial on a table next to her bed. "Please bring me some rosemary tea, to which I may add a few drops of this bitter stuff."

Evie bobbed a quick curtsy. "Yes, ma'am." She looked at Lucy. "Shall I lead you out, miss?"

Mrs. Whitby stirred. "No, no. She can stay with me until you return."

"Very good, ma'am. I will return in a few minutes with your tea."

Evie left, shutting the door behind her.

Mrs. Whitby sat up. To Lucy's surprise, she reached for the vial and took two quick gulps. "I do not mind the bitter," she said, hiccupping.

"Oh, ma'am!" Lucy cried. "That was quite a lot at once! If the physician said only a few drops, then—"

"Bah," Mrs. Whitby said. "The sooner I can forget, the better." A tear slipped down her face; she brushed it away impatiently.

"You were asking about my daughter. I do not know, truly," she said, sniffing. "Julia never had many close friends. Being a spinster . . . it wasn't her fault. Her father and I had hopes. She was betrothed twice . . ." Mrs. Whitby's voice trailed off. "The first man died of the galloping sickness. We all quite liked him, so it was a bit of a blow. When he died, her bloom began to fade, and her prospects grew slim. We were beginning to despair, until the son of one of my husband's friends offered for her."

Mrs. Whitby's eyes were looking in an unfocused way toward the ceiling. From her next words, Lucy thought she might have forgotten to whom she was talking. "He broke off the engagement even though the banns had been read. Found out about Jacob. His family would not stand for such heresy."

She moaned. Before Lucy could stop her, Mrs. Whitby lifted the vial to her lips again and took another quick swallow. "Oh, why did Jacob take up with those awful Quakers?" she lamented. "He made it worse for her! We were all but shunned ourselves! No one would speak to us! That is why his father cut him off, hoping that her engagement would be resumed. But the damage had been done!" She let out a little sob.

Lucy waited, feeling helpless, until she continued. "We were so hopeful when Julia renewed her childhood friendship with Elizabeth Wiggins. Well, she was still Miss Stirredge then, before she married Mr. Wiggins of Bishopsgate. She gave our daughter an *entrée* back into society. For a while we hoped—" She rubbed furiously at her eyes. "Unfortunately, after Mrs. Wiggins married and moved away, well, I am afraid invitations for Julia dried up." Mrs. Whitby turned her head to look at Lucy, although her eyes were growing more dilated. "Oh, where could she be? She must be with Elizabeth!"

"I thought the constable said they'd inquired at the Wiggins home. He said no one had seen her," Lucy said.

"Well, perhaps she is having a bit of fun with us. She must be there. She used to hide when she was a little girl, whenever she was upset or angry. She could be very naughty that way."

"Was she upset or angry, then?" Lucy asked casually.

Mrs. Whitby's voice was growing softer. "I know she was angry at her father for cutting off Jacob."

"That happened a while ago," Lucy said. "Was there something else she was upset or angry about?"

"What else could it have been?" Mrs. Whitby asked, turning onto her side, clutching a small lace-trimmed pillow to her chest. "Oh, what shall I do? I cannot very well send the constable after my daughter. I do not know what I was thinking when I sent for him in the first place. My husband is right. What must people think? Her reputation will be ruined if this gets out."

She clutched at Lucy's hand, looking up at her. "Could you go see Mrs. Wiggins? See for yourself if my daughter is there?" Her voice began to sound more slurred. "I do not know you, but

Jacob seems to have trusted you. I know, too, that Adam Hargrave was his friend, and I trust him."

She looked beseechingly at Lucy. "Please. Help me find my daughter. Bring her back to me. Lord knows she was a burden, but she's all I have now that Jacob is dead." Her voice breaking on the last word, she turned back toward the wall.

Lucy waited. In less than fifteen seconds, she heard Mrs. Whitby begin to snore, the sleeping draught having clearly done its duty.

After pulling the shutters closed, Lucy tiptoed out of the room. Evie appeared then, holding the tea.

"She is already asleep," Lucy whispered. "She took several swallows of the draught already. I think you should watch over her, to make sure she is all right."

"Whatever am I supposed to do?" Evie wailed. "I don't know how to take care of her! She's not in her right mind now, is she?"

"Your mistress has suffered a great loss. Her daughter's disappearance has only worsened her pain and stress," Lucy said. She continued in the same low voice, even though she was fairly certain that no one was around to hear her. "What do you think happened to Miss Julia Whitby? Did she run off with someone?"

The maid rolled her eyes and for the first time ventured a cocky grin. "Her? Not bloody likely. Not too comely and had a tart tongue when she wanted. I heard her talking to herself sometimes." Lucy noticed a doubtful look on her face. "And yet—" she started to say, before recalling herself. 'Twas unseemly to gossip about her employers in such a fashion, particularly with a stranger.

Although she wanted to press the girl further, Lucy instead sought to pretend she hadn't been paying much attention, hoping to reassure the girl that she'd committed no indiscretion. "Such a big house," Lucy commented, trying to ease the girl back into a pleasant conversation. "Are these all bedchambers?"

Evie relaxed, and her face lost its stricken look. "Yes, that one is the master's other chamber, and that one we use for guests. I think it used to be Jacob's, when he lived here. That one there is Miss Julia's." She pointed to a door at the very end of the hallway. "This, of course, is the privy."

"Oh!" Lucy said. Lowering her voice again, she said, "Would you mind? I've been holding my stream for some time. No need to wait. I can show myself out." When the servant hesitated, Lucy added in a firmer tone, "You must go in with Mrs. Whitby now."

"Yes, miss," Evie said. "I will." She turned and scurried back into the bedchamber they had just left, shutting the door behind her. Lucy found herself alone in the corridor, exactly as she had hoped.

·7·

After Lucy quickly used the privy, she opened the door a crack and peered down the corridor. No one seemed to be about, and Mrs. Whitby's bedchamber door was still shut. Saying a quick prayer, Lucy stole over to Miss Julia's door. After pausing to listen for any sounds, she stole inside.

The room was cold and dark without a fire in the grate. Lucy could see a slight light streaming through the shutters. Fortunately the sun had not descended into evening. Carefully she opened up one of the shutters so she could see the room more clearly. Besides the bed, there was a small table with a candle and a Bible, a large chest, another table with another mirror draped in black wool, a few shelves along the wall, and a small chair. Swiftly, she started at Julia's lace-covered dressing table, opening her small jewelry boxes fearfully. Her heart was pounding. If she were caught in here she'd be thrown in jail for certain.

There could be no reason for her to be in Julia Whitby's private chambers. Even her friendship with the constable could not save her.

She opened the walnut wardrobe and ran her fingers thoughtfully along Julia's dresses. They were fine, to be sure, but had been indifferently maintained, unlike her mother's immaculate mourning costume. She shut the door.

Next, she peered into the large chest by the bed, which seemed to contain mostly blankets. She didn't know what she was looking for exactly, except that she knew she was looking for some hint of the information that Julia Whitby had wanted to pass on to her brother.

Her eyes fell on a small wooden chest on the lowest shelf. Kneeling beside it, she opened it. Inside, she found a few scarves, ribbons, and the like. Moving those items aside, she uncovered two packets of letters, each tied in string. One appeared to be correspondence she had received from her friend Elizabeth Wiggins, née Stirredge. The other packet seemed to be letters she had received from her brother.

Still straining to hear any sound from the hall, Lucy untied Jacob's letters. A glance at the dates told her they had been written in the last few months, but she couldn't take the time to read them properly. She bit her lip. Then, without thinking, she thrust them into her bodice, where they could be concealed until she had more time to peruse them carefully.

Her heart pounding painfully now, she was about to close the chest when she saw that the green silk lining was bumpy and mussed, as if something had been thrust underneath it. Holding her breath, she carefully peeled back the lining.

There she discovered a few more papers all oddly creased and bunched up. The first two appeared to be Quaker tracts, one titled *A Lamentable Warning to London and Its Inhabitants*, published by Elizabeth Calvert at the Bull and Mouth, and the other was Humphrey Smith's *Vision for London,* a popular tract sold by many printers. Atop each title someone had handwritten the word "Behold!"

Lucy was familiar with one of the tracts, Smith's *Vision for London,* having peddled it for Master Aubrey herself. Because of its prophetic nature, describing how London and its sinners would be burnt up, yet printed several years before the Great Fire, the *Vision for London* was a piece that had been reprinted several times. When she used to peddle it, one fanciful passage had always struck her, and she found herself whispering the words from memory:

"All the tall buildings fell, and it consumed all the lofty things therein, and the fire searched out all the hidden places, and burned most in the secret places."

More prophetic words have scarcely been spoken. Indeed, she had learned for herself a secret that the Great Fire had so vividly exposed. The other tract she was not familiar with, but it appeared to be a standard warning to the citizens of London.

Lucy turned her attention to the third paper, which was a penciled sketch of some skill. A gentleman dressed in what looked to be a fine suit lay on the ground, propped up awkwardly against a grand column. His face was turned away, but his eyes were closed. A vizard, of the type worn at fancy masquerades, rested by one of his outstretched hands. Beside that, a goblet lay overturned, as though the man had spent a good night tippling the spirits. Though roughly drawn, there was real artistry there in the simple lines of the man's form.

Lucy was about to refold the drawing and place it with the Quaker tracts when she noticed a line that had been added in rough script at the bottom. *This is the dandy I told you about. Set upon and killed.*

Her eyes flew back to the image. With a start, she could see now that the man had a knife inserted deep in his abdomen, so that only the hilt was visible to the viewer. Initially the hilt had looked to be part of his ornate coat, which was why she missed it when she first examined the image.

Shocked, Lucy nearly let the small chest slip onto the wooden floor but regained herself in time. She wrestled with whether to take the picture or to leave it where she had found it. The packet of letters was already chafing against her skin, an uncomfortable reminder of her theft. Truly, what difference would taking one more piece of paper make? "In for a penny, in for a pound," she whispered to herself with a shrug, slipping the folded sketch inside her bodice. "I'll replace them later," she told herself. Although how she would do that, she didn't rightly know.

After replacing the chest on the shelf, Lucy eased open the door and peeked out. No one was in the corridor, so she stole out of the room and back down the stairs.

She found Adam still waiting where she had left. "I am ready," she said, and together they left the Whitbys' home.

She was not surprised when outside Constable Duncan rejoined them as well. He seemed to have been loitering at the end of the street, clearly waiting for them to leave the Whitbys'.

"Did you learn anything more?" Adam asked her. Turning to the constable, he added, "Lucy was kind enough to help Mrs. Whitby upstairs after the madness overcame her." His tone was amused.

The letters were now painfully rubbing against her. She wanted to tell Adam and the constable about what she had discovered, but truth be told, even the thought of telling them about this rash theft made her cheeks flame. She knew neither man would take kindly to her little theft. *Best be prudent,* she warned herself. *I will read through the letters first.* No point in telling anyone about her transgression unless she discovered in them some news to share.

Still, she could not help wondering. Why had Julia Whitby possessed those tracts? Had someone—perhaps her brother—given them to her to read? Seeing Mr. Whitby's angry response to the Quakers, it was obvious why she would have kept such pieces away from his eyes. But why keep them at all?

She realized both men were looking at her, waiting for her to reply to Adam's query.

Gulping, she spoke quickly. "Mrs. Whitby thinks her daughter is hiding at Mrs. Wiggins's," she said. "Or else that she has run off with the Quakers. Although I told her that seemed unlikely. Thankfully she didn't ask me why I thought so."

The constable looked up at the rapidly darkening sky. "I cannot make inquiries now, that's for certain." Stopping, he said to Lucy, "Perhaps Master Aubrey would not mind you selling out in Bishopsgate? I could come by for you around nine o'clock tomorrow morning. Is it not on Tuesdays when you make your longer journeys?"

Before Lucy could reply, Adam broke in. "Constable," he said, clearly irritated, "why ever would you expect Lucy to accompany *you* on such an investigation?"

Constable Duncan smirked slightly. "This is Lucy we're talking about." He turned to Lucy. "Tell me you weren't thinking of making this inquiry on your own."

Feeling slightly abashed, Lucy nodded. Indeed, she'd been thinking about how she could speak to Mistress Wiggins that very minute.

"Just so," the constable said, squaring his shoulders. "I think you would agree that Lucy should not go to this house unaccompanied."

Adam straightened up. "Well, that may be so. As it happens, I was planning to make the inquiries myself. I will accompany Lucy."

Lucy looked at him in surprise. He had not indicated anything of the sort when they were in the Whitbys' home.

Adam went on. "Indeed, I am sure that Jacob's mother would expect no less of me, as an old family friend." His emphasis on the last few words seemed deliberate.

"Are you not expected at the Fire Court in the morning?" the constable asked. His manner had once again grown stiff.

Adam looked slightly defeated. "Yes, I am. I thought I could see the Wiggins family afterward. But," he said, "I suppose we would not want to delay so long." Looking pointedly at Duncan, he added, "Good night, Constable."

Still smirking, Duncan saluted them with an exaggerated military gesture and strode off to the makeshift jail on Fleet Street where he'd lived since the Great Fire.

Lucy and Adam continued on to Master Aubrey's shop. The sky was darkening rapidly, although a few kind souls had put lanterns in their windows to assist those who dared venture out after nightfall.

As they walked, Adam drew her hand into the crook of his arm, carefully steering her around a steaming pile of manure in the road. She looked up at him, admiring the clean lines of his face.

He looked down at her, smiling slightly. "So you do not mind taking this journey with the constable?" His tone was gentle, not accusing. "I know he was glad enough to accompany you."

Mrs. Whitby's sorrowful face flashed into her mind. "I do not mind being with the constable," she said, without realizing how it might sound to Adam.

At his silence, she glanced up at him and saw that he had lost his earlier smile. Hurriedly, she sought to explain. "I mean, it is the least I can do for Jacob Whitby and his mother."

He frowned now. "Lucy," he said, "why do you suppose Jacob Whitby wanted to speak to me specifically?"

"You and he were good friends, were you not?" Lucy asked, not following. He seemed a bit perturbed.

"Well, that's just it," he replied. "Jacob and I were never very good friends. I knew him at Cambridge. He dined with us on a few occasions, too, although that may have been before you entered my father's employ. He and I"—he paused—"enjoyed different sorts of amusements. Indeed, we nearly came to blows once."

Lucy gave him a quick measured glance. "Over Sarah?" she guessed.

Adam frowned. "Yes. Do you remember how my sister was? A bit flighty? Impetuous? Do not mistake me. Jacob was never a bad man, but I did not like his interest in my sister." He shook his head. "I never dreamed he would become a Quaker. Of course, I still find it hard to believe that Sarah became a Quaker."

"You believe in their cause, though," Lucy said. "I remember that you wrote several petitions to the king and Parliament in the Quakers' defense."

"Yes, because I do not believe men and women should be persecuted for their religious beliefs. That is different than supporting their faith or the actions they take on behalf of their faith."

"Maybe that is why Jacob wanted to see you. He knows you've been a friend to their cause. Perhaps he wanted to make amends."

"Perhaps." But Adam did not seem convinced. Having reached Master Aubrey's shop, they turned to each other. Gazing down at her, he brushed away a strand of her brown hair that had come loose from her cap. She thought for a moment he might forget they were on a public street and kiss her. But honor and decorum won out.

"Be careful, Lucy" was all he said before walking off toward home.

At nine o'clock that evening, after she had finished cleaning all the pots from supper and had tidied up the workroom, Lucy finally was able to retire to her bedchamber. Closing the door behind her, she pulled out the packet of Jacob's letters she'd hidden under her straw pallet. Sitting at the table, a thin wax taper at her side, she carefully untied the string around the packet. There were six letters altogether, three that were dated, three that were not. All were in that same educated hand that reminded her of how the magistrate and Adam fashioned script.

In the first one, Jacob must have been writing shortly after he became a Quaker and was repudiated by his father. *Dearest sister,* he wrote, *I cannot tell thee how thoroughly thy letter did give me hope and comfort. It gives me great pleasure to know that thou hast survived the plague and returned to London, safe from harm. I do not understand why our father has forsaken me, but I know now to seek solace in the Lord and to be nourished by the Inner Light that resides within us all.*

It went on like this at great length, ending with a great flourish. *Thy Loving Brother, Jacob.* A quick read of the second letter revealed much of the same sentiment, describing how he exulted in the love of Christ, and then spoke of meeting George Fox, the founder of the Friends. The third letter was different in tone. Jacob seemed more despairing. *I thank thee, dearest sister, for trying to arrange reconciliation with our father. It is enough to know that we shall be reunited in heaven one day. Please, Julia, thou must ask Mother to stop paying tithes to the church on my behalf. It makes the other Quakers doubt my conviction, and I feel I must share in the same imprisonments as the others. If I do not have my faith, and the companionship of those who share my convictions, then I have nothing else.*

The next letter she read more slowly, a familiar name having caught her eye. This letter seemed more buoyant. Toward the end he described, with great rapture, a woman whom he had recently met. *Her name is Esther Grace,* he wrote, *and as her name suggests, she has transformed me, helped me regain what I believed I had lost. It may seem rather fantastical to say, but she has woven a spell—not of magic, but of God's love—over me, which I shall not likely recover from soon.* The letter continued in this vein for a few more sentences before his customary signature.

The fifth letter was the most ebullient by far. He and Esther Grace had gotten married. *By her suggestion, we moved to the house in which I have been living. We have talked about selling everything and starting our life together, maybe even in the New World. I should hate to leave thee. I would very much like for thee and my sweet Esther to meet.*

In the sixth letter, he seemed a bit sad, even apologetic. *I am sorry that Esther was unable to meet with thee. I should very much have liked her to make thy acquaintance. She was moved by the Lord to speak at the Devonshire Meeting. The movement of the Lord within us cannot be verily understood. I myself have been moved by the Lord to rid myself of my last possessions.*

Thoughtfully, Lucy retied the string around the letters. Unfolding the sketch, she stared at the dead man resting against the column. She could not keep herself from whispering aloud the words that had been scrawled at the bottom of the sketch. *"This is the dandy I told you about. Set upon and killed."*

Even as she blew out the candle and climbed into her bed, her thoughts continued to swirl. Who was this man? Where had he been killed? Who had killed him? And perhaps most unsettling of all: Who had sent this message to Julia Whitby— and why?

·8·

Hang on. Let me sell here for a b-bit," Lucy said to the constable the next morning, trying to keep her teeth from chattering. Although it was early March, it was still one of the coldest days she could recall. Certainly, no spring in sight. She and Duncan were still a ways from Bishopsgate, but they'd come to a small market where people were peddling spices, soaps, and baskets. She had stopped in a spot that gave them some protection from the bitter chill, since no innkeeper would let her hawk her wares inside his establishment.

Not giving the constable a chance to disagree, Lucy began to rifle through her pack for a few pieces that she knew would sell easily.

"The Constable Cozened!" she read aloud before hastily stuffing it back in her pack, hoping Duncan had not heard the title.

Glancing at another, she groaned. "*The Cuckolded Constable!*" She looked at another, her mortification growing. "*The Constable's Cod-Piece!* Lach!" She swore. "I am going to kill him!"

Constable Duncan peered at the pieces with a wry smile. "I take it that Aubrey's *other* devil packed your sack? I suspect these kinds of merriments are to his liking."

She rolled her eyes. "I was still typesetting another piece, and Lach offered to put my sack together. He said he'd put in some that always sold well." Sheepishly, she added, "These *do* sell well."

"Especially if I'm nearby? I suppose that's what he wanted. Perhaps I should stand here slack-jawed and stupid, so I can truly play the role of—what is it?" He looked at one of the penny pieces. "*The 'Confounded' Constable?*"

Lucy grinned. It was true that Lach had little admiration for the constable, or most authorities, for that matter. "If you wouldn't mind."

For the next thirty minutes, the constable watched her sell the pieces, but from a goodly distance away. Finally, when Lucy felt her sack had been significantly lightened, they were able to move. When they reached the Wiggins house in Bishopsgate a short while later, Lucy carefully hid her pack in a low hedge. It wouldn't help to have the Wigginses question her presence at their door before she'd even had a chance to explain.

A smiling maid answered the door, returning shortly to the drawing room with Mrs. Wiggins, heavy into her confinement.

"My maid said you have a message for me?" Mrs. Wiggins asked.

Duncan stepped forward. "Not exactly. The message is for your friend Julia Whitby. Your mother thought she might be here."

To Lucy's dismay, Mrs. Wiggins paled and sank down in a soft cloth-covered chair. "Are you all right, mistress?" Lucy asked. "May I get you some water, or some other refreshment? Do you need assistance?"

The woman waved her hand, then dropped it onto her bulging belly. "No, I'll be fine. I just felt a wave of dizziness. The baby is very active today." She flushed slightly, with a glance at Duncan. Respectable women were not supposed to discuss their condition, especially in the presence of men.

"I remember my wife's confinement," Duncan said unexpectedly. "Resting a short spell would often help her."

Lucy stared at him. She'd never heard the constable speak of a wife or child. When he met her gaze, his face was expressionless. She could not tell what he was thinking.

Anxiously, Lucy and Duncan waited in silence. When Mrs. Wiggins finally took a deep breath, her face had resumed a more healthy color. "I'm so sorry to tell you that I haven't seen my dear friend Julia Whitby in quite some time. I was ever so puzzled when I received that urgent message from her parents. I did send a reply with the same messenger, saying I had not seen her, nor, truth be told, had I invited her to stay with me." She looked from Lucy to Duncan. "What is going on? Why did her mother think she would be here?"

As she spoke, Lucy watched Mrs. Wiggins closely. The woman seemed genuinely anguished. She hated to distress her further, but she thought the woman might be able to shed some light on Julia Whitby's disappearance.

"I'm afraid Miss Whitby has fled her parents' home," Lucy said quietly. "She left a letter saying that she was planning to stay with you."

Tears welled in Mrs. Wiggins's eyes. "I wish she had come to me." She ran her hand along a porcelain vase on a low table next to her chair. "I knew something was bothering her, you see. I wanted to come and see her, but—" She waved expansively again toward her belly.

Duncan nodded. "Why do you think something was bothering her?" he asked.

"Because she wrote me a letter. I received it just three days ago, by messenger."

The same day Julia had summoned her brother to come see her, Lucy thought. The same day her brother was struck by the cart.

Mrs. Wiggins continued. "She was concerned about her brother, but she would not say why."

"Because—" Lucy began before Duncan cut her off.

"Because he was a Quaker?" Duncan asked blandly, darting a quick warning glance at Lucy.

Mrs. Wiggins didn't see their exchange. She was still gazing sadly at the vase. "No, I do not think so. Something else."

"Do you have the letter now?" Lucy asked. She knew that in many families, letters were passed from hand to hand, often until they were far gone from the intended recipient's keeping. Some people, though, would use the extra paper for kindling, particularly in this cold winter.

To Lucy's relief, Mrs. Wiggins nodded. "I do have it. I shall fetch it."

When she returned with the letter, she handed it to the constable. Lucy could not resist peering over his arm to read the message as well.

"*Dearest Elizabeth,*" Lucy read out loud, "*I so long to see you, not the least because of your—* What are those words?" She squinted, trying to make out Julia Whitby's script, which was hurried and difficult to read.

The constable continued where Lucy had left off. "*Not the least because of your confinement. I hope you are well and in good spirits. I should very much like to see you, but I fear I have some business I must attend to first.*" He broke off. "Madam, are you all right?"

Mrs. Wiggins had closed her eyes. "Yes. Pray, continue."

"*Something has occurred, however, that I should not like to detail for you, given your present delicate condition. Suffice it to say, I am very concerned for my brother*"—here Lucy and the constable exchanged a glance before Duncan continued—"*and there is something pressing I must address. I pray you do not go into your travail before this unfortunate matter is resolved, for I should very much like to join you in your lying-in. Yours truly, etc., Julia Whitby.*"

Duncan handed the letter back to her. "You have no idea about the matter to which she was referring?"

Mrs. Wiggins shook her head. "No, I wish I did. That's how Julia was, even when we were children. Always on the secretive side. That was just her nature." She placed the letter inside her bodice, beneath the ecru scarf that crisscrossed her chest. She patted the seat next to her. "Pray, sit."

"So you must have known her brother, Jacob, then?" Lucy

asked, sitting gingerly beside her. Duncan gave her a look before he stepped out of the room. *He must want to look around, to
see for himself whether Julia Whitby was on the premises,* Lucy thought.
She turned back to Mrs. Wiggins. "You grew up together?"
she prompted.

Mrs. Wiggins rubbed her extended belly. "Yes, but I didn't
know him all that well. He was a few years younger than us,
had his own tutors, went to Cambridge, and so on. I couldn't
have had more than half a dozen conversations with him in all
the time I knew him. He was a little on the wild side, as most
men are when they are young." She lowered her voice, looking a
bit mischievous. "Especially those university sorts. Not that we
ladies are supposed to know of such things."

Lucy paused. Although she had been about to ask Mrs.
Wiggins another question, her words died on her lips as she
pondered what the woman had just said. She'd heard enough
bawdy tales about the scholars and tutors at Cambridge and
Oxford to know that most did not comport themselves as they
did in the company of ladies. Not for the first time she wondered
how Adam had passed his time when not at his studies.

Duncan returned then, interrupting her thoughts. He seemed
ready to leave, and there seemed little else of importance to
learn from Mrs. Wiggins.

"Thank you for your time, Mrs. Wiggins," he said. "If you
do hear from Miss Whitby, will you please send me a note?" He
gave the location of his makeshift jail on Fleet Street before they
left. "And I will inform you, should we learn anything of her
whereabouts."

Once they were a few steps away from the Wiggins home, Lucy looked at Duncan expectantly. "Well?"

"Julia Whitby was not there, I am certain of that," the constable replied. "I talked to the servants—they had not seen her. I do not think she was hiding there, either."

"So she lied in the letter to her parents?" Lucy asked, shivering in the cold. "Where is she, then?"

Duncan shrugged. "Who knows? The question, of course, is whether Julia Whitby lied about where she was going and went somewhere else. Or did she truly intend to visit her friend and something—or someone—kept her from getting there?"

Since there was no answer to the question, they fell silent. As the bitter wind blew, instinctively they moved a bit closer together. Lucy's nose was running, and her feet were hurting a bit more than usual, another side effect of the cold. She could not help but look longingly at a covered hackney cab as it drove by.

"Can you imagine being able to hire a hack anytime you wanted?" she asked. "At any time, anywhere you needed to go? Maybe I would never walk anywhere again. What about you?"

Duncan scoffed. "I need to be on the ground to perform my duties. So I prefer walking to riding. As, I imagine, so do you. Or would you not still be a bookseller if you were rich enough to travel everywhere by hack?"

Lucy giggled. "I could just hire someone to push me about in one of those wheeled chairs. I could bid him to stop whenever I reached a street corner I liked."

Duncan glanced down at her, smiling slightly. "I could not see you in such a contraption. Or you could just marry well."

His hazel eyes grew suddenly intent. "Or perhaps if you marry, your husband will not want you to keep traversing the city, selling tracts."

"Oh, no, I love being a bookseller!" She gulped. "I do not think my husband, if I had a husband, would ask me to stop." Yet she knew that was not necessarily true.

"You know," Duncan said, "after my father left the army, he became a merchant and then married my mother. For many years she helped him, at first just managing the accounts, but later, when he grew ill, she took on much of the business herself. I always admired their partnership." He blinked and looked off.

Lucy wanted to touch his arm, but something kept her from doing so.

He looked back down at her. "A man is lucky indeed if he has a wife who brings some fortune into the marriage."

That reminded her of something he had said earlier. "Constable Duncan, were you—are you—married? I thought you were not, but you mentioned your wife's condition . . . ?" Her voice trailed off.

The look he gave her was inscrutable. "I am not married now, but I was."

Lucy looked down at the ground. His wife must have died, because a divorce was next to impossible for anyone to get. The Church was very clear on that point. She wondered if their child had died as well. "I'm sorry," she whispered.

"It was a long time ago. When I was still in York." He changed the subject. "I am ready for my noon meal."

Lucy nodded, having been hearing little complaints from her own stomach as well. They walked the rest of the way in silence.

When they neared the jail, Hank, the bellman, hailed the constable. He'd obviously been keeping an eye out for him. "A body has been found, sir," he said. He gestured to an older woman who had followed him out of the jail, a slight limp to her gait. "Found by this woman."

Perhaps in her sixties, the woman was dressed as a widow, in all blacks and grays, with not a frill to be found on her woolen cloak or dress. Her hood was drawn close to her face to ward off the chill, but the eyes that peered out were dark and unafraid as she regarded the constable and Lucy. Not a Quaker, Lucy decided. Friends would not voluntarily approach the authorities unless they wished to be cast into jail.

Taking in her stance, Lucy grimaced when she realized that the woman was gripping a bell in her left fist. A searcher! One of those fearful older women who spent their days searching and calling for the dead, all to make a few pennies on every body found. They would inform the local priests about any deaths that had occurred in their parish, whether from Divine Providence or from another's hand. "Bring out your dead!" they would call, ringing their bells. The parish priests would use the information to compile the weekly Bills of Mortality, to inform the public of all deaths that had occurred throughout London and its suburbs.

Though scarcely educated, and certainly with no medical

training, the searchers would nonetheless render judgment on the nature of death. "A necessary evil," Lucy had heard Dr. Larimer say once to Master Hargrave. "They would name every death consumption, should they find even a trace of spittle upon the victim's lips, for they know no other disease. But they dare traipse where a sane man would not go willingly."

During the plague the searchers were particularly ominous, as neighbors would watch closely to see who might be hiding bodies and how many had died in the house next door. Because there were so many deaths during that terrible time and city officials just wanted the corpses gone, the seekers were usually accompanied by rakers, who would cast the corpses into a cart, to be buried in unmarked mass graves in Houndsditch or burnt in the fields outside the city. As the death toll lessened, the number of searchers did, too, but there were still some about, checking on the dead bodies.

The bellman's next words confirmed her opinion. "She is a searcher. Sadie Burroughs, widow." In a lower voice, he said, "She did not want to speak to you, but I tried to keep her here so that you could talk to her."

Lucy winced when she caught wind of her. The woman frankly stank of something stale and horrid.

"Mrs. Burroughs, why bring your news here?" the constable asked, trying to hide his own grimace. "Your business is with the parish priest. We have no money to pay you."

"Ah." Mrs. Burroughs wagged her finger at the constable. "This body is different. A young woman, stabbed she was. Gentry, I'd reckon, from the quality of her dress."

"Where's the body?" Duncan asked, all trace of tiredness and hunger forgotten.

"Shire Lane."

Hearing this, Lucy felt a sinking feeling in her stomach. That street was not too far from where Julia Whitby had lived with her parents. "Mrs. Burroughs," she asked, "did this woman, this body, you found have light brown hair? Gray eyes?" She was imagining the portrait of Julia Whitby hanging in her parents' drawing room.

Narrowing her eyes, the searcher turned her whole attention toward Lucy. "Her hair was brown, from what I could see. As for her eyes, I could not say." She lowered her voice. "Not a pretty sight."

Lucy felt another lurch to her stomach. Before she could say even another word, Duncan turned to her. "No," he said. "You may not come." Gripping her arm, he spoke in a lowered voice. "I know what you are thinking, Lucy. But I also saw the family portrait. I know what Julia Whitby looks like. So do not even offer that as an excuse."

"That's fine," Lucy said, trying to disguise her annoyance at the constable's high-handed air.

"Why would the young lady wish to view a dead body?" Mrs. Burroughs asked, watching the exchange in interest. She barked a short mirthless laugh. "Seeing a corpse is hardly merriment at a fair."

"I know that!" Lucy said, feeling stung by the woman's comment.

"She is looking for someone who has disappeared," Duncan

said shortly. Seeking to mollify Lucy, he added, "I will send word to Master Aubrey's later."

Lucy turned away as Duncan walked off, a pace behind the searcher.

The rest of the afternoon, Lucy carried out her tasks in Master Aubrey's shop, setting letters, hanging papers, and other such chores. Lach tried to make fun of her once or twice, but when she ignored him, he stopped, looking at her in a puzzled way. She didn't know if she was angry or worried. Worried, she decided.

Around four o'clock, Lucy was preparing to shut up the shop when Duncan appeared in the entrance, looking weary. One look at his face and she knew what he had seen. "Was it Julia Whitby?" she whispered.

Duncan nodded, sinking down onto a wooden bench. "I am afraid so."

Master Aubrey came in then. "Constable? What brings you here?" With a jovial laugh, he added, "Got a murder for us?"

"Yes, he does," Lucy said in a small voice.

"Well"—Master Aubrey's voice gentled somewhat, taking in both their demeanors—"how about you tell us all about it over some ale? I've got a jug just over there. Lach, go pour the good man a mugful."

Frowning, the apprentice pulled out the jug. As he passed the mugs around, Lucy asked again breathlessly, "For certain, the body is Julia Whitby?"

Duncan nodded. "Yes, I'm afraid it was. Dr. Larimer said she'd been dead since yesterday at least."

"She didn't make it very far after she left her parents' house." Lucy took a deep breath. "How did she die? The searcher said she had been stabbed."

Duncan took a deep swig. "We found her just inside an empty establishment on Shire Lane. Yes, she'd been stabbed several times." Lucy waited. Duncan had always seemed fairly inured to the violence around him, and certainly he'd seen many dead bodies in his time. He seemed so protective, something truly unbearable must have occurred.

Without meeting her eyes, Duncan finished. "She was encased in a scold's bridle when she died. It had been affixed in such a way"—he swallowed—"that no one could hear her scream."

They all gasped. Lucy set down her mug, a shiver running over her. "A scold's bridle? What could that mean?"

Without thinking, Lach recited a bit of doggerel, probably from a ballad they had printed at the shop. *"Woman, woman, take your bridle! Best curb that tongue that speaks too idle!"*

At Lucy's glare, he fell silent, his grin fading.

"That bridle is meant to shame its wearer, that is for certain," Master Aubrey said.

Lucy agreed with him. There were many stories of women being forced by their husbands to wear the iron contraption as a punishment for nagging them. Usually this would happen behind closed doors, in the privacy of their own home. Sometimes magistrates would even order a woman to wear the mask publicly, usually standing in a public square to humiliate her. Only once, though, had Lucy ever seen a woman wearing one. She was being paraded through the streets as a warning to all those women who would gossip and tell tales. She winced at the terrible memory of the woman's mortification.

"Miss Whitby was not married. So not a nag," Lucy mused, still thinking about Lach's rhyme. "Was she full of idle talk?" She looked at the constable. "Both her mother and her friend, Mrs. Wiggins, called her a secretive, private person. Evie the servant said she heard her talking to herself sometimes. Said she had a 'tart tongue.'"

"Certainly, she knew something that she wanted to tell her brother," the constable reminded her. "Was it a coincidence that he was struck down before he could hear her message? I think not, given that she's also been murdered." He looked at her closely. "Lucy, tell me. Did Jacob say anything else before he died? Something you have not told us? Oh! I can see that is so! Tell me."

"I hadn't wanted to say anything because Sarah had asked me not to, but—"

"Yes?" Duncan asked. "Lucy, this is not the time to hold back."

"He said that his sister had told him, in the letter, that one of the Quakers was an impostor. But she didn't tell him who it was."

"An impostor?" The constable stood up and walked over to the door. "What did he mean?"

"I do not know. The ones I met all seem devoted to their faith."

"That tells me I need to learn more about these Quakers. I will speak to them tomorrow."

"You must not!" Lucy exclaimed. "They are so distrustful of the authorities. If you go in there asking questions, I know they will not speak to you at all." Seeing him frown, she knew she had gone too far. He did not like feeling limited in his investigations. "You have the right to do so, of course," she added hastily. "You could even haul them off to jail if you chose. But perhaps a lighter touch would help you get the information you need."

Duncan rapped his knuckles impatiently against the door. "What do you suggest?"

"I could talk to them again? See if I could learn anything more?"

Duncan looked down at her, considering her words. "Perhaps. You've certainly proved yourself to be very resourceful. Can you see a way in? A way that won't raise suspicion?"

"I was thinking I could go to a meeting, over at Devonshire," she said slowly. "I was, er, invited to attend the meeting at Jacob's funeral. I could take some tracts to share? While I make some general inquiries?" She glanced sidewise at Master Aubrey, who had a speculative look on his face. "If that is all right with you, sir."

"Oh, she thought to ask my permission, did she?" His words were jocular. Waving his hand he said, "Of course, why not? I have some of those last dying testimonials they always like to trade. Mind you, don't give them away. I want coin or kind." Something about his jovial manner made her look at him more suspiciously. She didn't think the printer was being sarcastic, but there was a gleam in his eye that she couldn't help notice.

"Of course, sir," she said. She turned back to the constable, who gave her a terse look.

"Don't put yourself into any danger," he warned. His hand on the door, he leaned in closer to her. "Just talk to them. See

what you can learn. Do not give any details about Julia Whitby's death. For heaven's sake, don't let anyone know that you are
making inquiries on my behalf."

A sudden shock of guilt coursed through her. "Constable?"

"Yes, Lucy?"

"Please wait. I have something to show you." She ran upstairs
to her chamber, returning a few minutes later. The constable
was still standing by the door.

Mutely, she handed him the packet of Jacob's letters and the
sketch she had discovered in Julia Whitby's bedchamber.

He glanced at them, his eyes widening. "Where did you get
these?"

Her head hanging a bit, she told him how she had acquired
the pieces. "I don't know if they mean anything, but in light of
Miss Whitby's death, perhaps you can find sense in them."

Crossing his arms, he regarded her with a scowl, then stepped
outside into the wintry sleet.

As she closed the door behind him, Master Aubrey stood up,
rubbing his hands gleefully. "So we've stumbled upon another
mystery, have we? I can see it now! *A True and Terrible Account
of a Scolded Scold*? Or perhaps, more simply, *The Scold's Last Scold*?"
His manner grew brisk. "I'll need it written and set in three
days."

Lucy bit her lip. She thought of Julia's mother, weeping in
her bed. Would the true account add to her grief? Lay open the
details of their daughter's murder?

Then a different memory came into her mind. Jacob Whitby,
pleading with Lucy to help him, trying to protect his wife even
as he lay gasping on his deathbed.

Surely Julia Whitby deserved more, too. It would seem that the scold's bridle had been used to punish her, perhaps because she had intended to tell her brother about who was the impostor among his acquaintance. Perhaps publishing the story of Julia's death would shake something out. Such a thing had happened before. She nodded at Master Aubrey. "Yes, I'll do it."

·9·

The next morning, Lucy pulled her cloak tight around herself as she hurried toward Chancery Lane. The cold was even more biting today than it had been the day before. She had convinced Master Aubrey that it would be worthwhile to sell down by the Fire Court, although now she had to wonder how many people would be outside and in a buying mood. Regardless, she had filled her pack carefully. She had included pieces about the Great Fire, of course, such as *The London Miscellany* and *From the Charred Remains,* two pieces that Lucy had helped put together in her first few months working with Master Aubrey. She had also brought along a few murder ballads, and the last dying speeches of three criminals, since those would be of interest to a court-going crowd.

As she turned down the lane, Clifford's Inn—one of the original Inns of the Chancery—loomed before her, a somewhat ominous vestige of London's medieval past. Stopping short, Lucy took in the building's crumbling majesty, a bit fearful of its grace and beauty. The temporary Fire Court, she knew, was being held deep within the great stone walls. It had been sitting since the last few days of February, so only a handful of cases had been tried so far, although they expected many more in the upcoming months.

Few people were outside the building. The cold had likely driven everyone inside, Lucy decided. She watched a young man in clerical garb scurry past her, one hand holding his wool hat tightly to his head while the other hand tried unsuccessfully to keep his robes from flapping in the wind.

Since there was no sense trying to hawk outside, Lucy followed the man inside Clifford's Inn to the courtroom, taking a seat at the back of the room after a quick look around.

She noticed Adam right away, seated on a low stool near the front of the room. He would speak neither for the defendant nor for the plaintiff, he had told her, but for the "people." Sometimes he might be asked to stand before the judges and read testimony that he had earlier taken from a witness who did not currently reside in London or who was physically unable to attend the session. Other times he might take the testimony of witnesses under oath and help ensure that the verdicts were issued properly by the court clerk.

A sleepy-looking jury was seated on benches on the side of the room, situated in such a way that the jurors had a clear view of the proceedings without getting between the judges and the defendants.

A man with a white beard rang a bell, and a judge dressed

in full magisterial robes strode into the courtroom and seated himself on the elevated bench at the center of the court floor. Although Lucy had never met him, she knew it was Sir Matthew Hale, one of the three judges authorized by King Charles to preside over the trials. Unlike some justices of the peace, he was not one who had ever frequented the magistrate's supper table. She knew that the magistrate did not approve of the Fire Court, and indeed had turned down the invitation to serve. When she had asked Adam about it once, his answer had been terse: "Father believes that the Fire Court will subvert the law, rather than uphold it." Nor had the magistrate been pleased when his son agreed to help. Although Adam did not say much about it, she knew that it pained him to be on the outs with his father in this regard.

Lucy shifted on the hard wooden bench, peering between a row of heads and hats, to better glimpse the proceedings. The first case brought Elizabeth Purnell, a vintner's widow, to the stand. Her late husband, she claimed, had furnished wine on the king's account to the Prussian ambassador. "As my husband's beneficiary, I am due the payment of £600," she declared. After several questions from the judges and a few supporting documents, the case was decided in the widow's favor.

The next case concerned a young violinist, one of His Majesty's concert performers, who had seen his salary withheld for not playing at recent performances. "My violin was burnt in the Fire!" the young musician exclaimed, tears in his voice. "I've not been able to purchase a new instrument, particularly since my salary has been held in arrears." Again, after a few questions, the jury and the judge found for the plaintiff.

About an hour had passed before the court took a brief recess. Making her way toward Adam, she was gratified by the way his face lit up when he saw her. "Lucy, what are you doing here? It is freezing outside!"

"Master Aubrey thought I should sell some pieces before the sessions—and I wanted to see you. I have something to tell you."

He looked at his timepiece, a gift from his father. "We have about fifteen minutes before the sessions resume." He began to move down the corridor. "I have something to tell you, too."

As they walked, she smiled up at him. "Do you find it humorous that the Fire Court is being held in *Clifford's* Inn?" she asked, emphasizing the name. Not too long ago, they had met a man named Clifford who had not been a particularly honest fellow. "Is this inn an honest place?"

"One would hope," Adam replied with a chuckle. "This inn, I can assure you, stemmed from the more honorable line of the Cliffords." Then he frowned. "On the other hand, as you may have noticed, there has been much dishonesty since the Fire."

"Surely there is something you can do? Is that not the charge of the Fire Court?" Lucy asked.

"How do we keep people from lying, you mean?" Adam sighed. "'Tis difficult, to be sure. In the case of the musician, he was able to find the ruins of his violin where it had been lost. He was also the third member of the king's concert that we've heard from. There are eighteen more musicians who have made similar claims, and I suspect their trials will be equally quick when it is their turn to appear in court." He went on, "Sometimes when I take their testimony, as I ask them questions, I know they are embellishing the facts or even lying outright. Many people stole so much during the plague and the Fire, sometimes I wonder if the world will ever be righted."

Nodding, Lucy remembered then how during the plague she'd seen a servant who had served in a nearby household sneaking out a side window, garbed in her dying mistress's clothes, even as the rest of the family was being boarded up inside, in the futile hope of containing the plague. She touched his arm. "If anyone will help put the world to rights, it's you."

Adam smiled down at her. "Ah, Lucy." She thought he was about to say something else, but after looking at his pocketwatch again, he changed the subject. "We must talk quickly. First, I looked for Jacob Whitby's will, but I could not find one with the clerk. To be honest, it is not so surprising. He was a Quaker, and they certainly do not put much stock in the government. Besides, he was a young man and surely did not expect that he would—" He broke off, looking sad.

Lucy completed his thought. "Die."

"As his widow, Esther Whitby will be responsible for the legal settlement of his debts. Since they had no progeny, she will inherit everything."

"There is very little left, I imagine. He seems to have given everything to their widow's fund."

Adam nodded. "That makes sense." He looked at her closely. "Now, Lucy. Tell me, what brought you here? I can see that you have some news."

Taking a deep breath, Lucy relayed the news of Julia Whitby's murder.

Though Adam was visibly repulsed by the nature of the hideous act, he did not look altogether surprised. "I thought it likely," he said, sighing. "Does Sarah know?"

"I asked Annie to give her a note. I will see her tomorrow, though. I was invited to attend Jacob Whitby's burial at Bunhill Fields," Lucy explained. "I intend to go."

"Why?" Adam asked. "Did Sarah ask you to accompany her?"

"No, the other Quakers did. I think they are hoping to convince me of their ways." Seeing a momentary worry in Adam's eyes, she smiled. "Do not worry. I have no plans to become a Quaker." She paused. "Adam, there is something that I did not tell you. Before he died, Mr. Whitby told me that his sister was concerned that one of their acquaintances was not truly a Quaker. That he or she was an impostor. I know he had been afraid for his wife's safety."

"What!" Adam exclaimed. When a few people in the corridor turned to stare at them, he lowered his voice. "Why did you not tell me this before?"

"Sarah begged me not to," she said. "She was concerned that you or your father would not allow her to commune with the Quakers if you knew the truth."

"Well, she was right!" Adam said grimly. "If Jacob believed his wife was in danger, then Sarah may well be in harm's way, too. I shall tell Father at once."

"No, Adam, please do not!" she exclaimed. "Sarah has chosen to be a Quaker. I know that you and your father are not pleased with that fact, but this is the life she has chosen. She might be pushed into a step no one wants her to take."

"She might go off with them again," Adam conceded. "Which I do believe would be a great blow to Father."

"And this time, she might not return." She hurried on. "I was thinking that we might be able to discover which Quaker is the impostor," she restated, trying to come back to the heart of the matter.

"Why would *you* make such inquiries, Lucy?" he demanded. "Would this not be better pursued by the constable? May I remind you that it is *his* job to make such inquiries, not yours?"

"The Quakers will not talk to him. Not as they would speak to me. But we must learn all we can about Jacob Whitby, and his sister, too."

Adam sighed. "I suppose that is so. Promise me that you will not make such inquiries alone."

Seeing his dark look, she added, "I was not going to attend the burial alone, of course."

"Who will accompany you? The constable, I suppose?" He looked at her intently.

"I am fairly certain that the constable is the last person who should attend one of the Quakers' meetings." When he didn't laugh at her little jest, she touched his arm again. "I imagine Sarah will be there. I can have Lach accompany me, too."

He moved closer to her. "It's cold outside," he said, pulling the hood of her cloak over her head. Somewhere a bell rang, and reluctantly he stepped back as people began to move past them, back into the courtroom. "Stay warm," he said before walking back inside.

———

Indeed, the bitter freeze continued throughout the rest of the day and into the morning of Jacob Whitby's burial. Lucy had not ventured outside since she first returned from the Fire Court, nearly frostbitten. Master Aubrey had taken one look at her and ordered her to sit by the fire with hot stones in her stockings for a full hour, until she was able to walk properly. "Not too useful to have apprentices with fingers and toes blackened and falling off from the cold," he had muttered. Lach and Lucy were both shocked, too, when Master Aubrey allowed them to have a good fire going the whole time, although he never stopped grumbling about the dear price of coal. Thus, they had spent the rest of the day indoors, printing, cutting, and folding, trying to ignore the terrible wind that blew fiercely at their shuttered windows and heavily latched doors. Lucy was beginning to think they would never be allowed outside again.

Thankfully, though, on the morning of Jacob Whitby's funeral, Master Aubrey changed his mind. "All right, lass," he said to her. "Stop fiddling with the press and get your pack ready for trading." He looked at Lach. "You, too. Take a second pack to trade."

Within the hour, Lucy had set off, accompanied by a mule-faced Lach, each carrying a sack of religious pamphlets and tracts. In the bitter cold, every step of the two-mile walk from Master Aubrey's shop to Bunhill Fields was torturous. Eerie shimmering icicles hung treacherously from the trees, and the wind whipped at them cruelly.

"Don't know why I had to go," the printer's devil kept muttering. "Like as not we'll be thrown into jail, taken for Quackers."

Lucy would not admit it, but she felt glad of his company,

especially when they reached the end of Grub Street and arrived at the large frozen field. From the Quakers' directions, she knew that the meetinghouse had to be near.

Uncertainly, Lucy looked around. They seemed to have stumbled upon one of the great Tudor estates built outside the city walls that had long ago fallen into disuse and disrepair. In the distance she could see a manor house, with some other ramshackle buildings. Only one seemed to be in use, for she could make out a distant trail of smoke whispering from the chimney. For the first time she wished she had asked a few more questions of Joan and Theodora before heading out here.

Lach gave her his usual mocking stare. "Meeting in a barn, are we? I'm sure the stained-glass windows are *lovely*." Naturally, then, he began to hum another bit of doggerel called "The Four-Legg'd Quaker." As instructed he was singing it to the "Tune of the Dog and Elder's Maid."

"In Horsely Fields near Colchester,
A Quaker would turn Trooper;
He caught a Foal and mounted her (O base!)
Below the Crupper."

Lucy elbowed him. "Shhh," she whispered. "They might hear you!"

"Ah, there's no one around," he said and, to her chagrin, continued the ridiculous ballad more loudly now.

"Though they salute not in the Street
Because they are our Masters

'Tis now Revealed why Quakers meet
In Meadows, woods, and pastures—

"Hey, ouch! What did you do that for?"

Lucy had elbowed him hard, pointing at a figure moving toward them.

"Oh, Lucy," Sarah exclaimed, pushing her woolen cap back from her face. Lucy could see her eyes were troubled. "How dreadful, that news about Jacob's sister. I was shocked when I received thy note. I did not know her. Although our brothers were friends, she and I were not acquainted." She paused. "Dost thou think her murder was connected to Jacob's death? Is dear Esther in danger? I must go to her! Has she arrived?" She started to move toward one of the outlying buildings.

"Wait, Sarah, please!" Lucy exclaimed. "Jacob told me he was concerned for his wife, but that he didn't know who the impostor was. What if she confides in the wrong person?"

Sarah looked thoughtful. "I suppose thou might be right. Still, I owe it to Jacob to make sure that his widow is kept safe from harm." Sarah looked at them curiously. "Why didst thou come here today, Lucy?" she asked. "Do not tell me that thy conscience has called thee and thy fellow *devil* to worship. Want to be a Quaker, do you?" She said the last to Lach, looking at him with the semblance of a smile.

"I'm no Quacker!" Lach said hotly. "Indeed, Master Aubrey sent us. Thought we could trade a few godly tracts and the like."

"Oh! I see," Sarah replied. "I don't know if the Quaker printers are here." A distant look crossed her face. "They need to bury Jacob first."

"I know," Lucy said softly, touching Sarah's arm. "That was why I wanted to come today."

The sound of hoofbeats caused them to look up. A cart, led by a single roan horse, had arrived. "Mrs. Whitby is here," Lucy said softly, recognizing the figures.

Esther Whitby was seated in the cart, with Joan beside her. Sam Leighton walked alongside the horse, guiding the animal carefully along the hard ground. Theodora walked at the right side of the cart.

At the sound of the cart, several other figures appeared from the barn. Lucy recognized a few of them as well. Devin. Katherine. Ahivah. Deborah.

As the cart approached, Lucy could see that it contained a long wooden box. Jacob's casket, she realized. Gervase was there, too, holding on to the casket, steadying it over the bumpy patches.

When the cart stopped next to them, Esther Whitby dismounted, extending her hands to Sarah. "I thank thee, for joining us in this final testament to my husband."

Taking the woman's hands in her own, Sarah said in a low voice, "Dearest Esther. I was so sorry to hear about what happened to thy sister-in-law."

A slight pucker appeared on Esther's forehead. "Thou hast heard about Julia?" she asked, glancing at the Quakers standing beside her. "I was only just informed myself. Pray tell me, how didst thou learn of her tragic end?"

Lucy shifted her feet. Sarah seemed to realize then the

awkwardness of her knowledge. "The constable told us," Sarah tried to answer truthfully. "Well, he told Lucy. She told me." Seeing the slight suspicion on their faces at her mention of the constable, she spoke quickly to reassure them. "Lucy is a friend of the constable."

Inwardly, Lucy groaned at Sarah's rash words. She could see the warmth in their faces chill considerably as they stared at her. Friends of the constable were not altogether welcome among the Quakers. Out of the corner of her eye, she saw Lach edge a few steps backward, as if to distance himself from her.

"Well, not friends. I was speaking to him about"—Lucy hesitated—"another matter when word came about Miss Julia Whitby's death." Not a lie exactly, but it wouldn't do to let the Quakers think that she'd been conversing with the constable about Jacob Whitby. The women were still looking at Lucy with guarded expressions. She continued, "I promise, I would never say anything to get you in trouble." Her words sounded limp to her ears.

"I see," Esther said.

Everyone was still staring at them speculatively. Lucy glanced at Sarah, who was twisting her fingers in her gray woolen skirts. She couldn't leave yet, not before she'd had a chance to speak privately with Esther.

"I trust Lucy with my life, I do," Sarah finally said. "She is not one to speak to the authorities about our goings-on. Indeed, like my brother, she has always been a friend to the Friends. She has a true and valiant heart, and would not betray us in any fashion." Her heartfelt words seemed to break the tension. Lucy smiled slightly at her friend as she felt everyone relax.

Gervase smiled at her. "Welcome, Lucy. We thank thee for joining us today. It is a sad day, but perhaps"—he waved his arms expansively—"thou wilt better understand the meaning of Jacob's life by being among those of us who loved him. Who better than thee, a lady writer, to appreciate him and to express our love in words?"

Lucy smiled back at Gervase, drawn in by his warm refined speech.

Sarah turned to him as well, a genuine smile cracking her tear-stained frozen cheeks. "Thank you, Gervase. That is very kind of thee to say that to my friend Lucy."

"What about him?" Theodora said, pointing at Lach, who had moved a few steps away. "The pup looks like he is about to keel over."

"Lach is with me," Lucy said. Indeed, Lach was looking quite miserable, stamping his feet, trying to keep warm in his thin clothes. "He is my master's other apprentice. My master had him accompany me with the hopes we might trade some tracts with your printer." She indicated the pack at Lach's feet. "When the burial is over, naturally."

"Tell the poor boy he can warm himself inside," Esther said, wiping her eyes. "My dear Jacob would have been troubled by his misery, and would not like to see him suffer so."

After giving Esther an adoring look, Lach moved quickly toward the building.

Theodora murmured something to Esther Whitby, who nodded. "Let us turn now to the sad task of burying our brother," she said.

Clicking his tongue, Sam nudged the horse forward. Seeing

that Mrs. Whitby had begun to weep more profusely, Gervase took one of her arms while Theodora supported her on the other side.

Along with the others, Lucy trailed behind the somber procession as they made their way, shivering, past the outlying buildings toward a collection of gravestones. Lucy could tell straightaway that this was where the nonconformists of London were buried. Unlike the mixture of ornate and religious statues in most church cemeteries, the gravestones here were all simple, and most looked like they'd been laid in the ground within the last few years. They weren't covered with moss, nor did they look particularly weathered or crumbling.

They stopped by an open grave, which was cut unevenly into the frozen ground. Sam positioned the cart alongside. With just a few grunts, Gervase grabbed one end, Sam the other, and together they slid the coffin from the cart and across the ground. Using only a single rope, they were able to lower the coffin.

Straightening, they joined the others at the edge of the hole. Bowing her head, Lucy said a quick prayer for the soul of Jacob Whitby, hoping that the Lord would see him fit for heaven. To think that his parents were not present to bid their son farewell! A tear sprang to her eye.

Lucy blew on her gloved hands, trying to warm them through the cloth. Opening her eyes, she realized that she was expecting someone to begin a eulogy or to say a few words about Jacob. Instead there was more silence. Finally Joan began to sing about the blessings of the Lord shining down upon them. It was like no hymn or psalm that Lucy had ever heard, although the words seemed to draw from the Old Testament. That was the Quaker way, she supposed, to be moved by the Spirit of the Lord to speak or be silent as commanded. Lucy, of course, had remained silent throughout.

Finally, after periods of silence and a few testimonials, Esther Whitby took a handful of earth and threw it on the casket. One by one the others did the same. When it was her turn, Lucy hesitated. Catching her eye, Sarah gave her a slight nod. Seeing this, Lucy threw in her handful and then a dried posy that she'd been keeping hidden in her peddler's sack. Gervase and Sam picked up the shovels and began to push dirt in earnest onto the casket. The funeral seemed to be concluded, and the mourners began to drift back into the barn.

Theodora and Joan remained near, moving among the other graves, talking quietly. Seeing this, Sarah began to do the same. Fallen acquaintances, Lucy thought.

Esther was still standing silently, watching the hole get slowly filled. She had stepped back to give the men more space to work. Lucy seized the opportunity to speak to Esther, repeating condolences for both her recent losses.

Esther gave her a grateful smile. "Indeed, I will pray much for my soul to be replenished."

Lucy took a deep breath. "Did you know your husband's sister, Miss Julia Whitby, very well?" she asked.

Esther shook her head. "No, I met her only once."

"I suppose no one else here knew her either?" Lucy asked.

Esther gave a short laugh. "Hardly." She looked at Lucy curiously. "Thou hast many questions."

"Several years ago, a dear friend of mine was murdered,"

Lucy said carefully. As she spoke those words, she felt a clenching in her heart and gut that she feared would never go away. "I still think about her all the time." Lucy struggled to hold back the tears that threatened to spill.

Seeing this, Esther patted her hand. "I'm truly sorry for thy heartbreak. 'Tis a terrible shame that such monsters walk among us. How sorrowful I am that my husband's family has had to bear such loss and misfortune."

"The constable thinks Miss Julia may have known her murderer," Lucy said softly. "Or, at least, that she may have been known to her murderer."

Jacob's widow looked taken aback. "Indeed?" she said. "I did not know that." Then she looked at Lucy curiously. "Why ever would he think that, dost thou suppose?"

Esther must not know of the scold's mask, Lucy realized, or its possible implications. "I'm not certain," she said, not wanting to disclose more information than the constable had already given her. Improvising, she added, "I believe that they found her pocket still upon her person. The constable didn't think she had been robbed."

"So her murderer wasn't in pursuit of her money," Esther mused. She leaned in toward Lucy. "Was her person otherwise violated?"

Lucy shook her head, feeling the heat rise slightly in her cheeks. "I don't know," she said truthfully, kicking a stick from the stone path. "The constable did not tell me."

"Nor should he have." Esther clucked her tongue. "My poor sister-in-law. My husband always spoke fondly of her. It wasn't she who had banished him from his home. That was their *father*," she said, practically spitting out the last word. "He would never understand that we had been called to the Lord, to spread our Inner Light."

"I'm so sorry that he was banished from his family home," Lucy murmured. She could not help but glance at Sarah when she said this.

Esther must have followed her thinking. "Sister Sarah must find following her conscience to be particularly troublesome, given that her father is a magistrate." Her violet eyes were kind, troubled.

"I have been worried," Lucy confided softly, "that Miss Sarah and her father will grow divided, as so many Quakers seem to have become divided from their fathers." Thinking that the conversation was turning a tad too personal, though, Lucy changed the topic. "Will someone be staying with you?" she asked.

"I imagine that Deborah and her aunt would like to stay. Perhaps Joan, too. I am glad for the company." Her eyes glistened. "Indeed, I will do as the Lord commands me. Recently, I have felt called to a new conviction. I will likely accompany the others when they return to the New World. They wish to leave in a fortnight, if the Lord permits." Esther hesitated. "Truth be told, I do not rightfully know. I am a bit afraid of such a venture. Yet I will do as the Lord wishes."

Maybe this would be the right time to reveal what her husband had whispered on his deathbed. "Do you feel safe? With them?" Lucy held her breath.

"Safe?" Esther looked puzzled. "Certainly. They took me in when I had no one. Why?"

"Oh, the journeys just seem so long and terrible. You must

take care that you choose companions with whom you may travel safely." Lucy broke off, uncertain how to continue. She could not simply say, *There is one among your acquaintance who may be a murderer, and you'd best take care.*"

Esther searched her face. "Why dost thou feel concerned for my safety? Is there something thou know? Something the constable may have said?"

"No, no," Lucy said hurriedly, seeing that the others were drawing near. "It's just that I worry for Miss Sarah's safety, when she travels with the others. She is unmarried, unprotected. I worry whether her traveling companions will be faithful to her. Whether they will watch over her and shield her." She gulped, hearing her long-standing fears expressed. "I imagine your husband would have been worried for you, too."

"Yes, I can understand that," Esther agreed, dabbing at her eyes with a bit of linen. "Thy words are true. Jacob was always anxious that some harm would come to me. I can't imagine how worried he would be if he knew." With a rueful laugh, she touched Lucy's arm. "I know he trusted and loved Sister Sarah, long before he knew me. Perhaps she and I could look after one another, even as we trust in the Lord to guide our path. Certainly that is what my husband wanted. I should do more to make sure his dying wish is fulfilled."

Sarah approached them then, a middle-aged man following her. He was one of the men who had gathered around them silently when Jacob was interred. Lach stepped out of the building as well and moved toward them, untying his pack as he walked.

"Lucy," Sarah said, "this is one of the Quaker printers. Robert Wilson. He's just arrived back in London. I told him that you were apprenticed to Horace Aubrey and that you and Lach had brought some tracts to trade."

Lucy opened her pack and began to untie the small interior sacks to show the printer what they had brought. Out of the corner of her eye, she noticed Esther walking off with Sarah, returning to the warmth of the Quakers' building. Jacob's widow had drawn Sarah's arm into her own, and the two were pressed companionably together, their heads bent in what seemed to be a closely whispered conversation.

Seeing their intimacy, Lucy felt a twinge of misgiving. Suddenly, she wanted to grab Sarah's hand and drag her forcibly from the group. Wanted to pull her back to the magistrate's home, where she would be protected and safe. Instead, Lucy remained silent and watchful as Esther opened the door to the Quaker house and the two women disappeared inside.

Hearing the printer cough, Lucy turned her attention back to the exchange. "I suppose you've known these Quakers well," she asked idly, her thoughts still on Sarah.

The printer was glancing through an Anabaptist tract. "Hmmm," he muttered, flipping through the pages before handing it back to her. "I knew Jacob Whitby and Sam Leighton a long while. Both good men. A few of the others from the meeting. Sam's wife. Joan. Ahivah. I had never met her niece, though. Still a few I didn't know. Say, do you have any pieces that might be a little more . . . entertaining?"

Reaching into her pack, Lucy pulled out another small sack.

Hesitating, she untied it and handed the printer the stack of tracts and ballads neatly packed inside. She studied the printer. "Are you interested in that one?" she asked in surprise.

Master Wilson was now examining *The Rogue's Masque,* a play about the romps that had been orchestrated in the court of a barely veiled King Charles. She'd brought along only a few of the merriments in case she had a chance to sell in the market on her return.

The printer grinned. He had a friendly twinkle in his eyes that Lucy liked. "Yes, I enjoy merry romps such as these. Rest assured, I will sell these to others than those present here. I'll take this one, too." He pointed to one of the murder ballads she'd kept at the bottom of the pack. "Everyone loves a good murder," he said, winking at her. "I have heard your own master say that on many occasions."

Lucy nodded. That was certainly one of Master Aubrey's favorite expressions. "You said you didn't know all the Quakers who were here today?"

Master Wilson shrugged. "To be honest, I don't know his widow all that well, although I had met her. That man Gervase. Deborah. Your friend," he said, nodding his head toward the meetinghouse that Sarah had just entered.

"Oh, she and Joan only just returned to London. They were traveling in the New World."

"Well, that explains it, then. Usually I get to know them at meeting. Though they must have all been recently convinced. All right now, let's make our exchange."

He pulled out a number of Quaker tracts and pamphlets from a peddler's sack that looked remarkably similar to Lucy's own. "We've had little success printing since the Fire, I'm afraid," he said apologetically. "These are some we saved before we lost everything."

Lucy glanced at them. She could tell that they had been handled more than the ones she sold. Most likely, he'd already passed them out among the Quakers so that they could read them, but had collected them back, hoping to make a few coins. Spying two that were familiar, she seized them with a sharp intake of breath. Humphrey Smith's *Vision of London* and *A Lamentable Warning to London and Its Inhabitants.* She had found copies of these two tracts in the chest in Julia Whitby's bedchamber. "I'll take these," she said.

Lach raised an eyebrow, but to her surprise did not say anything, although he watched her closely.

"Excellent eye, my dear," the printer said, giving her an approving nod. "Those two tracts sell extremely well to Quakers and non-Quakers alike. Not as well as murder sells, perhaps, but visionary tales can be difficult to resist."

"I do not suppose you would remember who had recently bought either of these from you?" she asked with little hope.

The man threw his hands in the air. "Heavens no, lass. Do *you* remember who you sell to when you are out and about?" When she shook her head, he chuckled. "I thought as much. Although—" He paused. "Now that you have pressed me, I do remember who mustered up a coin for them."

"Who was it?" Lucy asked.

"Sam Leighton. He purchased several a few weeks ago, including these. I remember him saying how he wanted these tracts specifically."

"Sam Leighton?" Lucy repeated. "I wonder why."

He grew more businesslike. "I do not know, nor, to be honest, do I particularly care. There are many reasons people seek out specific pieces, and I am sure I should not like to know most of them. Come now," he said, shivering. "Let us haggle. This freeze is starting to tear my bones from the inside."

After a few minutes of bargaining, Lucy and Lach left, having been relieved of all their penny merriments, a few religious pieces, and several last dying speeches of condemned murderers. In exchange they were bringing back a number of Quaker warnings to Londoners, including the ones she'd found among Julia Whitby's effects.

Although Lucy wanted to look at the tracts right away, a cold rain began to fall. Master Aubrey would be none too pleased if she let the tracts get wet and mussed. Sighing, she made certain that her pack was tightly knotted. Any secrets that the Quaker tracts held would have to wait.

·10·

Several hours passed before Lucy had the chance to look at the tracts. When she showed them to Master Aubrey, he was too distracted to look at them properly. It seemed the stationer had been late on a shipment of paper, and the matter needed to be sorted out. Lach was to accompany him to the stationer, having been told by the printer that "you must learn to deal with these deceitful rapscallions, lest you never have any paper when you have started your own shop."

For her part, Lucy was instructed to clean the typeset and break down the typeface. "Ensure that each letter, quoin, and woodcut has been returned to its proper place," he said, pointing to the great wooden trays stacked along the wall. "Mind you be finished by evening," he added as he and Lach prepared to leave. "Best be done before the light begins to fail. I will not have you wasting candles."

"Yes, sir," Lucy replied, eager to be alone in the shop.

When the door shut, she turned to the task at hand. Breaking down the typeface was quite tedious, but she had found ways to make the chore pass a little quicker. She liked to start with the largest font, picking out all of the same letters and placing them in their section of the tray. Then she'd pick out all the same letters in the next size font, usually picking out two that lay next to each other, to make the process quicker.

When the tiny font began to slip through her numbed fingers, however, she knew it was time to rest for a few minutes. Grabbing a red apple from the basket, she moved over to the bench below the shop window and sat down with the sack of tracts she had acquired from Master Wilson earlier.

After she slid the contents of her sack onto the table, Lucy picked out the copies of the two tracts she had seen in Julia Whitby's bedchamber and began to examine them more closely.

Why would Miss Whitby have hidden such pieces away? she wondered again. Both *The Vision for London* and *A Lamentable Warning to London and Its Inhabitants* were fairly typical warnings from the Quakers to the citizens of the city. Since she was more familiar with the *Vision for London,* Lucy set it aside and focused on the *Lamentable Warning* instead.

Right away she found the reading to be slow going. The tract described at length the terrible treatment that the Quakers had received under Charles's reign, but most of the interesting bits were only punctuations in a sermon as boring as what the ministers preached on Sundays. Lucy could feel her eyelids beginning to droop—the long walk from the morning was taking its toll.

Although she wanted to rest her head on the table, Lucy forced herself to turn the fourth page of the tract. Unexpectedly, a familiar name jumped out at her. Ahivah, the Woman in White.

Straightening up, Lucy read the passage out loud. *"As our own prophet* Ahivah, *whom our own King Charles did call his* Woman in White, *has warned: 'If ye have not sinned, get ye to a safe place, for the Lord's righteous anger will be soon upon us.' Heed Ahivah's words, for the Day of our Lord's judgment does rapidly approach."*

Startled, Lucy read the words again. *"Get ye to a safe place."*

She sat back, placing the tract on the table, trying to make sense of it.

Could it be coincidence that such words of warning had been delivered to Julia Whitby? Was it strange that the person who had uttered them was Ahivah, a Quaker in her brother's own close circle of acquaintances? More important, how had Julia Whitby read these words? Had she taken this message as a personal warning? Was that why she decided to flee the house?

"I need to show this tract to Duncan," she said out loud just as church bells began to ring in the hour.

Jumping to her feet, Lucy finished putting the type away as fast as she could, praying that she had not mixed anything up. She was not entirely sure when Master Aubrey would return, but she rather hoped that he and Lach would stop at a tavern for a bite and some ale. She had learned that the master printer liked to celebrate his victories over the stationer with a pint, and she hoped that this time would be no different. He'd be none too pleased if he came home to a cold hearth and empty stew pot.

Nevertheless, Lucy said a small prayer and left the shop, hoping to find the constable at the jail.

When she arrived a few minutes later, Lucy found Hank in the front part of the jail, looking unusually haggard. "Hank, are you well?" she asked.

The bellman tried to smile, but his eyes looked bloodshot and weary. "My wife and wee ones—they have all been sick. This deathly cold has been taking the life right out of them. I've been at home with them these last few days. The worst of it is over though, thanks be to God."

Lucy murmured her agreement. She hoped that the sickness did not return, although Culpeper said it was not uncommon for illness to linger in a household, even after it was believed to be gone. She turned her attention to the matter at hand. "Is the constable in?"

The bellman began to cough, a dry hacking sound, as he gestured to the back room. "Th-there!" he managed to sputter.

"Thank you," she said. "Best take some honey for that cough," she added as she passed him by.

She knocked on the door.

"Yes, come in!" she heard the constable call.

When she entered, Duncan looked up from his table in surprise. "Lucy!" he said, standing up. "What brings you here?"

"Constable Duncan," she said, crossing the room toward him, "look at these tracts." She handed him the two Quaker penny pieces.

The constable glanced at the tracts, and back at her. "Quaker warnings. What of them?"

Not replying, Lucy boosted herself up onto one of the overly large barrels that the constable kept in the room, smoothing her skirts after she did so. The barrels had been salvaged from the ruins of the Cheshire Cheese, an old tavern that had burnt down during the Great Fire. A few months ago, a body had been found inside one of the barrels, a knife through its chest. Having been one of many Londoners helping with the cleanup of the Great Fire, Lucy had been there when the body was discovered. The memory still made her shiver. She almost asked the constable if the barrel she had perched herself on was *the* barrel, but she opted against it.

Instead she answered his question. "I found them both in Julia Whitby's bedchamber. Well, not these exact ones," she added hastily when he frowned at her. "These are copies. I remembered their names. I saw them today when I was trading tracts with a Quaker printer, Master Wilson, and I thought we might learn something from them. And I did—" She was about to explain when he cut her off.

"*When* did you see these tracts?" he asked, his voice stern. "Did you return to Julia Whitby's home?"

"I saw the tracts the first time I was there," Lucy said, growing flustered by his tone.

"Why did you not speak of these tracts to me when you handed me the letters and the sketch? Why were you keeping this secret from me?"

Lucy tried to explain. "I saw them, but I did not think to

take them. I remembered them later and I thought they might be important." Growing exasperated, she added, "Which is why I am here. Do you not wish to know what I found?"

He took a step closer, looking up at her. "What is it?" he asked.

"Well, the tracts had been carefully hidden in the chest, I imagine by Julia Whitby herself," Lucy said.

"Maybe she was thinking about becoming a Quaker," he said.

"That is possible. Yet I remember that someone had written the word 'Behold!' on both of them. Someone wanted to draw attention to the tracts."

Constable Duncan looked thoughtful. "Is that so uncommon? Do people not write on such tracts? Julia could have written the word herself."

Lucy took a deep breath. "Or it could be that someone was deliberately sending Miss Whitby a message from the Quakers." She directed Duncan to the *Lamentable Warning.* "Look at the part about Ahivah," Lucy said. "Do you think it's a coincidence that Jacob's sister has a tract in which there is a warning from one of the same Quakers who sat at Jacob's deathbed? A strange happenstance, would you not agree?"

"Perhaps. I don't know." He looked down at the tract again, as if seeking more clues. "Maybe they all know each other."

"Moreover," she continued, "Master Wilson, the Quakers' printer, told me that Sam Leighton was the one who purchased the tracts from him."

"He remembered that, did he?" Duncan said. "That seems a peculiar thing to recall, don't you think?"

"He said that Mr. Leighton had been looking for those specific titles." Lucy paused. *Had Sam Leighton known those tracts would end up in Julia Whitby's possession? Had he sent them to her? If so, for what purpose? What if we asked him?* Lucy started to express these thoughts to Duncan.

"I wonder if I could speak to the Quakers again," she mused. "Maybe speak to Mr. Leighton."

At this, he frowned, and the tension had returned to his voice when he spoke. "No more of this piecemeal information, Lucy. If you know something, you need to share it with me. At once! I will not allow you to dangle bits and pieces before me as the whim strikes you."

Lucy stared at him. Duncan had never spoken to her in such a way before, and she did not care for it. "I shall leave, then," she said, hopping off the barrel. "I have no wish to dangle anything before you. I already explained myself, and I see there is no point in us conversing further."

She had not taken a step when she found her way barred by the constable. Duncan had placed one hand on the barrel by her hip and his other hand on the wall, so that she was effectively trapped. She did not feel afraid, though her heart began to pound at their closeness.

"Lucy, I did not wish to anger you," he said, searching her face, all traces of his earlier temper gone. "Yet I must know. Please! Have you told me everything now? No more secrets?"

"I have no more secrets to share," she said. "Please let me by."

He dropped his arms to his sides, but he still stood before her, just a few inches away. She could have moved around him, but remained where she was, looking up at him.

"I just think that secrets are what got Julia Whitby killed. Maybe Jacob Whitby, too," he said.

Lucy nodded.

He looked at her intently. "That is why I worry about the secrets that you keep. Lucy, I cannot abide the thought of you being injured—" He broke off then. The lopsided grin he gave her seemed a bit rueful, maybe even sad. "I know it is not my place to say."

"Duncan, I thank you for your concern." She put her hand on his right arm, closing the gap between them.

Unexpectedly, he reached up with his free hand and covered her fingers, so that they fit neatly within his own. His hand was rough but warm.

The move surprised them both, and he stepped back, dropping his hand. "Beg pardon," he muttered.

"'Tis no matter," she said, her hand still tingling from the brief contact. Adam's face rose in her thoughts, and she could almost hear him saying, *The constable's interest in you is quite keen, I fear.* Then her own voice, from deep within, asked, *Is Duncan's interest unwelcome, Lucy?*

To cover her flurried thoughts, Lucy thought it best to change the subject. "Did you learn anything from the letters and the sketch I gave you?" she asked hurriedly.

A long moment passed before he replied. He seemed to be considering her. Perhaps he had expected her to leave, Lucy thought. Indeed, she was not sure why she had not left the jail. She had been ready to leave just a minute earlier.

"Not anything other than the obvious," he finally replied.

Then his manner regained its customary briskness. "That reminds me, though—"

He opened the door. "Hank!" he called. "Come look at these." To Lucy he said, "I haven't had a chance to show him the sketch."

When Hank came in, the constable handed him the sketch. "What do you make of this?"

Hank picked up the sketch of the dead man with some trepidation. *"This is the dandy I told you about,"* he read. He looked up. "What dandy? Where did you get this sketch?"

"I found it at Julia Whitby's," Lucy said matter-of-factly, admitting her theft once again. "I don't know where she got it or what it means."

Hank continued to study the piece. "I think I know who drew it," he said.

"Who?" Duncan and Lucy both exclaimed.

"The searcher. Sadie Burroughs. You met her the other day. She likes to draw the strange deaths. Don't know why, but she does."

"So does that mean that Mrs. Burroughs knew Julia Whitby?" Lucy paused, puzzling through an idea. "She is the one who reported her body. We need to speak with her! Find out what she knows about Miss Whitby!"

Duncan frowned. "She would not have been able to recognize Julia Whitby, since the scold's mask had been affixed to her face. Still, I do not like such coincidences. I agree, we need to speak with her. How to find her, though, that I do not know."

"How can that be?" Lucy asked. "She does work for you, does she not?"

The constable shook his head. "No, she does not. She would work for a parish. I have not known her long, and I have no record of her address. Likely as not, she reported natural deaths to the Parish of St. Giles before the Fire. Now she has nothing to report since no one is living in the burnt-out areas yet." He looked at Hank. "What about you, Hank? Do you know anything about her? I know you've spoken with her more than I have."

Hank looked at the ceiling of the old candlemakers' shop as he tried to recall his conversations with the searcher. "I recall her once saying that she liked to take her evening ale at the Bow and Arrow. Down on Fetter Lane."

"I know where it is," Lucy said. Spending her days peddling books on the streets of London had given her extensive knowledge of the locations of most alehouses, churches, and coffeehouses in the area. Fetter Lane was one of the first streets to the west that had not been ravaged by the Fire. "Let us go! Perhaps she will be there."

Even as she spoke these words, a vision of Master Aubrey's face arose before her eyes. *What will he say when I am not there when he returns?* she thought, feeling a twinge of apprehension. *Well, I cannot worry about that now.*

"I do not think she will speak to me," Duncan said slowly.

"Let me talk to her, then," Lucy said.

"Some dangerous sorts there, at the Bow and Arrow," Hank said to Duncan, with a meaningful nod at Lucy.

Seeing the constable frown, Lucy said hastily, "Perhaps Hank could accompany me. If, as you say, she speaks to him more than she speaks to you—?"

Hank inclined his head respectfully toward the constable. "I could take Miss Campion there, if you like. Ask around. If she's there, she might give us the information we seek."

With Duncan's reluctant approval, a short time later, Hank and Lucy were regarding the Bow and Arrow cautiously. Hank hadn't been jesting when he said that some dangerous sorts frequented the place. Lucy did not even object when Hank told her to wait across the street, near a little broom-maker's shop that looked to be closing for the evening. A few minutes later, he came back out, a grim look on his face.

"No luck?" she asked.

"No, she's there. She wants to speak to you, inside. Wants us to buy her an ale." Lucy understood the source of his frown. He likely had to save every hard-earned penny from his occupation as bellman.

"I've got enough for three pints," she said, with an inward groan. Like Hank, she hated to give up any coins.

"That will do," he said. "Come on."

Once inside the Bow and Arrow, they seated themselves across from Sadie Burroughs at a dirty wooden table that had clearly seen better days. Hank waved for the tavern miss, who banged three pints of strong ale down before each of them. Lucy smelled her ale cautiously. Catching Hank's warning eye, she took a great swallow to steady her nerves and laid the tankard back down.

Although clearly suspicious of them, the searcher took a swig as well, wiping her mouth with the back of her hand. "Can't say I expected to see you again," she said to Lucy in her harsh and raspy voice. "Whatcha want?"

"Did you know Miss Julia Whitby?" Lucy asked, trying to keep her voice from quavering. Even though Hank's presence beside her was comforting, there was something about the woman's dark eyes that made her nervous. "The dead woman in the scold's mask?"

Sadie Burroughs chuckled, exposing great gaps in her yellow teeth where the tooth-puller must have had his way. She took another deep drink of her ale. "Maybe I did, maybe I didn't. Just because I find them don't mean I killed them."

Lucy pulled out the sketch of the dead man and laid it on the table in front of the searcher. "Did you draw this?" she asked. "We think you did."

Mrs. Burroughs straightened up a bit. "Now, how did you come by that?" she asked. "You'll have to pay me more than just a pint. After all, I'm a searcher. By law, I am forbidden 'to engage in any public work or employment,' nor may I 'keep any shop or stall.' Do their dirty work once and it keeps me from honest employment forever after." Again her laugh was bitter. "Can't keep an old woman from making a few bits, can you?"

Lucy looked helplessly at Hank, who shrugged. His look said it all. He couldn't make her talk. With a huge sigh, Lucy pulled up her skirts under the table and felt for the secret pocket she kept buried within her lining. She had a few coins there. Reluctantly she pulled out one of her two crowns and pushed it across the table to the searcher. "Please. Tell us. Who was this man?"

"I found him. Two years ago." Mrs. Burroughs answered after pocketing the coin. "He was already dead. I sketched him."

"Who was he?"

The searcher shrugged. "Don't know who he was. I never know their names. I don't care to, either. I just make my report to the parish priest. Or sometimes the constable, when I find them that get themselves killed."

"Well, where did you find him?" Lucy asked, growing more impatient.

Mrs. Burroughs sneezed, wiping the snot onto her arm. "I find a lot of dead bodies. I can't remember them all." She smirked, though, clearly hiding something.

"Hank?" Lucy looked at the bellman, mutely imploring him for help.

Understanding, the bellman reached over and gripped the searcher's frail arm. "Now we've paid you for some information. Tell us where you found the body."

"Fine. All in due time. No need to be brutal. Just having a bit of fun with you, is all." Shaking off the bellman's grip, she took another deep swallow. "I found him in Lincoln's Inn Fields. At the theater there."

"At the theater?" Lucy exchanged a puzzled glance with Hank. "How odd," she said.

The searcher shrugged. "Is it? I don't know. I find stiffs in all manner of places that others might find peculiar. One time I found a body coming straight out of a tree trunk."

Lucy shook her head, trying to remove that image from her mind. "Tell us why you gave that sketch to Julia Whitby. *'This is the dandy I was telling you about.'* Why were you telling her about this dead man?"

When Mrs. Burroughs didn't answer, the bellman grasped her forearm again, his beefy fingers easily encircling it. The searcher's face tightened slightly in pain, though she didn't cry out.

"Your Miss Julia Whitby sought me out. Me. A searcher. Said she'd heard about a murder in a theater, wondered if I knew anything about it." The woman's lips twitched. Lucy looked at her closely. Was the woman lying?

"Do you know why she asked you about it?" Lucy pressed.

Once again, the searcher extracted herself from Hank's firm grip on her arm. She scowled at Hank again before quaffing her ale deeply. "I do not know. Don't care either."

"We know that someone told her that one of her brother's acquaintances was an impostor," Lucy added desperately. This conversation was taking them nowhere.

"Is that so?" Mrs. Burroughs said, downing the rest of her pint. She wiped the foam off her mouth. "I would not know." For the first time, the searcher dropped her mocking tone. "It certainly seems, however, that her questions may have brought about her own demise, would you not agree?" She stood up.

Desperately, Lucy pulled out another coin. Seeing this, Hank's eyes widened, and he shook his head at her. "Is there anything else you can tell us about Julia Whitby? Did she ask you about anything else? Anyone else? Please!" Another question occurred to her. "How did you know about her body? Miss Whitby had only just been killed. Her body didn't smell yet. Did someone tell you about the murder?"

The searcher laughed down at her, a dry, mirthless chuckle. "You are persistent, aren't you?" She took the coin and sat back down on the bench. "No one had told me about her body. I found her on my own."

"But how?"

Mrs. Burroughs shrugged. "The same way I usually hear about bodies. I heard tell that a woman had gone missing, so I thought I would just take a peek around, to see what I could see. That is how I came to find her, all alone, with that thing over her face. Lucky the rats hadn't started on her. At least, not to any great extent."

She laughed when Lucy shuddered. "Perhaps you would like to see how I found her," she said. Opening her leather bag, the woman pulled out a sheet of paper and laid it atop the old wooden table. It was another sketch. "I will sell it to you for a small sum."

Lucy and Hank leaned in to look at it more closely, recoiling when they looked at it. The sketch depicted a finely dressed woman lying on a wooden floor, limbs askew, a knife in her chest and the leather and iron of a scold's mask obscuring the details of her face.

"Is this Julia Whitby?" Lucy exclaimed. "Why did you draw this?"

The woman shrugged. "I sketched it when I found her. I did not know who she was, naturally, since she was wearing the scold's mask and all. I always draw the interesting deaths. Pen and ink. Sometimes chalk. My little merriment." She barked her cheerless laugh again. "If I'd had a bit of red chalk, I'd have sketched the blood in proper."

Lucy was unable to keep her eyes off the image. She could see now some faint horizontal lines, suggesting that the sketch had apparently been drawn on the reverse side of a broadside or printed petition. "Why would I want such a thing?" Lucy asked. "I'm not one for the macabre."

The searcher snickered. "We both know that's not true. Your sort always has questions. I could see it in your eyes when you were with the constable."

Seeing Lucy flinch, the searcher ran a gnarled finger along the sketch. "I'm an old woman. I must pay for food and lodging, now musn't I?"

Lucy turned the macabre sketch over, paying attention to the petition that had been printed on the other side. She read the title out loud. *"The Quakers' Final Warning to the King and Mayor of London and the Sinners of the City."*

Another fairly common piece, describing the ills and troubles that would befall those unrighteous Londoners who persisted in their sinful ways. Unlike most Quaker pieces, this was a one-sheet broadside, perhaps intended to be nailed to a wall in a tavern or even to the door of a church. Underneath, there was another title, in smaller font. *Behold your final judgment, all ye sinners. If ye have not sinned, get thee to a safe place, for the Lord's righteous anger will be upon you.* Ahivah's warning again.

Lucy looked closer, trying to see if anything had been written on the piece. She did not see any words, but when holding the petition up to the light, she could see that someone had faintly underlined *get thee to a safe place.*

She looked up at the searcher. "Where did you get this broadside? Did you have it with you?" She gulped. "Or did you find it with Julia Whitby's body?"

Unexpectedly, the woman seemed genuinely amused, as if delighted by a smart child. "I found that paper with the body. Found it in her pocket, under her skirts. Didn't think anyone would miss it. No coins, though, more's the shame."

Sadie Burroughs stood up. "That is all I have to say. Do not bother looking for me again. I will not be coming back here."

Angry now, Lucy stood up as well and stalked toward the door. She'd lost two months' earnings and had little enough to show for it.

To her surprise, as she passed Mrs. Burroughs, the searcher grabbed her arm and pulled her close. "You know nothing about the people you're dealing with," she hissed. "I suggest you keep your distance. Let the devils lie where they are buried. Do not seek to resurrect the dead."

Before Lucy could say anything more, the searcher released her arm and limped out of the tavern, in her hobbled painful way.

·11·

"Miss Campion?" a young boy called, poking his face into the printer's shop. Two days had passed since Jacob Whitby's funeral and Lucy's conversation with the searcher. Lucy and Lach were both engaged in small tasks set them by Master Aubrey. Seeing Lucy's startled nod, the boy moved to where she was standing by the printing press. "I have a message for you. Already paid." He handed her a note that had been sealed with red wax and left the shop. From the elegant script bearing her name, she knew the note was from Adam.

Before Lucy could read the message, however, Lach snatched it from her hand, breaking open the seal. He skimmed the contents, despite her indignant protests. "Quack, quack, quack! More stuff about the Quakers." He tossed her the note.

Lucy threw a wooden block at him, which narrowly missed his head. She picked up the note, reading it to herself.

Sarah has just informed us, Adam wrote, *that she can no longer stifle her conscience. As we feared she might do, she has left my father's home and has taken up residence with Esther Whitby. We are hopeful that she will return soon. If she does not, perhaps you might be so good to stop by the Whitbys' tomorrow after church, and do what you can to prevail upon her to forgo this independent spirit. We should like to mend this divide before it is too late. Yours, etc., Adam Hargrave.*

"I do not know that I can help them," she said softly. Though her words were not intended for Lach, he heard them anyway.

"Why bother? Quackers quack the loudest when people try to silence them. Why not let her leave? Be done with her?" Lach said, beginning to quack like a duck again.

"Lach! Stop that nonsense!" she said, putting her hands on her hips. "If you could only see how Sarah's decisions have pained the magistrate and Adam, you would not mock them. If you cared about anyone other than yourself, you would understand how they worry when she is away, walking unprotected in the world." She stared down at the note. "I will do what I can to help them." She looked back at Lach. She knew her voice was rising. "And I will not let you mock them or me for doing so!"

The apprentice just shook his head at her. "Adam Hargrave is besotted with you, Lucy. Why, I have no idea. But I know he will not be besotted forever, if you stay the harping shrew you are now."

She was about to retort when the constable opened the door to the shop and stepped inside. His eyes flitted from one to the other, and Lucy wondered if he had heard any of her conversation with Lach. Their odd encounter from the other day still entered her thoughts, and she did not know what—if anything—it could mean.

Naturally, at the sight of Duncan, Lach immediately began to hum a mocking tune.

"The Constable Cozened, Lach?" Duncan asked, his eyebrow raised. "I think I have heard that one."

Lach grinned impishly. *"The Constable's Cod-Piece,* actually."

"Ah!" Duncan replied. "So many. It is hard to keep them straight. I suppose you know them all, though."

"I do indeed," Lach said. "Shall I teach you the words?"

Getting up from her stool, Lucy kicked the apprentice in the ankle as she walked toward the constable. "Lach," she asked over her shoulder, "did Master Aubrey not tell you to fetch the ingredients from the cellar to make a new batch of red ink?"

He rubbed his ankle, glaring at her. "Don't have to do it now, do I?" he asked.

She glowered back at him, hands on her hips. "Lach!"

"All right, all right! Remember what I told you!" The printer's apprentice began to sing as he moved toward the steps descending to the cellar below. "Oh, harping shrew! Harping shrew! Who in the world will marry you?"

Lucy looked back at the constable. "I seem fated to always apologize for that scoundrel," she said.

"No matter," Duncan said. He seemed amused.

She set down the cloth she was using to clean the press, taking in the constable's appearance. He was not dressed in his usual uniform; instead, he was in the nondescript clothes of an ordinary tradesman. He seemed to be off duty. She'd rarely seen him this way, and she was not sure what to make of him.

"Constable," she said, "what has brought you here?"

"Fancy going to the theater this afternoon?" he asked.

Taken aback, Lucy searched for a reply even as Lach let out a great whooping sound from the cellar stairs. Apparently he had remained near the top in order to eavesdrop on them.

"The plays!" Lach whooped again. "Oh, that is rich! Whatever will your poor besotted suitor say to *that*?"

"Hush!" Lucy hissed, her cheeks flushing. "I, er . . . do not have a day off today," she said hesitantly.

"Hank informed me about the conversation you had with Mrs. Burroughs," the constable said, his easy manner growing brisk. As he spoke, the door behind him opened and Master Aubrey walked in, a question in his eyes when he saw the constable.

"Some of our questions about Julia Whitby's murder may well be answered by a visit to the Lincoln's Inn Fields Theater," Duncan continued. "I should like you to accompany me, if you would. With two sets of eyes and two sets of ears, I am less likely to miss something important." He looked toward Master Aubrey, who seemed a bit puzzled. "That is, if you would allow it, sir."

"You wish to take my apprentice to the plays?" he asked, looking from one to the other. Clearly, *The Good Master's Guide to the Godly Training and Disciplining of Apprentices* could not possibly explain such a situation. Lucy nervously stifled a smile.

"In truth, we would not be attending a performance," he said, glancing at Lucy. To her surprise, the constable then explained what they had learned from the searcher. "I thought we might be able to speak to the players. This is why I am not wearing my uniform."

Lucy could see that Master Aubrey still needed some convincing. "We shall include what we learn for *The Scold's Last Scold,*" Lucy said. "This information will help the tract about Julia Whitby's death sell even better."

Master Aubrey's brow cleared. "Ah, yes, by all means, go," he said, rubbing his hands together. "We'll get the jump on Roger L'Estrange yet, when we write the strange tale of the scolded scold!" Then he frowned. "A murder at the plays, you say? I seem to recall—"

He ran his fingers over the press while he was thinking, pushing a temperamental bodkin into place. "I seem to recall selling a piece about that very murder." He straightened up. "Let me check."

As the master printer disappeared down into the cellar, where he kept old printed pieces, Lach turned indignantly to her. "I suppose you want me to finish your work as well," he hissed at Lucy. "While you are escorted about by your *other* suitor." He jerked his head toward the constable.

If she had not already been flushed, she certainly was now. And Lach's emphasis on "other" had certainly not been lost on the constable either.

Master Aubrey returned then. "I could not find the piece I was looking for. No matter." He waved his hand at them. "Off you go. Lach will take care of cleaning the press."

Lucy hesitated, seeing Lach's downcast face. "Master Aubrey, perhaps Lach could accompany us," she said. "We would not be gone very long, and certainly we could sell along the way." She did not look at the constable to see if he was disappointed.

Master Aubrey sighed. "I suppose." He seemed a bit defeated. But then he wagged his finger at them both. "I expect you to figure this out. I'll not have L'Estrange putting something out about Julia Whitby's murder before I do!"

A short while later, after some squabbling between Lucy and Lach, the three arrived at the Lincoln's Inn Fields Theater. Neither she nor Lach had ever been there, although the constable seemed to be familiar with the building.

"This playhouse was originally Lisle's Tennis Court," he explained as they looked up at the building. "William Davenant owns it—you can see his house, just there." He pointed to a smaller building adjacent to the theater. "I saw *Hamlet*, by the Bard, played here, four years ago when I first arrived in London. Now they've been playing *The Humorous Lovers,* by Cavendish. The company is called the Duke's Players." Seeing Lucy's look of surprise, he added, "I like to keep track of the goings-on in the community."

As Lucy and Lach began to walk toward the front entrance, the constable pointed to a side door. "Let's try that one. They are unlikely to be open to the public. I am sure they are rehearsing, or at least sleeping off a night of tippling down."

Sure enough, the door was open. As they stepped inside, Lucy looked around in amazement. She'd been to a theater down in Southwark, on the other side of London Bridge, but never one like this. Long wooden benches stretched across what used to be the tennis court floor, interrupted by aisles that ran the length of the playhouse. Three tiers of box seats rose along on the sides and facing the stage, with the middle tier likely offering the best view of the stage. For the nobles and wealthier gentry, Lucy surmised. See and be seen. One box close to the stage looked particularly lavish, full of embroidered pillows and satin seats.

"For the king," the constable said by her ear, having followed her gaze.

The stage itself was quite elaborate, with doors on either side, for quick exits and entrances by the players.

"Look," she whispered, pointing at the great columns on either side of the stage doors. "That looks like the column that the searcher drew in her sketch."

"That would mean the murder happened on the stage," the constable said thoughtfully, in his regular voice. It carried easily through the entire theater.

"That, indeed, is the sad truth of the matter!" came a great sonorous voice from behind them.

Lucy jumped, turning around to find a portly man standing there, regarding them with an amused look on his face. He was wearing the elegant ensemble of a gentleman, which Lucy suspected was a costume, not his own dress.

"The vicious event happened right there on the stage! Luckily, there wasn't so much blood." He lowered his voice now, in a conspiratorial way. "Cleaned it up, right quick. We didn't even have to cancel a performance." The man appraised them in a friendly way. "It's been a while since we've had any blood-seekers touring the playhouse. When it first happened, two years ago, we had them in droves."

"Oh, we're not—" Lach began to say when Lucy pressed his foot in warning.

"Thank you! We've only just heard about his untimely demise. Who was he, anyway?"

"Basil Townsend. One of the duke's own players. Missed, to be sure. Though there were many others, including myself, who could play his parts."

"Oh, my! Are you one of the Duke's Players, too?" Lucy asked, looking up at the man under her eyelashes, with what she hoped was a coquettish smile. She didn't spend a lot of time looking in mirrors, so for all she knew she could be looking at him as if struck by indigestion. Out of the corner of her eye, she saw Lach and the constable exchange a glance, and then each take a casual step away.

The man gave a lavish bow. "Herbert Bligh, my lady," he said, taking her hand and kissing it with an exaggerated flourish. "I've been one of the Duke's Players for four years, and I was here the day that poor Basil Townsend was struck down by that villain."

"What happened?" Lucy asked breathlessly, resisting the urge to snatch her hand away. Instead, she touched the man's sleeve and was rewarded by his tucking it in his arm companionably. She allowed herself to be led down the aisle to the stage, the constable and Lach following a half step behind them.

"Two years ago, it happened," Mr. Bligh began, his voice so loud that Lucy was sure that it could be heard from every seat in the playhouse. "Two weeks before the plague struck and the

king shut down the theaters. Poor Basil was standing there"—
he pointed at the column—"when a ruffian entered the theater,
demanded his money, and stabbed him. There he died." He made
a terrible choking sound to illustrate his point.

"Did anyone witness this terrible act?" the constable asked.

"Yes, several of my company, including a female player," he
said. "Basil, it seemed, had been making wagers with the wrong
people. Eventually, one of them came to collect their money."
He turned back to Lucy. "Now enough about the past. Let us
talk about the present." For the next few minutes, he pointed
out the different machines and scenic devices and trapdoors. Lucy
was just wondering how they might be able to break away when
he turned to her again. "Would you care to see me perform tonight? You could be my special guest. We could get a bite to
eat after the performance." He leaned in a bit more, all the while
rubbing his thumb across her fingers. "I promise, it will be well
worth your while."

The constable jumped in then. "Alas, we must be off. Thank
you, sir, for your time. Our visit has been most . . . interesting."
Taking Lucy's other arm, he pulled her away and rushed them
both out of the playhouse.

"So what connects Basil Townsend's murder to Julia Whitby?"
Lucy mused, lifting her face to welcome the light mist upon her
cheeks. The theater had been a bit warm and stuffy. "The searcher,
Sadie Burroughs, said Julia Whitby had come to her and asked
her about it. Why was she interested in a murder of a player that
happened two years ago?"

Lach pushed past them then, jostling them against each
other. "You are missing an even stranger question."

The constable and Lucy exchanged a glance. "What?" Lucy asked. When the apprentice just gave him an impudent smile, she stamped her foot. "Lach, tell us! What are we missing?"

"How did Julia Whitby know to ask Sadie Burroughs anything at all? Why her? It's not like she is the only old woman out there searching for dead bodies."

Stopping short, Lucy put her hand to her forehead. "Lach, you are right." The more she thought about it, the more odd it was. "Julia Whitby knew something that connected Sadie Burroughs and that player's murder."

Duncan shook his head. "There seem to be many links on a chain that we cannot see."

Whether that chain would ever become visible, Lucy was beginning to have her doubts.

·12·

The next day, after the Sunday service concluded, Lucy made her way over to Esther Whitby's home as Adam and his father had requested that she do. At her knock, Joan opened the door.

"Welcome, daughter," the Quaker said. "I am glad that thy conscience has bid thee to come here."

Lucy smiled weakly. She wasn't *trying* to pass herself off as a Quaker, she told herself. If letting them believe she wanted to join the sect would give her access to Sarah, well, she would not gainsay the claim.

Joan led her into a room that had likely once been a drawing room—the same room where Lucy had spied the conventicle, if that's what it had been. Sarah and Esther were sitting together, sewing with Theodora and Ahivah, the latter still garbed all in white. *Perhaps I can speak to Ahivah later*, Lucy thought, remembering how the Quaker's warnings had appeared in the tract found in Julia Whitby's effects.

Deborah was sitting beside the women, a torn garment in her lap, although she did not appear to be sewing. Sam, Gervase, and Devin were all there as well. Sam appeared to have been reading a tract out loud, which he set aside when she entered the room.

"Lucy?" Sarah asked, standing up. "What has brought thee here? Did my father send thee to convince me to come home? If that is why thou hast come, then I beg thee to leave now."

"I-I wanted to see for myself how you fare," Lucy said, a bit stung by Sarah's words. She turned to leave.

Esther Whitby stood up. "No," she said to Lucy. "I cannot let thee leave in such a forlorn state. Pray, sit down, Lucy. Yes, there by the fire. Joan, wouldst thou be so kind as to fetch a hot drink for our guest? She looks half frozen and could stand to be warmed up some." Leaning over, she patted Sarah's shoulder. "Sarah, my dear sister, thy family has been blessed with friends who care for thee."

Lucy sat down gratefully next to the stone hearth, warming her hands over the low fire. Although she would have preferred to speak to Sarah in private, it seemed that she would not be able to do so.

Awkwardly, she leaned toward Sarah, speaking softly. "Your father and brother are concerned for your well-being, as am I." Hearing her words spoken out loud, though, Lucy looked around at the Quakers in chagrin. "I do not mean to offend you. I am sure you are treating her well."

However, no one looked offended. Indeed, the Quakers were

regarding her with approval. "Thy words do not offend us," Joan explained. "Rather, they lift us up and nourish us. Such friendship should not be cast aside, even if thy father has cast his daughter out. 'Tis a blessing to us all that thou hast joined us here."

"I do not think your father has cast you out—" Lucy began, before being stopped by the intensity of Esther's sorrowful gaze.

"She will be cast off soon enough," Esther said firmly, "as so many others have been who are called to be handmaidens and servants of the Lord." The others nodded at the authority in her voice.

"Lucy, I know that my family has been castigated by the other judges. He is all but harboring a criminal in his household if I am there," Sarah said. "There is no use denying it. My very existence puts him at odds with the law. 'Tis better for everyone that I did not remain in his household. Indeed, I feel certain that the Lord has moved me to be here."

"I think your father would rather you return home to keep you safe," Lucy said in a low tone.

"It sounds like he wants her to go against her conscience," Sam said. "It is better that she stay here with us."

"You know that he does not approve of the way Quakers have been treated and—" Lucy pleaded. As she looked around, she could see the other Quakers looking at her skeptically. "I know that her father is a magistrate, but he does not wish them to be persecuted or injured."

"He does nothing to change the laws, does he?" Theodora said, apparently voicing what everyone in the room was thinking.

"Let him stop punishing the Quakers," Gervase agreed, making a dramatic flourish with his hands.

Lucy stood up then. "I am so sorry that you will not return home," she said, blinking back tears. She left the room quickly.

She had walked only a short way down the corridor when Sarah called her name. Lucy did not turn around.

"Lucy!" Sarah whispered fiercely, grabbing her arm. "Dost thou not apprehend why I am here?"

"I understand what you just said and—"

"No, you do not!" Sarah interrupted. "I have moved to Esther Whitby's home because I am worried about her. She is the widow of my dear friend. I believe the Lord has called me to protect her." Tears filled her eyes.

"Why did you not tell your father this? Or Adam?"

"I know that if I were to tell them that I had been moved to protect Esther against an impostor, Father would remove me for certain." She searched Lucy's face. "Can you not see how terrible it would be for the Friends if one of them were forcibly removed by a magistrate? I fear that the uneasy truce would be gone."

At Lucy's nod, she continued. "If there is an impostor here, he or she must be led to understand that I have spurned my father." She took Lucy's hand. "Thou wert present when Jacob had me promise to keep his wife safe from harm."

Miserably, Lucy nodded again. "The deathbed promise," she whispered, feeling the goose bumps prickle across her flesh.

"If thou must call it that, yes," Sarah said. "I think of it as a promise to a friend. A last promise to a man that I . . . once loved."

Lucy stared at her. Sarah went on, her voice lowering more. "Thou said it thyself—Esther Whitby could be in danger. To think that someone close to her could wish her ill turns my stomach. Thou canst see how good and kind she is." She paused, looking up and down the quiet hallway. "Some of the people whom Esther calls her 'dear acquaintances,' I do not think are so dear at all."

"What do you mean?"

"Some of the men watch her hungrily. Sam, Gervase, Devin— other men, too. I fear this hunger toward her. Men do desperate things when they are consumed by such passions."

"She *is* a beautiful woman," Lucy said thoughtfully. "Gervase is unmarried, I know. But I have met the other men's wives." *And their wives are all wan and drab in comparison,* she thought, but did not say out loud. "What of the others in her acquaintance? Theodora? Deborah? Ahivah? Do any of them raise a concern for you?"

Sarah wrinkled her brow. "No. Truth be told, I think the danger to Esther comes from another source." Lowering her voice, she added, "Esther told me that someone has been follow- ing her."

"Who is it?" Lucy whispered.

"An old woman, always carrying a bell. I have seen her my- self. Quite a frightful figure, to be sure. Esther was quite beside herself with fear the last time we spied the woman watching the house. Both Devin and Gervase have run her off. Still she returns, lurking—watching."

Sadie Burroughs! Why was the searcher watching Esther?

Lucy was about to tell Sarah about the searcher when her friend took her hand, changing the topic. "Dearest Lucy," she said, "I am ever so grateful that thou hast come to see me today.

I am sorry that I spoke ill to thee when thou first arrived. Indeed, aside from Joan and Esther, thou art the dearest friend I have." She sniffed slightly. "I am grateful, too, that thou wert with my family these last few years. I know my father misses thee now. Do not shake thy head, 'tis true."

For a moment, Sarah stood silently, gazing at a cobweb above the doorframe. "I remember how thou wert the only one who would answer my father's questions when he would read to the family." She laughed, looking for a moment like her old self. "I am afraid that my responses used to make him sorely angry with me." She sighed deeply, returning to the source of her earlier sorrow. "My father and I seem doomed to be at odds. But he must understand that he is asking a fish to live in a tree."

Joan appeared then, carrying a small steaming kettle with two mugs.

"Child, please do come back inside and sit with us a spell," she said to Lucy. "Perhaps if thou couldst understand us better, thou might be able to help Sarah's family understand the people with whom their daughter is now living."

"Thank you, Joan," Lucy replied, thinking that if she stayed, she might be able to speak to Ahivah. Or, if she were able, ask Esther about why the searcher might be watching her. "I should very much like to do so."

They returned to the drawing room. No one commented on Lucy's return, but they all gave her small welcoming smiles. Now that she no longer seemed to be trying to separate Sarah from them, they were friendly again. Lucy returned their smiles, but vowed silently to remain watchful.

Joan, Theodora, and Ahivah had returned to their sewing.

Even Sarah, it seemed, had learned to sew, though Lucy could see that her skill with the needle was even worse than her own. Only Deborah just sat there, halfheartedly pulling a thread through the material when anyone looked in her direction.

Lucy plucked a garment from the workbasket and began to ply a needle. Deborah raised an eyebrow. "Idle hands are the devil's tools," Lucy murmured, offering the old adage by way of explanation. It was difficult for her to just sit without doing anything to pass the time, and besides, by sewing she could easily listen to the others without looking like she was doing so.

The next hour passed in a fairly companionable way. Sam first read a passage from the Old Testament, which the others then discussed with some animation. There was something Lucy admired about their ease of speech and the manner in which they listened to each other. What would it be like to be on the outs with society? To always be unwelcome in most communities? Clearly, though, they had each other, which was saying something indeed.

Afterward, they began to discuss what seemed to be typical Quaker business. Recent imprisonments, in London and elsewhere. Petitions that had been written. How the funds, victuals, and clothing they had collected should be dispersed to widows and orphans, or to those temporarily without a parent or spouse. The plight of Quakers still languishing in jail, mostly, it seemed, for nonobservance of the Lord's Day, for being vagabonds, and for failure to take the Oath. Again and again, the same refrain. "The magistrates are harassing us."

Unexpectedly, Esther began to speak, an exalted look on her face. "Oh! The mighty power of the Lord broke in amongst us and tendered our hearts," she called. "So also it hath continued with us unto this day, which I desire may never depart from us!"

Although Lucy did not know what Esther was talking about, the woman's passion was obvious. The others were all nodding and murmuring, clearly transfixed by her words.

"Let us remember," Esther proclaimed, "that the preserving hand of the Lord is time after time witnessed to keep us and nourish us, and"—here her voice dropped—"his intent is to do our souls good." She slumped in her chair then, as if all her energy had been spent.

"Thank you, dear Esther," Sarah said softly. "I needed thy words."

As the room had begun to darken, Esther moved a candle closer so that she could better see her stitches. In the candlelight, her features took on an ethereal quality, enhancing her beauty, and the outline of her form could be seen through the thin garment she was wearing.

The effect was not lost on the others in the room, or at least not the men. Sam, Gervase, and Devin all seemed to be stealing glances at her, their faces displaying a shared longing. Lucy thought about how Sarah had described the men's attention toward Esther. They did look ravenous.

Unbidden, a phrase from a popular merriment popped into Lucy's head: *The rich Widow weeps with one eye and casts glances with the other.*

Esther Whitby certainly was not rich. Could she be planning to marry again? Such was the expectation, even when there were no children who required a father. For her part, however, Esther seemed oblivious of the men's sudden attention.

The other women might not have been so unaware. Theodora laid her hand on Sam's arm and murmured something to him. He nodded, but he still seemed distracted. Deborah yawned and stretched, breaking the spell.

This seemed like a good moment to speak to Ahivah. Lucy turned to her, asking quietly, "May I ask you a question? Is Ahivah your given name?"

The woman smiled sadly, shaking her head no.

"She does not speak," Joan said.

"My aunt *cannot* speak," Deborah corrected. "Ahivah's name was given to her by the Lord, when she became his handmaiden."

Seeing Lucy's puzzled look, Joan explained, "Like the ancient prophet who spoke to Jeroboam the king of Jerusalem, our sister Ahivah shared her vision with the king. She became known to him as the Woman in White."

Lucy nodded. This she knew. "I have seen tracts that speak of her prophecies and warnings," she ventured, looking casually around.

Joan nodded eagerly. "Her warnings must still be heard, even though she can no longer speak."

"Ripped out her tongue, they did," Deborah said. She sounded almost triumphant.

"What?" Lucy stared at them, putting her hand to her mouth, feeling the bile rise in her throat.

Ahivah gave her a gentle smile. Then she spread her lips, baring her yellow teeth. Slowly, she opened her jaw as wide as she could. Where her tongue should have been was a great gaping hole.

Gasping, Lucy could not keep herself from shrinking back

from the horrifying sight. "What—whatever happened?" she exclaimed. "Who did that to you?"

"A Boston magistrate." Deborah shrugged again. "One of the many who are frightened of the Truth."

The Quakers around her all murmured their thanks to the Lord in response.

Joan then addressed Lucy directly. "Didst thou know, my child, that when the Anglican priests fled their pulpits, 'twas the Quakers who stayed, preaching to the sick and the dying?"

Lucy murmured something but did not know what she said, still shocked by what she had just witnessed. Unheeding, Joan continued on about the early Quaker preachers. The Valiant Sixty, she called them.

As Joan spoke, Lucy watched Esther stretch and stand up, moving to close the shutters. For a moment she stood in the window, her face beautifully illuminated by the candlelight.

Then, as Lucy watched, Esther's face changed, taking on a fearful expression. Her knuckles clenched as she gripped the shutter. Gervase, who had been watching her, moved beside her and peered out the window as well.

"That woman!" Lucy heard Esther whisper to Gervase, her voice shaking a bit. "She is back. Why does she plague me so?" She had started to tremble as well.

"I will take care of her," Gervase replied in a low tone. "Stay here." She saw him turn toward Sam and nod.

The two men left the room then. Esther stayed by the window, looking anxiously outside. Lucy slipped out as well, murmuring something about needing the privy.

As silently as she could, Lucy tiptoed out and opened the

front door, hoping that no one would see her. Her cloak was still in the other room where she had left it, so she shivered deeply in the chilly March air.

She looked up and down the quiet street. It had grown terribly foggy, and she could only just make out three figures. They appeared to be talking, but she was too far away to hear them. She wanted to draw closer, except she was worried that someone would notice her absence. As she went back into Esther's house, she heard a bell ring, its tinny sound almost lost in the rising wind.

Shutting the door behind her, she ran into Deborah, who was coming from the direction of the kitchen.

"Were you outside?" Deborah asked curiously. Lucy noticed that she did not use the Quaker's plain address. "Whatever were you doing, without your cloak?"

"Just wanted a breath of fresh air," Lucy replied as pleasantly as she could, all the while wishing the young woman would lower her voice.

"Oh, don't I know it!" Deborah replied. "It's stuffy in here, all right. I would not be here a minute if I did not have to be."

"Do you have to be here?" Lucy asked. "Can you not leave? I thought Quakers roam as they please, following their conscience."

A curious flutter crossed the young Quaker's face. "Well, I have nowhere better to go. Not received the calling and all that. Besides, my aunt Ahivah needs me here." She looked down at Lucy's boots. "I wish I had boots like yours. I just have these old things." She kicked disdainfully at her somber buckled shoes.

"My brother gave them to me," Lucy said, growing more curious about the young woman. Although she did not know too many Quakers, surely most did not admit to coveting the worldly possessions of others. "Have you been a Quaker long?"

Deborah shrugged. "A while, I suppose. Well, a few months. Or has it been a year? I cannot rightfully recall." Unexpectedly, she gave Lucy an impudent wink.

"Deborah!" Joan called to her as she descended the stairs. "Please come in."

Esther came out behind her. "We are about to start readying for supper now. Lucy, wouldst thou care to join us? Though it be meager fare, thou art most welcome to stay."

"Thank you. You are most kind. I fear, though, I must return to Master Aubrey's to fix his evening meal. Lach has likely burnt the roast, which will make my master very cross indeed."

"We do not want thy printer to be cross. One day, perhaps, thou wilt not have to call another man your master." Esther smiled, and then, to Lucy's surprise, the woman embraced her warmly. "Thou art welcome any time. Sarah has said that thou wert once like a sister to her. I know we should be very glad to see that dear acquaintance resumed."

To her delight, Sarah smiled at her as well. "Any time, Lucy. Thou art a good friend, and as Esther says, a sister, too. Let us not have my differences with my father come between us." As they embraced, Lucy felt a glad tiding rising in her heart.

Moving from the warm companionable house into the increasingly blustery wind, she felt something that was almost akin to loss. What would it be like to experience such companionship? Such friendship? Such a sense of spiritual equals? Pulling her cloak closer, Lucy could only wonder.

———

A heavy fog had descended, making the narrow street far darker and more fearful than she expected. She was thinking about returning to the Whitbys' home and requesting a lantern when two figures emerged at the end of the road. Since the dark often brought out cutthroats and thieves, she thought it prudent not to draw attention. Lucy pressed herself behind a tree, thinking to let the figures pass her by before she resumed her journey home.

As they drew nearer, she recognized Sam and Gervase, conversing in low tones. She was about to step from her hiding place when she caught a snippet of their conversation.

"I am rather afraid that Sarah's companion, Lucy, has learned something she ought not to have," she heard Sam say. "We must hope she will not tell the magistrate."

Lucy felt the blood drain from her face. What was it they thought she knew? Their next words made her almost fall, and it was all she could do to refrain from shaking. She was wary of cracking a single stick beneath her feet.

"Esther seems to trust her. So we must, too. At least thou hast dealt with that searcher," Gervase said. "The nonsense that woman speaks!"

"Oh, the Lord will stop her evil tongue," Sam replied, tapping his leg. The two men were within three feet of her now. "Of that, we can be certain."

To her surprise, Gervase laughed then, a deep, resonant sound. "That is so."

As they moved away from her, Gervase spoke again, sounding

more serious. "Sam, let us stay silent about thy dealings with the searcher," he said. "I should not like to further burden our sister Esther, for she is already quite overcome with grief and fear. She might not understand what thou hast done."

Sam said something, but Lucy lost his words in the wind. She stared at the retreating figures, sickened by what she had heard. It was all she could do to refrain from running to the door and demanding Sarah return with her. Instead, she stumbled away, with only glimpses of the moon to guide her home.

·13·

As she waited for Annie to meet her at Covent Garden the next day, Lucy could not dispel the sense of unease she'd been feeling since leaving the Quakers. The conversation she had overheard between Gervase and Sam disturbed her greatly. Several times during the night, she had thought about writing a note, but she did not know what to say, or, truth be told, whether she should send it to Adam or Duncan or one to each man. So she sent no notes at all.

Even the first hints of spring could not lift her low mood. Most of the recent snow and slush had finally disappeared. The temperature was milder, the great fog had finally lifted, and the sun was shining brighter than it had in days.

Idly, she watched a woman heavy with child trying to sell letter-writing supplies to passersby who were largely ignoring her. Since the Fire, the city was still in desperate need of poor relief, more than what the parishes could provide.

"Buy a wax or wafers!" the woman called breathlessly, the loud chant obviously a strain to her body. Wincing, she put a hand to her back, brushing away a tear. Catching Lucy's eye, she asked weakly, "Buy a pen, miss?"

Lucy sighed. The woman was unlikely to be licensed by the Stationers Company, yet given her state, Lucy could not bring herself to turn away from her pleading gaze. Without thoroughly examining them, Lucy bought one pen for a penny.

Annie came up then, nearly colliding with a woman carrying a basket of hot coddlings in her haste. As they began to walk among the stalls and carts, Annie's bright chatter helped dispel Lucy's anxious feelings.

Finally Annie realized that her conversation was one-sided. "Lucy, what ails you?" she asked.

"I am terribly worried about Sarah," Lucy confided.

Annie's face fell. "I still can't believe that Miss Sarah has gone to live with the Quackers, I mean, Quakers." Her voice dropped. That Sarah had defied the magistrate in such a fashion clearly still awed Annie.

"She cannot stay with them! I know that now. But she can be so stubborn. She thinks she is helping Esther," Lucy said, beginning to walk faster, moving past the vegetable stalls. Her thoughts were moving even more rapidly. "There are some questions we never asked."

"What questions? What are you talking about? Hey—Lucy! Where are you going?" Annie called, panting after her. "I've barely anything on my list. Cook will kill me if I forget the raisins and ginger. She's making—"

Lucy interrupted her. "Annie, please, will you come with me? I need to speak with someone, and I promised"—she paused, remembering Adam's fervent words—"someone that I would not look into these things on my own." Without waiting for Annie to agree, Lucy began to move out of the market, back onto the muddy cobblestone street. Annie followed behind her, a bit helplessly, her empty straw basket swinging on her arm.

As they walked, Lucy told Annie about Jacob Whitby and his sister, everything she had learned so far. She also told her how Sarah believed that it was her duty to safeguard Esther, because of her promise to Jacob. She even told Annie about the conversation she overheard between Sam and Gervase the night before. All the while, Annie listened openmouthed, but did not say anything.

"We need to know what Julia Whitby knew," Lucy declared. "What was she going to tell her brother?"

"She was going to tell him the name of the impostor," Annie said, stating the obvious with authority.

Lucy threw her arm around Annie's bony shoulders and gave her a little squeeze. "Yes, I think that is right," she said, smiling. It felt so good to share all of her worries with someone else who understood the family. "Perhaps there was something else, too. Something more to discover, which will shed light on this question."

They turned down the street where Julia Whitby's family lived. In a tremendous stroke of good luck, a familiar figure was out front. It was Evie, Mrs. Whitby's maid. She was clearing away the ruined rush matting from the street in front of their house. All the traffic from the carts and carriages had destroyed the matting, and the recent icy sleet had made it a slippery mess.

"Ho there!" Lucy called amiably. "How does your mistress fare?"

Straightening up, Evie squinted at her, taking in her bookseller's pack. Lucy could see that her eyes were still red from weeping. She looked at Annie, too, who gave her a friendly smile. Puzzled, she asked, "You were the one who came here the other day? With the gentleman?"

Lucy nodded.

"I must thank you, then, miss," Evie said, giving a little bob. "For helping with the mistress the other day. A blessing it was." She gave a little sniff. "A sore week it's been."

Lucy smiled gently at her. "I'm sure the blessing is in the care you have taken of your mistress." She set her pack down heavily. "Ah! It's nice to set this down."

"You're a peddler?" Evie asked.

"Bookseller, and printer's apprentice," Lucy replied, a hint of pride creeping into her voice. "Annie here works for the magistrate, you know, the Whitbys' old friends. She holds the same job I once held. Chambermaid." She held her breath when she said the last. She was gambling that Evie would feel more comfortable speaking to one of her own station. She knew, too, that the opposite was sometimes true as well. Servants could be even snobbier than their masters, looking down on those who did the most menial tasks. She knew she was taking a chance. To her relief, Evie seemed to relax when Lucy revealed her former occupation, rather than holding it against her.

"Terrible news about Miss Julia," Lucy said, kicking a bit of the rush matting toward the pile that Evie had been creating with her broom.

"Gar!" Evie replied. "That it was. When the constable came to tell the mistress, I never seen her take on so." She continued sweeping, a bit harder now, her face growing red with the effort. "Awful the way Miss Julia died." That she didn't add any details showed the girl was not a gossip.

Lucy murmured something in consolation, even as a sharp memory from the past overcame her. Almost two years ago Constable Duncan had appeared at the magistrate's own door, bearing equally distressing news. That was the first time she had met him. So much had happened since then.

She could see now that the girl was trying not to cry. Annie, who had been watching, quietly took the broom from the maid's bare hands and continued the task of pushing away the rush matting. Lucy held out a small linen cloth she kept tucked away in her skirts. Evie accepted it with a watery smile and blew her nose loudly.

"My head ached so," Evie said. "The mistress was wailing and the master was shouting. All the while they kept asking me questions. What did I know? I didn't know anything. Cook said they'd toss me out if they found I wasn't telling the truth. I told them over and over I didn't know anything. She only wrote that note. I couldn't even read it." Tears began to threaten again. "Only the constable was kind. He spoke in a nice soft voice. Didn't yell at me."

"He is kind," Lucy agreed, with what she hoped was an encouraging smile. "Did you tell him anything?"

Evie shook her head. "Didn't know anything. I'd have liked to have talked to him more, though." She made a funny clucking sound. "He's a handsome sort, ain't he? No tongue-pad, trolling about, that's for certain. A good man, I could tell."

"Evie," Lucy said, trying to ignore the girl's simpering, "could you tell me something? The other day, when I was helping tend to your mistress, you told me that you thought Miss Julia had received some letters of late. Letters that had put her in a strange state. Could you tell me more about them? Where'd they come from? Who sent them?"

Evie looked back up, her eyes suspicious again. "Why do you want to know that? What business is it of yours?"

"Please," Lucy said, seeing how skittish the young woman was growing. This could be the only chance she had to speak with her. "You must not feel you are betraying Miss Julia by telling me what you know. Indeed, you are doing her the greatest service, if you can help bring her murderer to justice. I am sure the constable would appreciate it." Even though she felt a quick flush of shame over using the girl's obvious interest in the constable, Lucy continued to look at her steadily.

The servant's face had grown pinched. "Do you think those letters had something to do with what happened to Miss Julia?" she asked. "They just kept asking me if she'd said anything to me. I told them the truth. She hadn't said anything. My mum always said I couldn't put two thoughts together; always said the Lord had not given me a whit of good sense." She looked at Lucy in great consternation. "I should have told the constable, do you think?"

"Perhaps. I don't know," Lucy said, trying to contain her excitement, mindful of the maid's fragile emotions. The girl could know more than she realized. "Please, Evie. Who gave you the letters?"

Evie hesitated. "They were not letters. Not really. Printed pages, though. Like the kinds you buy."

Lucy pulled a tract out of her bag and showed it to Evie. "Like this one?"

Evie nodded.

"Could you tell us who gave them to you?" Lucy asked.

At Lucy's encouraging smile, the young servant sighed. "I told Miss Julia that there had been a knock at the door, and when I opened the door the letter was there, under a rock." She looked down, red rising up in her sallow cheeks.

Annie and Lucy exchanged a knowing glance over her head. "Someone gave them to you, to give to her?" Lucy asked gently. When Evie didn't answer, she continued. "Was it a man?"

The tears that had threatened to break now dripped down Evie's face in earnest. She began to sob out something about a man who'd approached her in the market several times. Though the lass was scarcely coherent, Lucy managed to piece it together. Three times a man had passed one of the tracts to Evie to give to her mistress, the last time right before Miss Whitby had left in a state.

"Did you look at them?" Lucy asked.

"Nah, he told me not to. He promised me things, laces,

ribbons, and the like, if I gave them to her without telling any-one." She frowned at the memory. "She told me not to speak with the man again. Even though *she* was not giving me extra coins or such fancy trappings. So I lied and said they'd been pushed through the door. When I asked her if I should take them to her father, she grew quite affrighted and remorseful like."

"What did the man look like?" Lucy asked, holding her breath.

The servant pursed her lips. "Handsome. Kept a wrap around most of his face—it was so cold, you know. Shopkeep, I'd wa-ger. He'd been out selling different things. One day spices, the next day perfumes. From the Orient they were. Struck me as odd, it did. He was a sweet talker, though." Evie frowned. "Said he was an admirer of Miss Julia. Nearly knocked me over when he said that. Being that she was a dried-up old spinster and all."

"Have you seen him recently?" Lucy asked. "Is he here now?" She gestured toward some of the street-sellers at the end of the street.

The servant looked around. "Come to think of it, I haven't seen him since the last time I gave her the message. Not fifteen minutes after that, she said she had to leave. To see Mrs. Wig-gins." She stopped, looking puzzled. "She never had a sweet-heart, you see, so I thought perhaps she was going to run off. Lord knows she could have some diversion in her life."

Thoughtfully, Lucy thanked her. As she walked Annie back to the market, she resolved to stop by to see the constable on the way home.

———

Arriving at the jail a little later, Lucy called out, "What news, Constable Duncan?" as she stepped inside.

The constable did not smile in return. "I cannot talk now, Lucy," he said as he tossed Hank a beating stick. "We've just received word there is a scuffle over at Jackson's coffeehouse. A couple of shifty fellows, knocking each other about. We need to restore order."

Since there was no one in any of the cells, they simply locked the jail and hurried down the street. Lucy trotted after them.

Seeing that she had accompanied them, the constable frowned. "Go home, Lucy," he said sternly. "A brawl is no place for a woman."

Lucy did not slow down. "Fiddle-faddle," she replied. "I need to speak with you."

"I mean it, Lucy," the constable said more tensely, glaring at her over his shoulder. "Hank, could you ensure that Miss Campion finds her way home?"

"He is mad who quarrels with women or beasts," Hank said, quoting an old proverb by way of reply. "Besides, I think you need me here," he added as Lucy smirked at the constable.

Her smirk fell away then when they began to hear terrible shouting. This was not the tussle she had assumed. This looked like an out-and-out brawl.

"Please, Lucy," the constable said to her again. Hearing the slight note of pleading in his voice, she relented.

"I promise I will stay back," she said.

The constable and Hank looked at each other. "Ready?" the constable asked, his voice tight and hard. The bellman nodded grimly in return.

Holding their beating sticks in the air, they moved into the fray. "Break it up, break it up," they began to cry, pushing the crowd away.

Lucy watched anxiously from a safe distance. She could see the flash of their clubs as they moved through the crowd. At first, when the spectators caught sight of the constable, they began to jeer and laugh. Seeing a constable brought down would be as entertaining as the men brawling, it seemed. However, as he and Hank continued to wield their sticks with strength and purpose, it became clear who would remain standing. At that point, the crowd began to disperse, their sport ending.

Now she could see just a few bloodied men at the center of the spectacle, still landing tired blows upon each other. At least their fight seemed to be only with fists. She saw the constable and Hank nod at each other before each grabbed one of the men and wrestled him to the ground. They pulled the men's arms behind their backs and laced them tightly together with a bit of rope.

Hauling them up at the same time, Hank managed to knock the heads of the two ruffians together, causing them both to groan loudly.

"Clumsy me," he said, broadly grinning all the while.

"What was this fight about?" Constable Duncan demanded.

Both men looked at him with sullen expressions.

"Ale," the scrawnier of the two men said.

"Coffee," the burlier man said.

At that point, the two men began to shout loudly at each other again. It seemed that the new coffeehouse had taken up residence directly next to the alehouse that had been there at least a hundred years. The tavern-keep was angry that the owner of the coffeehouse was stealing his customers. They were then arrested for disturbing the peace.

Hearing the church bells chime for the hour, Lucy knew she had to get back to Master Aubrey's. As Hank single-handedly wrestled the two men back to the jail, the constable turned to Lucy. "All right," he said. "Tell me what's so important."

She told him what she had learned from Evie, as well as the conversation she had overhead between Gervase and Sam. "I am worried that they did something to the searcher," she said.

He nodded. "I will look into it."

As she started to go, he touched her arm. "And thank you, Lucy. For telling me, and not keeping these secrets to yourself."

·14·

The next morning, Lucy showed Master Aubrey all the testimonies about Jacob Whitby she had painstakingly assembled over the last few evenings.

"I was thinking that we could call it *The Last Dying Breath*," Lucy said, showing him her handwritten pages. Her script was still not overly neat, but she had rewritten anything that looked particularly strange or illegible.

"See, this first part tells how he was struck down, in the prime of life, by Mr. Redicker, cloth merchant," she explained, her nervousness making her speak quickly. "In the next part, I have Jacob Whitby's sinner's journey, what he told me in his own dying words. After that, I have the words from his wife and his dearest friends, speaking of his spiritual conversion, lamenting his death and the loss of his good works."

Both Lach and Lucy watched Master Aubrey peruse the

tract. He did not say anything as he read, so Lucy continued to speak in a breathless way. "Naturally, in this piece, I did not mention anything about his sister Julia's death." *Or Jacob's belief that he had been pushed in front of the horses,* she added to herself.

"Hmph," Master Aubrey grunted. "I was planning to sell at the Fox and Hound this morning, and then meet a few chaps there for my noon meal. I was not planning on composing the type today."

"We can do it, sir," Lucy said.

Lach frowned at her. "*I* can do it, sir. She can help me."

Master Aubrey looked at them. "All right, then." He gave some quick instructions to Lach about the length of the quarto, and what to include on the recto and verso. "I expect the first two parts to be set by the time I return this afternoon."

"Yes, sir," they both dutifully replied.

As soon as Master Aubrey had departed, Lach turned to her. "I will compose the piece. You can clean the hearth and take care of the pots." When she made an indignant sound, he added, "You can help with the typesetting, of course."

"I am sure that Master Aubrey expected me to compose the piece," she protested, picking up a quoin. "*I* wrote it, after all."

"I am sure he did not," Lach said curtly. "Not when you think composition starts with simply putting quoins together."

"Well, show me, then," Lucy said, setting the quoin back on the table. When he didn't reply, she added, "I'll do your chores for the rest of the week."

He grunted. "Starting with those pots!"

Lucy stood beside him then to watch the composition process unfold. Even though she had worked for Master Aubrey for six months, she had not yet measured and laid out a tract from the very beginning of the process.

Lach began to work, composing the different sections so that it would become an eight-page piece. Although she didn't like the high-handed way he ordered her about, Lucy had to admit that he was very deft in arranging the parts of the tract. Within the hour, Lach had sectioned off the different parts, assembled the various woodcuts and necessary plates, and used the quoins, wedges, and crossbars to separate the text and images accordingly. They used the plainest type, all ten and twelve font, which seemed appropriate to tell a tale of a sinner's journey. Only the title would be in the more elaborate Gothic font.

For the next thirty minutes, they worked, Lucy trying to ignore the ache in her lower back. Setting type was always difficult, painstaking work. Sometimes she sat for a while on one of the tall stools, but bending across the type was still a bit painful.

As she pieced together the words of the tract, putting in each letter backward as she had been trained, she recalled how each person had testified about Jacob's spiritual journey. She thought, too, about Julia Whitby. What had she known?

Without her realizing it, Lucy began to slow down.

"Lucy!" Lach cried harshly.

The quoin she was filling with the tiny lead type flew out of her hand, spilling onto the floor and skittering in every direction. She stared in dismay first at Lach and then down at the mess.

"Lucy!" Lach growled.

"I am sorry, I am sorry," she said. "I will take care of it." She began to scramble around. To her surprise, Lach put down the quoin he'd been filling and began to help her, even though he grumbled under his breath the whole time. Finally they had picked up all the pieces. Still sitting on the floor, they leaned back.

Lach mopped his sweaty brow with a dirty bit of cloth. Rather than wiping his face clean, unfortunately, he had smudged ink all over his cheeks and forehead. The result made him look ridiculous.

With great effort, Lucy refrained from laughing. Instead, she stood up and went over to a small basket she kept on one of the lower shelves that was full of laundered scraps of cloth. She had even put a lavender sachet in the basket to make the cloths smell good. She placed a cloth in front of him without a word, then turned back to the type she was setting.

From the corner of her eye, she could see him stare at the cloth before dabbing gingerly at his face. He hesitated, then buried his face in the cloth, breathing the lavender scent in deeply.

He turned to her then. "All right," he said. "Spill it. What have you learned about all this? It is easy to see that you've been woolgathering this whole time."

Excitedly, she set down her printer's tool and told him everything she had learned so far.

As she spoke, Lach shook his head. "I cannot believe no one has asked him."

"Who? What? What are you talking about?"

Impatiently, Lach pointed at *The Last Dying Breath*, now laid out neatly and waiting to be pressed. "The driver of the cart who struck Mr. Whitby. James Redicker. Maybe he saw something!"

"He said he didn't . . . ?" Lucy said doubtfully.

"People always tell the truth?" Lach returned.

Of course, Lach was quite correct. Lucy could have slapped herself. Remembering her promise to Adam, she added, "You will have to come with me."

Lach shrugged. "Best that I come anyway. I will have the truth out of the man in two shakes of a goat's tail."

Lucy raised her eyebrow. "We shall see, will we not?"

After they closed the shop, Lucy and Lach walked the half mile to see Mr. Redicker. When they arrived at his shop, Lucy could tell that his establishment was new. She could see that there had been another business there once, perhaps a smithy, although she could not know for sure. If she had to guess, Mr. Redicker must have been one of the many shopkeeps whose businesses had been disrupted by the Fire. Unlike most, he looked to have his own stable in what was once a small courtyard. They could see a horse and a small cart from the street.

A boy, maybe about fifteen or sixteen, came out then. "Seeking some new woolens?" he asked cheerfully, looking at Lach's worn cloak.

"We were hoping to speak with Mr. Redicker," Lucy replied.

"Inside," he nodded toward the stable. "He is tending the horses. He will be in there a while. Perhaps you would like to look at some woolens while you wait? Nice for blankets—where are you going?"

Lucy was pulling Lach to the stable. "Our master expects us back soon, I am afraid. You do not mind if we speak to your father now? Our master is *very* rich and is looking to get new materials for his summer home. I do not wish to offend you"—she smiled at the boy—"but he would prefer us to speak to your father directly. You understand."

Before the boy could protest, Lucy pulled opened the stable door. A man—whom she assumed was Mr. Redicker—was standing beside a chestnut brown horse, speaking quietly, his hand stroking the horse's long mane.

At the sound of their entrance the horse jumped nervously, rearing backward and whinnying. Lucy stepped back, pressing upon the stable door. The black horse in the next stall began to stamp fearfully as well.

The man glanced at them. "What are you doing in here?" he asked tersely, trying to calm the horse down. The horse had stopped rearing but was still stamping. The black horse had started to whinny now.

To her surprise, Lach stepped forward, murmuring something to the black horse that Lucy could not quite understand, for he was speaking with an uncharacteristic brogue. She thought it might have been "There, there, little bairn," but could not be sure.

The horse looked at Lach and brought his head over to smell him. Slowly, Lach yawned. While Mr. Redicker and Lucy watched, Lach leaned up and placed his own head against the horse's and began to breathe at the same time. The horse immediately began to calm.

Mr. Redicker looked at him. "Thank you. How did you know how to do that?"

Lach shrugged. "Grew up on a farm, sir."

The cloth merchant looked them over, his eyes expertly gliding over their garments. "Purchasing something for your mis-

tress, lass? Or perhaps your master?" he asked, correctly deter-
mining their station.

"Yes, sir. Our master is interested in some woolens," Lucy
said, nudging Lach. She did not want to leave the stable, and she
wanted to stay on the topic of the horses.

To her surprise, he understood what she wanted him to say.
"Are your horses usually so skittish, sir?" He continued to stroke
the horse's nose and murmur quietly to her.

Mr. Redicker's face paled, and he wiped some sweat from his
brow. "No. Something terrible happened to my girls last week.
They have not been the same since."

Lach continued to stroke the black horse. "They are both
beauties, sir."

Seeing a bag of apples, Lucy picked one up and offered it to
the chestnut horse. She glanced at Mr. Redicker over her shoulder. He had sat back on a low stool, watching them. His face
was drawn, and he had huge bags under his eyes. She recognized that look. She had seen it before, on men who had faced
death or great loss. Indeed, he looked haunted.

"What happened to the horses?" Lucy asked, trying to sound
innocent.

"They . . . I . . . I . . . We ran over a man last week. In my
cart." He looked away. "It was the worst day of my life. Worse
even than when my wife died. She died in her sleep, painless.
This man—" He shut his eyes. "I can still hear him screaming."

"How terrible," Lucy said quietly, not wanting to break the
spell. "Did he trip? Or just not see your cart and horses?"

Mr. Redicker shook his head, wiping his brow. "I could not
say for sure what had happened. How could he have not heard

my cart? He must have heard my cart." He stood up and began to pace around. Sensing his nervousness, the horses began to pace again as well. "I thought my eyes were deceiving me. A break in the fog, you see."

Lucy and Lach exchanged a glance. Lach began to stroke the horses' manes, trying to restore their sense of calm.

"Did you see something then?" Lucy asked, trying not to sound excited. "What was it?"

Mr. Redicker looked heavenward. "I've been a God-fearing man my whole life. Never missed a day of church, never failed to pay my Sunday bits. I read the Bible, and I live as the Lord intended. Every day I ask myself, Why did he step into my path? Was it the will of God, asking me to better myself?' Why was I given this terrible burden?"

Lucy waited for the man to stop. "So no one else was there, then?" she asked, disappointment washing over her. "He did trip?"

Mr. Redicker paused. He seemed so lost in his nightmare. "It looked like another figure crept up behind him and pushed him before my cart." He closed his eyes again. "I was so intent on the screaming and what had happened to my poor horses that when I looked again, the figure was gone. Could that have happened?"

"Did you tell that to the constable?" Lucy asked quietly as if speaking to one of the horses, not wishing to spook him.

Mr. Redicker's weariness seemed almost palpable now. He gave a tired chuckle. "Lord help me. I lied to that constable."

"What?" Lucy and Lach exclaimed in unison. Lucy was grateful that for once Lach kept his jest-spewing tongue still.

Mr. Redicker began to speak more quickly, with the air of a man trying to remove an enormous weight from his chest. "The devil tricked me into this evil. I took money to say that that poor man tripped. I pray that the Lord will forgive my weakness."

"Who paid you the money?" Lucy whispered.

"I was heartsick, you understand." To their chagrin, the man began to weep. "I did not know what I had seen in the fog—I could not say whether it was a trick of the light. So I told everyone the man must have tripped. To think otherwise . . ." His voice trailed off. "And yet, I did wonder."

He took a deep breath, trying to control himself. "That same night, I heard a knock at my door. A man said he was there on behalf of the chap's widow. He said that she was worried about how I was feeling, and that they wished to give me money to fix my cart or to buy a new one. I was indeed bitter about the ruin caused to my cart and horses, and I readily took the money offered to me."

"That was very generous of his widow," Lucy said.

"Yes," Mr. Redicker said. "A charitable act indeed. To think that I, who had taken everything from her, who dealt her husband his fatal blow, would benefit so from her largesse. I felt guilt then, of such magnitude as I had never before experienced. So I told him that I wondered whether her husband had been pushed." His voice broke again.

"Yes, what did he say?" Lucy asked.

"He said no good could from disturbing the man's widow with so wild and strange an accusation. He told me that they were assured that it was an accident, and they knew I was assured of that truth as well. Then he passed me the money." He swallowed. "I knew then, you see."

"You knew what?" Lucy asked, confused.

His brow furrowed. "I knew then that I had made a pact with the devil. The money he had given me. It was far more than what was necessary to fix my cart and tend to my horses." He stood up and started stroking his horse again.

"You must tell the constable what you just told us," Lucy said.

Mr. Redicker's brow furrowed. "I have no wish to discuss this heart-sorry mess again."

"But what of your conscience? Do you not owe it to this man, and his widow, for the truth to be known?"

He gulped. "I have given more than my fair share to the church. I hope the good Lord will see fit to absolve me of my sin."

"Please, sir, just one more question. What did the man look like? The one who came on behalf of the man's widow?"

Mr. Redicker turned dull eyes toward Lucy. He now seemed spent and listless. "Why ever would you ask such a thing?"

Lucy and Lach looked at each other, not sure what to say.

"You are not here to buy woolens, are you?" he said wearily. He seemed resigned. "Why are you here? Did someone send you?"

"Please, sir. Absolve your conscience. Please describe the man who paid you the money," Lucy urged him. "I promise you, it is important."

Mr. Redicker spat on the ground. "His frame was not overly large, I should say." His tone grew dismissive. "The cut and quality of his cloth were quite poor. Never seen a tailor, of that you may be certain. Indeed, I remember being surprised that a man in such shabby clothes would have so many coins."

"His hair, what color was it?" Lucy pressed. "Brown? Black? What about his eyes?"

"Not sure. He was one of those damn Quakers. I could tell by his hat. He did not remove it when he spoke to me. No respect for his betters." He spat again.

Lucy sighed. The description was so vague.

Then Mr. Redicker spoke again. "I do remember, though, that his hand shook when he spoke. I could tell he had a tremor. Same as my grandfather."

The clothier turned away. "Please leave. I do not have the heart to speak of this matter again. I see it over and over again in my dreams. I do not need to revisit it in my waking hours as well."

Before she walked out, Lucy turned back to him. "It was not your fault, sir."

He just shook his head numbly. "That may be true, but it does not take away the screams."

Lucy and Lach hurried out, past Redicker's boy. Once they were at the street, Lucy turned to Lach. "Someone tried to hide the fact that Jacob Whitby was deliberately pushed in front of poor Mr. Redicker's cart. We must tell the constable."

Lucy fully expected Lach to start singing *The Constable Confounded* at the top of his lungs. Instead he just nodded and stayed silent all the way home.

———

When they entered the shop, Lucy was relieved to see that Master Aubrey had not yet returned. Working quickly, she and Lach finished typesetting Jacob Whitby's *Last Dying Breath* within the hour. After that, Lucy began to pace, occasionally popping her head out of the door, looking to see if Master Aubrey was making his way along Fleet Street. She was itching to tell the constable everything she had learned, but she also wanted to make sure the piece was correct before she requested an hour away from the shop.

"I'd send a message to the constable if I could find a lad to run it over to him," she said, sighing. The street seemed unusually void of boys lagging about, eager to earn a quick penny.

Finally Master Aubrey returned. He'd scarcely hung up his hat before Lucy pulled him over to show him the completed typeset quarto. Holding her breath, she watched as he looked it over. Lach, too, was watching him carefully.

At last, mopping his brow, he looked at them and smiled. "Good, good," he said. "A fine piece. We can print it out first thing tomorrow." He looked at Lach. "Well done, lad."

Lach grinned. For a moment Lucy bristled in indignation that she had been left out of the praise, but unexpectedly, the apprentice gestured toward her. "Lucy was, er, very helpful, and, er, the piece was a good one." He nodded meaningfully at Lucy. *Ask him,* his glance seemed to say.

"Master Aubrey, sir," Lucy said, trying not to sound desperate or pleading, "could I please have an hour's leave to speak to the constable?"

"What's that?" The printer eyed her. "Whatever for?"

"I've got some news. About Julia Whitby's death. We could use it for *The Scold's Last Scold*," Lucy replied. Truly her news related to Jacob Whitby's death, but that distinction did not seem to matter at the moment. "But first I need to speak with the constable."

Master Aubrey looked at Lucy with the same bemused expression he often had when considering her requests. "Female apprentices, bah!" he muttered. But he let her go, and for that fact she was grateful.

Hearing about her conversation with Mr. Redicker, the constable swore, a more vile oath than she had ever heard him express. "I am sorry, Lucy, to use such language before you. To think that Mr. Redicker lied to me angers me greatly. I should arrest him as an accomplice to this murder."

They were standing in the makeshift jail. Today two ladybirds were sitting dourly on the bench inside, one half asleep, the other watching them with mild interest.

Lucy put her hand on his arm. "Please, do not arrest Mr. Redicker, I beg you. He is heartfelt sorry about his lie."

"That may be so. Still, this means I need to investigate Jacob Whitby's death more fully." He paused. "I agree, though, it may make no sense to arrest the man. I will certainly press him for more details."

Lucy nodded, although frankly she doubted that Mr. Redicker would have more information on the matter. The poor man seemed to have expressed all he knew in that one tortured outbreak; she did not think he would likely break down again in the presence of the constable.

Duncan was still mulling over what she had told him. "From his description, you believe it was one of the Quakers who spoke to him? The one who paid him for his silence?"

"Yes," Lucy said softly. "Mr. Redicker said as much."

"Then I believe it is time that I pay Mrs. Whitby and the others a visit. Quaker conscience be damned."

·15·

Over the next two days, Lucy could not keep from fretting about everything she had recently learned. Her head ached constantly, and she felt snappish and out of sorts. She was not alone in her ill humor, though, for it seemed much of London was feeling a strange wave of lethargy. The physician Larimer would have said they were all phlegmatic, needing wine to restore balance to the humors. Certainly, a bone-chilling rain had brought much sneezing and nose-blowing—so much that some called it the return of the plague. Anyone who had lived through the great sickness, though, knew that the dreaded Black Death had not returned. Master Aubrey blamed their collective peevishness on the looming Ides of March, and Lucy was not completely sure that he was wrong.

They spent much of the morning printing, drying, folding and cutting the quartos, so there were thirty complete copies of

The Last Dying Breath as the Quakers had requested. In the early afternoon, Master Aubrey sent Lucy to Esther Whitby's home to deliver the tracts and collect their agreed-upon fee.

At Lucy's knock, Esther Whitby opened the door and looked out. Seeing Lucy, she raised one of her finely arched eyebrows. "Yes?" she asked.

"Who is it, Esther?" she heard Theodora call from inside the house.

Her beautiful purple eyes still trained on Lucy's, Esther turned her head slightly. "It's Lucy. Our printer's apprentice."

Theodora appeared behind Esther then. Her face looked particularly mottled and suspicious. "Why hast thou come here?"

"I-I have brought copies of Jacob Whitby's *Last Dying Breath* for you," Lucy said, wondering at the cool reception. After all, the other day they had treated her like a valued acquaintance. She gestured at her pack. "They are here."

"Let me see one," Theodora said, sticking her hand out. "We won't pay for filthy lies."

"N-no, of course not," Lucy stammered, increasingly confused. What would Master Aubrey say if they refused to pay? She handed a copy to Theodora. "I only wrote down what you told me. They are mostly your husband's own words," she said, turning back to Esther, "straight from his lips."

As Theodora perused the tract, Esther suddenly smiled at her, all traces of the earlier unfriendliness gone. "Oh, Lucy, we did not mean to frighten thee," she said. "It's just that the constable was here since we last saw thee."

"Oh! Is something the matter?" she asked. Esther seemed to be watching her carefully.

"I should say so!" Theodora cried. "Full of a false authority, mercilessly wielding his power against the handmaidens and servants of the Lord!"

"I do not understand—" Lucy began, but Esther broke in.

"He questioned everyone who was here, particularly the men," she explained, quietly and still watchful. "The constable said that the poor clothier who ran over my husband had come to believe that someone had pushed Jacob into the path of those wretched horses! He said, too, that someone had paid him to lie about what he had seen."

"Oh!" Lucy said, hoping she looked sufficiently startled by the news. "Indeed, we wrote nothing about Jacob having been pushed," she said. "Or that the clothier believed such a thing to be true."

Theodora glanced up sharply. "Thou hast heard tell of this ridiculous lie, then? Did the constable tell thee?"

"No, the constable told me nothing of the sort," Lucy said. At least that part was true. She was the one who had passed the information on to the constable, not the other way around. "Why would you think such a thing?"

"I am afraid that Theodora and I assumed that he might have told thee about this terrible accusation," Esther explained, "because we know that he and thou have some sort of friendship."

Her comment was made without insinuation, and yet Theodora looked at her in a knowing way. Wishing to change the subject, Lucy said, "If the tract is to your liking, I should like to receive my payment. My master will be waiting."

"This is fine, Lucy. Thank you. We are indeed indebted to

you," Esther said. "Theodora, dear sister, pray fetch Lucy her coins. I should not like her to have troubles with her master."

Theodora still seemed a bit surly, but she duly went away to get Lucy's payment.

When she disappeared, Lucy looked at Esther Whitby. "Please, how is Sarah?" she asked. "May I see her?"

Esther looked sad. "I am sorry to tell you that Sarah was quite upset after the constable stopped by. Much of her anger was directed at thee."

"At me?" Lucy exclaimed. "Why ever for?"

Esther looked around and then stepped outside beside Lucy, pulling the door behind her, so that it was almost completely shut.

"Lucy," she whispered, "Sarah told me everything."

"She did?" Lucy asked, feeling a bit stunned. What was Sarah thinking? "W-what did she tell you?"

"Sarah told me how my dear husband was so worried for my safety when he died, and how he passed that worry on to thee," Esther said, wrapping her arms around her chest to keep warm. In the cold air, her eyes had grown shiny and luminous. "Is that so?"

Lucy nodded cautiously, being unsure what else Sarah had confided. "But why is she angry at me?" she asked.

"She thinks that thou told the constable and that is why he came making inquiries. She is concerned that this rash action may have put me in more danger, and she is angry that thou wouldst willingly send authorities to her door." She touched Lucy's arm. "Let me assure thee, I do not see the situation as Sarah does. I do not believe that someone near me wishes me harm."

"But your husband—?"

Esther smiled kindly. "My husband suffered a terrible accident, an accident which confused him in his dying moments."

"What about his sister? Miss Whitby? She was killed, too!"

"That such a terrible thing happened to my dear sister-in-law will always bring a deep pain to my heart. A senseless tragedy, but one, I am sure, that is wholly unconnected to us." She smiled slightly. "I simply cannot believe that I am in danger from any of those I call a friend." Her smiled faded. "If anything, I have seen a woman who stalks me. A woman with a bell who communes with the dead. She watches me, day and night." Her teeth began to chatter, and her lips were turning a bright blue.

"How terrible!" Lucy said, pretending she knew nothing of it. "Has she hurt you?"

"She has never touched me, praise God." Esther gripped her arm. "I never walk alone. Sarah or someone has always accompanied me. I believe I am safe. But a more loathsome foul creature thou couldst scarcely imagine."

Recalling the ominous words she had overheard Sam say the other day, Lucy asked as casually as she could, "Have you seen that woman today? Or yesterday, perchance?" Stumbling under Esther's curious gaze, she added, "Is she still stalking you, do you think?" *Or has she been killed by one of your acquaintances?* Lucy could not help but think to herself.

Esther hesitated. "I do not recall seeing her these last few days. 'Tis no matter, though, for soon we will be rid of the woman's sickening gaze altogether."

"Oh?" Lucy asked.

"Yes." Esther smiled, her eyes shining yet more brightly. "Some among us have once again been called to resume our travels. We shall be leaving London very soon."

Theodora returned then with the coins, looking at them curiously. "Esther, get inside before thou dost freeze to death," she scolded.

Dutifully, Esther went inside, after bidding Lucy a warm farewell. It seemed that her earlier chill had been dispelled for good.

As Lucy accepted the payment for the tracts from Theodora, she could not help but ask. "You are leaving? Will Sarah go, too?"

Theodora stared at her, an unreadable expression on her face. "We will not all go. I have not received the call, but the others have and shall be leaving soon. Within a few days." For a moment she almost seemed sad. "It will likely be many months, even years, before Sarah and the others will return to England."

With that, Theodora shut the door, leaving Lucy standing awkwardly on the stoop. "I must inform the magistrate," she said to herself.

As she crossed a small field, she spied an old tree trunk that served as a fair enough table upon which she could write a quick note. Luckily, she still was carrying paper, ink, and the pen that she had purchased from the illicit stationer at Covent Garden.

Dear Sir, she wrote awkwardly. It still seemed so presumptuous for her to write a letter to someone so far above herself. Moreover, her poor handwriting was all the worse for writing on a tree trunk. She hesitated. What could she write that would not alarm him but would let him know how important her message was? Hoping her words were not too atrocious, she wrote another line. *I have reason to believe that Miss Sarah will be leaving England again. I am fearful that—* She bit her lip, hesitating again. What to say? Then she finished the sentence quickly. *—her traveling companions may not protect her as they might. I know not what else to tell you. I pray that there is something that can be done, although I know she Has Been Called.* She underlined all the words in the last sentence and then ended the note. *Your faithful servant, Lucy Campion.*

Lucy wished she had some sealing wax. Spying a bit of sap oozing from the tree trunk, she dabbed a bit on. While a bit sticky, the sap effectively sealed the short letter.

Seeing that the sky was growing dark from the impending rain, Lucy picked up her belongings and moved as quickly as she could to the Hargraves' household. When she discovered that the magistrate was not at home, she pressed the note into John's hand, bidding him to give it to the magistrate as soon as he could.

She looked up at the sky with a sigh. Not wanting to be caught without a lantern to guide her along the dark and treacherous path, she broke into a run and did not stop until she reached the printer's shop.

"Your note has put Father into a terrible state," Adam said the next afternoon, having appeared at the printer's shop without warning. "Quite cryptic. How do you know that Sarah is leaving? Did you determine who the impostor is? Is it one of her traveling companions?"

Lucy set down the cloth she had been using to wipe some

spilled ink off the press. "Indeed, I do not know for certain. I am gravely concerned about who your sister will be traveling with to the New World." Quickly, she filled Adam in on everything she had learned from Evie, Mr. Redicker, and the searcher. She also told him about the strange words she had heard Sam say to Gervase. He listened without interrupting, all the while watching her face closely.

Finally, when she was done, he spoke. "I must speak to Sarah," he said. "Bid her to see reason. She cannot go on in this way. I will tell her to return home tonight."

"Oh, Adam, I do not know if that will work," Lucy said. "Your sister has been stubborn. I know she feels she is protecting Esther—indeed, that she has been called by the Lord to do so. I do not think she can be compelled to return to your father's home just because you bid her to do so."

He smiled, although there was still a shadow in his eyes when he looked at her. "Lucy, I must try. I am so concerned for her well-being, even if there is not a so-called impostor lurking about," Adam said. "Lucy, I fear we are losing her."

"I think she will come around," Lucy said stoutly.

Adam looked down at her. "I have lost so much already. The city. The courts. So much has fallen apart, I can hardly bear to lose anything else."

"But we are rebuilding," Lucy said, wondering at his tone. Suddenly he seemed to be speaking about something other than the loss of his sister to the Quaker cause. "*You* are rebuilding."

Adam looked at her, smiling slightly. "Thank you, Lucy. I am ever struck by your faith in me. It renews me. I should hate to lose it."

"I do have faith in you," she said, looking up at him.

Unexpectedly, he pulled her to him in a rare embrace. She found her cheek pressed against his elegant wool coat, and she breathed deeply. Without another word, he leaned down and kissed her, still holding her tightly to him. For a moment she forgot everything that she had been so worried about.

Unfortunately, the feeling was soon dispelled when she heard distant church bells toll. She stepped back slightly. "I should get back to work," she said reluctantly.

Adam nodded. He seemed to be searching for words.

"What is it?" Lucy asked.

"The inquiries you make for Duncan," he said, then stopped, his face still holding an unusual expression.

"Yes?" Lucy asked. Inexplicably, she felt her heart beginning to beat a little faster. "What about it?"

"You seem to enjoy helping him. Spending time with him."

"I make those inquiries on behalf of your sister!" Lucy said. "I told you, I am worried about her, living with those Quakers. As I know you are worried about her, too. Besides, I felt that I owed it to your friend, Jacob Whitby, to help sort out the truth."

"Yes, I know that is so, Lucy." He was still looking at her in the same puzzled way. "It is just that I am not always sure any-more of"—he hesitated, looking a bit embarrassed—"of your heart."

"Oh!" Lucy said, startled. Given their relative stations, his uncertainty was a bit charming. Before she could stop herself, she stood up on her tiptoes and kissed him again quickly, try-ing to prove to them both what was difficult for her to say. She tried to push the image of Duncan, unexpectedly holding her hand, out of her mind.

Adam grinned more fully then, looking a bit relieved. "I missed that," he said. "For now, I will bid you good afternoon. Let us hope that I am able to convince my sister of the danger that surrounds her."

·16·

On Sunday afternoon, Lucy entered the magistrate's kitchen, breathless. John had stopped by with a note from the magistrate that morning, inviting her to join them for their noon meal after the church service was done. Master Hargrave had, it seemed, invited Sarah to dine as well.

She had run the whole way from church, fearing she would be late, only to find that the family had not sat down to the meal.

"Sarah has not arrived yet," Annie whispered. "Do you think she is going to come at all?" She nudged Lucy. "The master said I was to inform him when Miss Sarah arrived. I think he plans to remain in his study until then."

Lucy nodded. She was not altogether surprised that Sarah had not come. She wondered if Adam had spoken to his sister and, if so, whether she had listened to him.

"Just look what Cook made for us," Annie said. Both looked longingly at the cold mince pie, chicken, and bread that were laid out on the table. There was even a cheese and apple tart, no doubt made with sugar. "I am hungry," she added, pulling a crumbled piece off the edge of the bread.

"Not a taste, not even a crumb," Cook said, slapping Annie's fingers. "Not until Miss Sarah gets here. Or until the master gives his leave."

For a while they all sat waiting, John sharpening knives one by one. They made small talk for a while, until the sound of distant church bells chiming the hour reminded Lucy of the time. Standing up, she put some mince pie and a bit of the tart on a wooden tray, along with a cup of mead. "How about I take this to Master Hargrave," she said, nodding at Annie. "He's still in his study."

She was about to proceed with the tray when the magistrate emerged. As always, his quiet dignity subdued them. "I see my daughter has not arrived," he said. He waved the tray away. "I was lost in my own thoughts and did not hear you come in, Lucy. Let us eat."

After Master Hargrave said a quick prayer, Cook passed around the food. Annie sat awkwardly, not comfortable enough to speak in her master's presence. The magistrate asked Lucy a few questions as they ate, mostly about her time at Master Aubrey's. He seemed to be listening with only half an ear and did not even seem to notice when she stopped talking. They finished the meal in silence.

When they finished, the magistrate turned to her. "Lucy, I thank you for joining us today. I should very much like to ask for a favor from you," he said with his unfailing courtesy. He gestured to the door leading to the corridor.

The chicken bone on which Annie had been loudly sucking made a soft popping sound as she pulled it from her mouth.

"Anything, sir," Lucy replied, following him out of earshot of the others.

"As you know, I had asked Sarah to dine with me today, since I knew she would not be attending church. Indeed, I had hoped that she and I could discuss our differences while calmly breaking bread." He rubbed his hands together. "To be truthful, I had hoped that you might help persuade her to stay."

"Oh, sir, I—"

"I know, Lucy, that you were a good and loyal companion to her, no doubt keeping her from many a scrape. I've long prided myself on being a good judge of character. Though you were just a girl yourself, I never felt my faith in you—or your good judgment—to be misplaced."

He waved away her stammered thanks. "I should very much like to see Sarah. To let her know that she has a home with me. I am very concerned by what you and Adam have told me, that she is planning to leave England again. That you are troubled by the companions with whom she is traveling. I should very much like to reclaim my daughter before I lose her forever."

Hearing the sadness in his voice made her feel wretched, and the heartfelt simplicity of his request could not be refused. "How may I help, sir?"

"Will you please accompany me to Jacob Whitby's home? Now? I should like to see my daughter and"—he broke off to collect himself—"bring her home if I can. A father can only pray, and hope that her conscience will lead her back to the family fold."

A short while later, Lucy and Master Hargrave reached Jacob Whitby's home. A few flakes of snow had begun to fall from a grayish sky. Winter seemed to have returned once again, tricking all the flowers that had finally begun to poke their buds during the spring thaw.

A sense of trepidation passing over her, Lucy knocked loudly on the door. Master Hargrave, she noticed, stayed out of the direct line of sight and had pulled his hat down low on his head. Theodora opened the door and stepped outside, looking at Lucy. Remembering their tight exchange the other day, Lucy firmed her stance.

"Yes?" Theodora said curtly, peering past Lucy.

The magistrate stepped forward. With quiet authority he said, "I would like to pay my respects to Mrs. Jacob Whitby for the loss of her husband and sister-in-law. I should also like to speak to my daughter, Sarah Hargrave, if you would be so good."

Theodora's eyes widened. The horror of admitting a magistrate into the house was evident on her face. Still, she managed to rally. "If she doesn't want to see her father, I'm not going to make her do so," she said to Lucy, looking past the magistrate. Nevertheless, she could not keep from darting her eyes at him. She turned back to Lucy. "Pray do not bring a magistrate to our doorstep again."

Theodora started to shut the door, but Master Hargrave placed his foot in the door's path, effectively keeping it from closing.

"Which do you prefer? A magistrate, speaking amiably to *his own daughter* and paying respects to the bereaved widow of an old family friend?" His tone was measured and even, yet Lucy could see the slightest clenching to his jaw. "Or perhaps you would prefer if I called for some constables to go inside and bring my daughter out to me? You have nothing to hide, do you?"

"We do not." Theodora sighed. "I will let Sarah and Esther know that thou art here." She stepped aside so that they could wait inside.

"Thank you," the magistrate said, shutting the door behind him. Upon entering the house, he removed his hat and tucked it carefully under his arm. Lucy stood at his elbow, rubbing her hands together.

Before Theodora disappeared up the stairs, she shut the door to the drawing room as she passed. The magistrate frowned slightly. Lucy wondered if he'd noticed the Quaker's surreptitious action and guessed, as she had, that a secret conventicle might be meeting there. They could hear Theodora's heavy steps on the corridor above them, and then some muffled conversation, followed by an indignant squeak.

Sarah stomped forward, followed by Esther, Theodora, and Joan. "Father!" Sarah exclaimed. "How could you threaten my friends in such a way?"

From behind her, Esther said, "Pray, Sarah, do not trouble thyself. We have all encountered angry fathers before, although most of them are not able to use the law to force themselves into our homes." Her gentle smile softened the impact of her brazen words. To Lucy's surprise, Esther extended her hand graciously to the magistrate. "Welcome," she said simply.

The magistrate studied her while taking her hand. "Mrs. Whitby, I am truly sorry for your loss. My son and daughter have lost a friend in your husband, Jacob. I myself remember his more madcap ways, ere he turned Quaker. A terrible thing to happen to a man in his prime. The loss is immeasurable."

Esther Whitby inclined her head graciously, accepting the magistrate's condolences. "I did not know him then, as I was still in service to my tailor until recently. Thou wilt be glad to know that he did repent of his scandalous ways when his Inner Light began to nourish him and called him to the Lord."

"Yes, yes, of course," the magistrate said. "You were once a needlewoman, then?"

"Yes, with a Dutch family. Beetners. All died in the plague, they did. I was the only one to survive. 'Twas not very long afterward when I met my good husband."

"I see. Again, let me express my condolences for your loss."

"I thank thee for that." She hesitated. "We will take good care of thy daughter. She is our sister now. We will not let her come to any harm."

"Sarah," he said, turning to his daughter. Instinctively, the other women stepped in closer to her, as if protecting her. "Will you come speak with me? Privately?"

Biting her lip, Sarah shook her head. "No, Father. I love thee dearly; however, I must follow my own path. That path leads me to stay here, not in thy home."

"Sarah," her father said, great anguish in his voice.

"I'm sorry, Father, I am. I just cannot allow thee to run the risk of harboring a Quaker in thy own home." She gulped.

"Father, indeed, I cannot bear thinking that thou wouldst be imprisoned or lose thy property for my convictions."

"That would not happen! They would not dare seize my assets or throw me into prison," her father declared, although Lucy could hear an unusual note of uncertainty in his voice.

"They might! What would happen to John and Cook and Annie if you could no longer support them?" She had dropped the Quaker speech, Lucy noticed. "If you do not care about your own career, what about Adam's prospects? Such a thing could ruin him! No," she cried, "I will not be responsible for destroying our family."

He winced as if he'd been struck. "Sarah, I would protect you."

She stepped in closer to the women. "They will protect me. Please, Father. Please go. You should not be seen here."

As they walked out of the home, the magistrate slipped on a patch of ice. His face was gray, and he was breathing heavily. Were his humors out of balance again? Lucy could not refrain from worrying, having seen the magistrate nearly lose his life during the plague. "Are you all right, sir?" she asked, taking his arm as if he were her own father. "Let me help you."

He allowed her to take his arm, and they walked unsteadily down the street. The light snow seemed to refresh him, and she was grateful when he soon seemed to resume his normal color.

"Lucy," he said, "I know not what to do. For the first time, I am deeply afraid for my daughter."

Tears rose to her eyes, although she refused to let them fall. "I understand, sir. I'm afraid for her, too." She wanted to say more, except that she didn't know how to put into the words the source of her fears.

"Thank you, Lucy. That may be so. However, the pain of a father who has failed in his duty to his daughter is a difficult burden to bear." He seemed to be considering his next words carefully. "What do you know of Mrs. Jacob Whitby, Lucy?"

Slowly, Lucy recounted everything that she had learned about the life of Jacob's widow when she was writing his last dying testimony. He clicked his teeth as he listened.

Then he turned to her and looked at her intently, his gray eyes dark and piecing. Unexpectedly, he asked, "Why do you fear for Sarah, Lucy? What is it about her companions? I sense there is something that you haven't told me." When she bit her lip, he added, "Did she tell you not to tell me something?"

Her eyes flew to his, shocked that he had read her thoughts so easily. Why was she so surprised? After all, it was his considerable skill in reading people that had made him so formidable on the bench.

When he raised his eyebrow—waiting—reluctantly she told him everything. What Jacob had whispered to her as he lay dying. About Julia's unseemly death. About what she had found hidden in Julia's room. She blushed quite a bit when she told him about her theft, but he just waved her on. Finally she told him about the sketch she had purchased from the searcher.

At the end of her flustered, faltering tale, he put his hand to his forehead. "This is all so fantastic and strange, Lucy." Still shaking his head, he added, "I truly wish you had told me all of this before. Sarah, Adam . . . do they know?" He was still.

Lucy nodded. His disappointment was hard to bear. "I know,

sir. I am hoping, though, that if Miss Sarah and Mrs. Whitby can look after each other, perhaps they will be able to protect one another."

"That is just it, Lucy," the magistrate said, starting to walk again, his gait now strong and purposeful. She did not take his arm as she had before. "I've met Esther Whitby before. And not under pleasant circumstances, either."

"What?" Lucy asked, scrambling a half step behind. "How did you meet her?" Hearing her question spoken aloud, she clapped a hand over her mouth. "Oh! Begging your pardon, sir," she said. "I should not have asked you about a private matter."

"Nonsense, Lucy," he said. There was nothing left of the beaten man he had just seemed. "I know that you are concerned about my daughter's well-being. We must return home at once. I am certain that Esther Whitby came before my bench once. I recognized her. What's more—I think she recognized me, too, though she hid it well."

Lucy frowned as she carefully skirted a dead bird on the street. "Well, that's easily explained, isn't it? She came before you as a Quaker. Under the Conventicle Act."

The magistrate shook his head. "No, that's not it. I certainly would have remembered if a member of the Whitby family had been tried in my court. She would have had to say that she was wed to Jacob Whitby. I would have known her then."

"So she was tried before she married Jacob Whitby," Lucy said, rubbing her nose. "Yet she couldn't have been accused of breaking the Conventicle Act, since she had only become a Quaker after she met Jacob. She must have come to you when she still bore her maiden name. Esther Grace."

The magistrate rolled the name on his tongue and shook his head. "Not familiar. I need to remember for what crime she was accused."

"Just because she was accused does not mean she was guilty," Lucy exclaimed without thinking. Unbidden, the image of her brother, wrongfully accused of murder, had risen with nauseating clarity in her mind. Belatedly, she realized what she had uttered. "I beg your pardon, sir. I spoke in haste."

Once again, the magistrate seemed to have followed her thoughts. Dismissing her apology, he said, "The law tells us to assume guilt. However, I have found from experience that many men who came before my bench, having been accused of a crime, were innocent." He coughed. "Of course, more often than not, those who are accused are indeed guilty."

As they arrived at his house, the magistrate turned to Lucy. "I should like to examine my notes from the sessions I presided over. This puzzle is deeply maddening to me, and I should like to glean what I may about Esther Grace Whitby's background."

"Yes, sir," Lucy replied. Hesitating, she added, "I should very much like to learn what you discover."

"Perhaps you could help me, if your master could spare you a little longer," he said. "I can't imagine that even old Horace would expect his apprentices to labor on the Lord's Day."

"No, sir," Lucy said, smiling. "I think he would not."

"It's decided. Stay an hour or so more. I'll send John around with a note."

"Thank you, sir," she said.

After John had been dispatched to Master Aubrey's, Lucy

followed the magistrate to his study. "How may I help you, sir?" she asked.

Going to the corner of the room, he knelt by a large wooden chest, covered by a white linen cloth that had been painstakingly embroidered with bright colors by his late wife. With one finger, he traced the Latin words that she had stitched into the cloth, nestled on a bough of apple blossoms, between two chirping birds.

"*Ius est ars boni et aequi,*" he said softly. " 'Law is the art of the good and the just.' It is a phrase I try to remember every day. It is so easy for men to turn the law as they would please, to become tyrants, whether as a king of the realm or a judge in his courtroom. We must stand against such temptations and remember our reason for law and order."

Lucy nodded, watching as he carefully folded the long piece of linen and set it carefully on a nearby bench. After opening the lid, he pulled out several leather pouches, each one with a date inked on the outside. As he examined each bag, he muttered to himself. "Sixteen sixty-six, no, that would be too recent. Sixteen sixty-five—those proceedings were interrupted by the plague. We did not hold sessions then." He looked up at Lucy. "When did you say the Whitbys were wed?"

"Just after the plague, I believe. Before the Great Fire, though."

"Just so," he said, beginning to untie one of the pouches. "Then let us begin with the late sessions in 1664 and move our way forward." From the pouch, he withdrew a pack of papers that had been folded in three, all tied with a bit of string. Smoothing the first sheet on the surface of the table, he began to study it.

From her angle, Lucy could see the dense rows of handwritten script, though she was too far away to read any of the words. Venturing a bit closer, she could see that the script had been written in different hands. One she recognized as the magistrate's meticulous script. The other, equally fair, was larger and more ornate and took up much of the top of the page. She tapped on the paper. "Did the clerk write the first part?" she asked.

"What? Oh, yes." He peered more closely. "Yes, this was recorded by young Daniel Malloy, if I'm not mistaken. A promising lad, to be sure." He sighed, and a shadow crossed his face. "Unfortunately, he did not survive the plague." He cleared his throat, returning to the matter at hand. "You can see where he recorded the name of the defendants, along with the charges, as each came before the court."

"Ellsbeth Bourne, for the charge of—?" The clerk's words were difficult to read.

"Illegal craft work," Master Hargrave said. "Ah yes, I remember this case. She had illegally assumed her father's trade as a glassmaker. The Worshipful Company of Glaziers came down on her rather heavily, as I recall. They wanted to make an example of her. Poor woman. She'd likely been helping her father along for years while he hid the black tumors that had been growing inside him."

"How terrible!" Lucy exclaimed, looking at the woman's name again. She wondered what the woman had looked like, who she had been, what happened to her. "Her father must have trained her, even knowing that she would not be accepted by the guild." Rather like her own circumstances, she thought. She'd never be a true apprentice, let alone a master in her own right. Once again, she pushed away the little shiver of misgiving she felt every time she wondered what would happen if Master Aubrey chose not to keep her on.

The magistrate sighed. "The guild may well have known of the Bournes' destitute circumstances, only they chose to step in when her father died. When it was obvious that someone other than a licensed master was making glass, they had to intervene. They had to protect their standards, you see."

"Do you know what happened to her?"

"No," he said, glancing through the rest of his notes. "She was sent to the debtors' prison in Cheapside. Hopefully she had paid her debt to the guild before the Great Fire broke out."

Lucy shuddered. No one spoke much about what had happened to all the prisoners in the jails that burnt down. There were some who said they had been freed before the Fire reached their gates. But she feared most had been left to die.

Master Hargrave pointed at another sheet of paper. "Several trials may be listed at once, as they are on this next page. If you look through these"—he handed her a few folded pages, leaving another stack in front of him—"and I'll look through these, we can see if anyone named Esther appeared at my bench."

Lucy looked through the names of the accused. Mary Dinkle, fortune-teller, accused of theft. Nathanial Clarke, dish-turner, accused of poisoning. Gray Fitch, shoemaker, accused of drunken battery. The names and offenses went on. They looked through the session notes from 1663 and 1662 as well.

Finally the magistrate frowned at the darkening room. "I have kept you for too long, I am afraid, Lucy. You should be off. I can only try old Horace Aubrey's patience for so long, keeping his apprentice away." He began to carefully refold and stack the last set of papers they had just reviewed. "I just can't understand it. I know I couldn't have seen her between 1660 and 1663, because I was serving as a judge on the circuit courts for many sessions." He tapped his head. "Yet I can remember her before me at the Old Bailey. I remember her violet eyes, so cold and defiant." He shook his head. "It will come to me, I know it."

·17·

As Master Aubrey and Lach scrubbed the ink off their hands, using the harsh lye soap they kept by the basin, Lucy ladled a bit of leftover rabbit stew into three wooden bowls. The conversation she'd had with Master Hargrave the day before was still weighing heavily on her mind. Sarah was convinced that Esther Whitby was in danger. What if she had it backward? What if Esther Whitby was the one causing the danger?

Lucy pulled out Jacob Whitby's *Last Dying Breath*, reading through the now-familiar bits. *I met Jacob Whitby when I was living with the Beetners,* Esther Whitby had told them. *Before the good tailor and his wife succumbed to God's Will and the plague.*

"Master Aubrey," she said when the printer had taken his seat, "do you think it's unusual for a tradesman to leave his trade and all his movables to a servant? One who had only been with them a short while?"

He gave her a suspicious look. "Let me say the prayer, lass," he said. Obediently she set aside the tract and, like Lach, bent her head while the printer said the prayer. Never one to let food grow cold, Master Aubrey said the benediction and slid his spoon into the stew.

After swallowing with an appreciative murmur, Master Aubrey raised an eyebrow. "Planning to do away with me, are you?" he asked.

Lucy smiled. "No. I am not the servant in question. However, I should be interested in your thoughts, sir. What would you think if one of your friends did such a thing? Would you think that servant must have been particularly good and loyal?"

"Perhaps," he said, taking another bite. "Likely not."

"Why do you say that?" she asked.

"A man just does not do such a peculiar thing," he said with finality, as if that explained everything.

"I see," she said. Refolding the tract, Lucy resolved then to learn more about the Beetners and Esther Grace's former life. "Master Aubrey," she said, handing around slices of thick bread, "I was thinking I could sell out by Smithfield. We've not sold there for a while."

"Good Lord, this bread is hard," the printer said, banging a chunk on the table. It sounded like a rock. "Didn't you just get it from old Liddell this morning?"

"Yes, at quarter cost. Day old, Liddell told me. Try it with the stew," Lucy said, making a dunking motion. "It will soften in no time."

"Hmmph. Made Saturday, I'd wager. I'm all for your penny-pinching, but I like my bread fresh, miss." Nevertheless, he did as Lucy had suggested, sopping a bit of the hard bread in his stew. "Smithfield? In this cold?"

Lucy shrugged. "I don't mind." She ignored Lach's suspicious look. "There's a printer out there, isn't there? Master Blackwell? I saw his name on a tract."

Master Aubrey wiped his mouth. "Blackwell? Yes, I know him. Good sort. Why?"

"I was just thinking that he might like to trade a few pieces with us, too. Like we did with the Quaker printer."

Master Aubrey continued to chew thoughtfully. "See what he is peddling, hey?"

Lach snorted into his hand. "Wasn't Lucy supposed to help with *The Three Witches of Dorchester* today? And we still have not finished the *The Scold's Last Scold.*"

"I can sell along the way," Lucy said hastily. "And I can finish off what you started this morning. I'll be back in three hours, and I can work later, too, after supper."

She held her breath, watching Master Aubrey cock his head back and forth as he contemplated her request. He had a keen business mind, Lucy was coming to realize. Unlike other masters, who might be loath to give their apprentices much liberty, he did not govern them with an overly firm hand. Indeed, so long as they managed to bring in an extra shilling or two, let alone a crown or a sovereign, he was sure to be pleased.

Unexpectedly, though, he leaned over and lightly boxed Lach on his right ear.

"Hey!" Lach yelped, jumping away. "What was that for?"

The printer wagged his finger at him. "About time you start coming up with some good ideas, too. Right now, we need to reset that last tract, as the frontispiece was smudged. I think the typeset must be off."

"Wouldn't it be better if I accompanied Lucy?" Lach asked, a shade too innocently. She could read his thoughts. Even accompanying her was better than the tedious task that Master Aubrey had laid out before him. "Help her carry the packs."

"Oh, would you?" Lucy asked, with a similarly feigned sweetness. "You are *such* a dear."

Master Aubrey looked at him. If Lach had stopped there, the printer might have let him go. Instead Lach had to add, "I should very much like to keep Lucy safe."

Since he had been unable to keep the sarcasm from his voice, sure enough, the master printer scowled. "Bah! None of your larking about," he told Lach. "Lucy can manage fine on her own. Just don't load the pack too heavy," he warned, turning back to Lucy. "I don't want you dragging the sack like I've seen this imp do. And I expect you back in three hours' time, so you had best not gad about either."

Within the hour, Lucy was now closing in on Hosier Lane, where the Beetners had lived, a heavy bag hoisted over her shoulder. As she walked north, she could still smell the residual smoke that arose whenever debris was moved about. Nothing was actively smoldering, of course, though the smoke still lingered in the fog and remained trapped below the remaining rubble. Finally, as she neared Smithfield and St. Bartholomew's, she passed by Pye Corner, where the flames of the Great Fire had stopped and turned back upon themselves on that fateful third day.

Hosier Lane was not a very long street, consisting of a few homes and a few shops. Though it had long been associated with stocking-makers, now she saw only one sign that indicated cloth and thread. There was an instrument-maker's shop and at the corner a printer's shop as well, which she noted with great interest. "So that's where Master Blackwell works," she said to herself.

Passing by the shop, Lucy knocked. No one appeared to be in. No doubt he was out selling. She continued on, resolving to stop in the printer's shop on her return, since she had promised Master Aubrey that she would do so.

She walked up to the hosier's shop first. This shop was much older than the others on the street, more like a merchant's stall. The merchant had hung cords from the edge of the shutters to a pole several feet away. Along the cords hung all sorts of woolen and embroidered silk stockings for men and women, as well as children. There were even some tiny ones for infants, although only the richest sorts would purchase such finery for babes still in arms.

Seeing Lucy, a man standing beside the shuttered windows called over to her. His face brightened when he saw her. "New stockings, miss? Some hose for your master?" he called, his tone friendly if a bit pleading. "Some warm woolens for yourself? Couldn't hurt on a day like today!"

As if confirming his words, the wind picked up then, blowing a few stockings from the line. Bending over, Lucy helped pick up a few stockings that had fallen so that they would not grow sodden in the mud. She handed them to the merchant.

"I was wondering, sir," she said. "Did you know the Beetners? They used to have a shop here on Hosier Lane."

"Can't say I ever knew 'em," he said cheerfully. "Bought this establishment a year and a half ago. After the plague was sorting itself out, and before the Fire. Young woman sold me the place and the livelihood. I'd just become a master, you see, though I had not yet had a chance to establish myself."

Lucy couldn't explain it, but from the look on the man's face, she suspected he was lying. Probably he wasn't truly a master in his own right. Since Guildhall had succumbed to the Fire, it was unclear how many of the guild records had survived. Fishing out a coin, she bought a pair of bright red woolen stockings.

Taking the coin, he relaxed a bit and became more talkative. "From what I understand, the Beetners succumbed to the plague. Only their loyal servant survived. They had willed everything to her when they knew they were likely to die. She then was able to sell everything to me."

"Did you know her name?" Lucy asked eagerly. "The woman who sold you the place? How did she approach you?"

Instead of answering her question, he blew warm air onto his hands. "Sometimes I don't know what I was thinking, buying this place. Not too many sales in winter, I can assure you of that." He said the last meaningfully.

Lucy took the hint. If she wanted more information she would have to buy something else. Looking through a straw basket on the floor, she picked out another pair of gray woolen stockings that she thought would suit Will.

Accepting the coin Lucy passed to him, the hosier smirked at her. "Her name was Esther Grace. We met at the Ivy and the Oak. Burnt to a crisp now." He held up his hand to ward off her next questions. "That's all I can tell you."

Thoughtfully, Lucy went into the instrument-maker's shop next door. Unlike the hosier's shop, this store was not quite so old. She was able to press open the door and walk in. The welcome warmth of the room engulfed her, and she breathed in hungrily. Somewhere in the house, someone was making bread.

She looked around the quiet room, noting the instruments hanging from nails on the walls, stacked in the corners, and laid out on the overfull shelves. "Good day!" she called out. "Is anyone here?"

"Yes, yes, here I am," said a voice from a far corner near the hearth. Peering behind a great harp, she spied an old man sitting in a soft embroidered chair, a lute or some other stringed instrument in his lap. A large dog lay companionably at his feet. "Are you interested in a musical instrument, my dear?" the man asked. "Or were you hoping to warm yourself on this chilly winter's day?"

"I am very cold," Lucy admitted, looking longingly at the fire in the hearth. "I was also wondering if you knew the Beetners? They used to own the shop next door."

"The Beetners! Oh, a lovely family, they were. Oh, where are my manners? Pray warm yourself by the fire. Martha," he called to someone in the back room, "we have a visitor! She wants to know about the Beetners."

"Well—" Lucy started to say, although before she could finish her thought, an old woman came out.

"The Beetners!" she exclaimed. "Dear me! Sit down, my dear! I'll bring you something warm to drink."

Before long Lucy was settled on the low bench by the fire, appreciatively sipping a mug of hot mead. The honey soothed her throat. The old man and woman, she had learned, were the Fletchers, and they had owned their shop for nearly thirty years. They had lived above the shop for the same length of time, having survived the plague as well as the recent exodus from the city following the Great Fire.

"I did not actually know the Beetners," Lucy began, wanting to make her intentions clear from the start. "I was just interested in someone who used to work for them. Esther Grace?"

The Fletchers exchanged a glance. "Yes, we knew her." They looked disgusted. "What do you want to know of her?"

"Well, her husband passed away recently and—"

"Did she kill him?" Mrs. Fletcher interrupted with a humorless laugh.

"Now, now, Martha," her husband chastised her while Lucy stared at her.

"Why ever would you think that?" she asked.

"Because I'm fairly certain she killed my dear friend. May she rot in hell."

"I thought the Beetners died in the plague," Lucy said, gripping her cup more tightly.

"So *she* claimed!" Mrs. Fletcher said, crossing her arms. "All I know is that I had stopped in the night before to see her, find out where they planned to go. Mr. Fletcher and I were planning to leave London, stay with my kin out in Bath. I knew they had no other relatives in England, being Dutch, you know. We'd heard the sickness was bad in Holland, too, so we didn't think they'd be going there."

She stopped, closing her eyes as she recollected those dreadful days. Lucy remembered them, too, and it was all she could do to keep her own terrible memories clouding over her. Though her own mother and sister were safe, countless other acquaintances had not survived the scourge.

"You saw them and—" Lucy prompted gently.

"I saw them and they were not the slightest bit sick. Not a bit of it. You can't tell me that they all succumbed so rapidly. All I know is, when the searchers came by, ringing their bells, she declared all three bodies. The Beetners had an older unmarried daughter, Gretchen, who'd been living with them. Recently back from service, she was. We saw the bodies laid out, in their sheets. Dumped onto the back of the cart, taken to the plague-pits." Mrs. Fletcher sniffed. "Not even a proper burial. Good God-fearing folks they were. They deserved better, even if they were foreigners." Tears filled her eyes.

Something wasn't making sense. "If they were shrouded, why did you think they were murdered?" Lucy pressed. "The plague could take its victims rapidly. I saw that myself. Sometimes a body looked healthy, even though it was not. The sickness had already sunk in."

Master Fletcher glared at his wife. "Martha," he said, "let the dead lie. No good can come from speaking now. Pray, keep silent."

"I've been silent for too long!" Yet after that outburst, she clasped her hands tightly in her lap and pursed her lips, clearly heeding her husband's admonishment.

Lucy was looking back and forth between them in bewilderment. "Please," she said, unable to keep a slightly desperate note from climbing into her voice. "I promise that I am not here to take your time with idle gossip. I sought you out because I am concerned for someone I hold dear."

The Fletchers glanced at each other. At Mr. Fletcher's nod, his wife continued, speaking now in a low, angry tone. "I will tell you, I could not understand it. I wanted to look upon their faces. She told me not to, that the Black Death had done terrible things to them. She said it would be better to remember them as they'd been in life. I thought that was true." Her voice trembled. "As we waited for the raker, I asked her what she planned to do. She pulled out the Beetners' will. It seemed they had left everything to her. Livelihood, shop, movables. Said she'd met a nice man who wanted to marry her, so she thought she'd sell everything off and leave. That's exactly what she did, too. Got a taker for the business even in the middle of the plague!"

"Of course, we didn't know that until we returned a few months later," Mr. Fletcher interjected. "We had a new hosier then. Doesn't seem to know much about the trade, though. Seems to be selling everything the Beetners made before they died. Not seen him do any sewing or weaving, or even mending, for that matter."

"Probably not a member of the guild," Lucy murmured. It seemed her assumptions about the new owner were correct. Louder, she said, "I can see why Esther Grace's actions seem suspicious, but murder? Why did you think such a thing?"

"I tell you, I know the Beetners were murdered!" Mrs. Fletcher declared, her voice shaking from deep emotion. Standing up, she looked down at Lucy, tears filling her eyes. "As the raker hoisted Miss Gretchen's body into the cart, the sheet fell off her face. I could see her throat had been slit, or my name isn't Martha Fletcher!"

Lucy gasped. "What?"

Mrs. Fletcher went on, her trembling voice growing in strength. "The plague didn't take Miss Gretchen! Nor do I believe it took her parents! Their throats were likely cut, too!"

Lucy looked back and forth between the pair, her heart starting to pound. Mr. Fletcher nodded sadly, confirming his belief in his wife's story.

"What did you do? Did you tell anyone?" she asked.

"I started to call out to the raker, to tell him that there had been a murder," Mrs. Fletcher said, a remembered terror shining from her eyes. "Then Esther Grace turned to me and stared at me with those cold violet eyes. She put her finger to her lips and—I'll never forget this—smiled at me. Smiled! That's when I knew for sure she had killed them." She sat back down and grasped Lucy's wrist. "Then, still smiling, she said to me, 'You'll be off now, I suppose? Get yourself out of harm's way. If you stay here, who knows what will happen to you?'" Lucy felt Mrs. Fletcher shudder at the memory. "I remember her voice was so pleasant, so friendly. Yet I know what she was telling me: If I said anything about what I had seen to anyone, she would kill me. We left that afternoon."

She slumped back in her chair. Reaching over, Mr. Fletcher patted his wife's hand.

"Did you ever tell anyone?" Lucy asked.

"No," Mrs. Fletcher replied. "When the cart moved away, I

knew it would be too late. Even if I had been able to summon the constable, the bodies would have long been dumped in the plague-pit. There was nothing we could do, nothing we could say." She took a long sip of her mead, clearly trying to steady her nerves.

After a pause, she continued. "Tell me," she said to Lucy, "you said her husband had just died. *Was* he murdered?"

Both Fletchers looked at her expectantly.

Lucy weighed whether to tell them her thoughts. Then, after a long moment, she nodded. "I think so. On the first of the month, he fell in front of a cart." She hesitated. "Before he died, he told me he'd been pushed."

"Was it her?" Mrs. Fletcher asked, sounding a bit short of breath. "Expecting to live off her husband's fortune, I suppose?"

Lucy shook her head. "No, she was nowhere near him when it happened. Besides, he was worried about her, to be truthful. I do not think he suspected her at all."

Mrs. Fletcher looked doubtful. "What was her husband like? She must have married well. She's the sort that could trick a rich man, with scarcely a second glance."

"Oh, no," Lucy said, thinking of Jacob Whitby's plain home. "I mean, Mr. Whitby was a gentleman, to be sure. It's just that he became a Quaker, gave up all his finery and all that. She became a Quaker, too, and—"

She was interrupted by a great burst of laughter from the Fletchers.

"Esther Grace, a Quaker?" Mrs. Fletcher exclaimed.

Shaking his head, her husband added, "That just doesn't seem possible. Although"—he cocked his head thoughtfully—"I remember her going over to the Bull and Mouth a few times. That's where the Quakers gather, you know," he said to Lucy, who nodded. "Though she was no Quaker, I can assure you, when she lived next door. Too fond of her trifles, she was."

"If you don't think Esther Grace killed her husband, what brought you here?" Mrs. Fletcher asked.

Lucy remained deliberately vague. "I'd just like to know more about her. Could you tell me when she started working for the Beetners? Anything else about her?"

"She was a hoity-toity sort. Lord knows how she became a Quaker," Mrs. Fletcher said, refilling Lucy's cup. "She'd only been with the Beetners for about six months. Convinced them to take her on, she did."

"How did she do that, do you suppose?" Lucy asked.

Mrs. Fletcher snorted. "Had Mr. Beetner wrapped around her finger right quick, she did. Of course, this was before Miss Gretchen returned from service."

"Esther Grace did know the trade," Mr. Fletcher said.

Mrs. Fletcher nodded. "That's true," she said grudgingly. "She knew her stitches. I know they were pleased with her when she first came. Mrs. Beetner had been having trouble with the finer handwork, you see. Noblewomen and soldiers alike used to seek them out, and Mr. Beetner was anxious that they not lose the business of good-paying and steady customers."

"How did they come to hire her?" Lucy asked, taking a sip.

"Well, it's a funny thing, that," Mrs. Fletcher said. "Mrs. Beetner said she just came to the shop one day, seeking employment. A bit of saucy baggage she was, too. Still, Mr. Beetner hired her."

"How odd," Lucy commented. "Who had referred her, do you know? Did she have a letter?"

Mrs. Fletcher shook her head, snorting her head again.

"Batted her eyes at him, she did," Mr. Fletcher said.

"More than that," his wife returned crossly. "I'm of the opinion that Mr. Beetner already knew her." She lowered her voice and leaned in toward Lucy. "In the biblical way, at that."

Lucy set down her cup. This was not what she had expected. "Do you have any idea where she and Mr. Beetner could have met? How they might have become, er, acquainted?"

Mrs. Fletcher shook her head. "I don't. I have my suspicions, of course. I do know that, within not two weeks of her moving into their home, he began to bed her. My dear friend was beside herself!" She clutched her hands together. "Her husband was lovesick. Besotted, she said. Oh, the tears she would spill in that very chair you're sitting in now." She nodded toward Lucy, who shifted uncomfortably. "That's why Gretchen returned. Her mother had summoned her. I think she was hoping that with Gretchen there, she'd have the strength to cast the vixen out."

"Instead the Beetners died. Or were killed." Lucy was silent, thinking about everything she had just learned. She looked at Mrs. Fletcher. "You said you thought you knew where they may have met."

"I think it was fairly obvious, my child. They met at a brothel." She sniffed contemptuously. "Had to have been so. Mr. Beetner was not charming or handsome enough to get a woman without having to pay. She wasn't in love with him, that's for certain." She looked at her husband. "You're quiet, Hiram," she said, nudging him with the side of her hand. "Do you know anything more?"

Her husband shrugged, looking a bit embarrassed. Still, despite his discomfort he answered them. "He told me once that he fancied a cathouse over on Leather Lane. A big house, at the end of the street. Can't say that's where he met her, of course."

"Thank you for the mead," Lucy said, rising. "I must be heading home now." She began to wrap her scarves around her body, in preparation for her cold journey home.

Mrs. Fletcher clutched her hand. "I hope you stay away from that Esther Grace," she said. "No good can come from crossing that woman."

Thoroughly shaken, Lucy hurried away from the instrument-maker's house. She was horrified by what Mrs. Fletcher had told her. Could it be true? Had Esther Grace killed her employers' family? A far-fetched notion, to be sure. The woman scarcely seemed able to kill a mouse. Still, there was definitely something suspicious about how she'd come to the Beetners' household. How *had* Esther Grace come by the Beetners' trade? The more she thought about it, the sicker she felt.

Lucy walked back down Hosier Lane as she had come. As she passed by Blackwell's shop, she stopped. Although the store looked closed, she thought that perhaps Master Blackwell had known the Beetners. Maybe he could answer some of her questions. Knocking again, she felt the door move slightly. It appeared to be shut, not locked, and she was able to open it.

As Lucy stepped into the shop, she nearly gagged at the wretched smell. As in Master Aubrey's shop, there was a press at the front of the room, and great cases stacked high on tables, most likely full of lead type and woodcuts. That's about where the similarities ended, though—printer's tools were strewn about the room, and there were no great sheets drying. And while Master Aubrey's shop was certainly no haven of cleanliness, it would seem practically godly in comparison. There was a general forlorn quality to the shop, as if no one had been in there for some time.

"Master Blackwell," she called, still trying not to gag. Her teeth began to chatter. If possible, the shop seemed colder inside than it was outside. "Master Blackwell?"

Cautiously she moved into the back room, and that was when the smell became overwhelming. On some level, her nose and mind informed her of the obvious. Master Blackwell was dead. She began to back away, and that was when she saw him, a dark shadow in the corner, lying in a makeshift straw matting bed, covers pulled up to his shoulders. Drawing up her courage, she peered more closely at him, still holding her nose. She saw no obvious signs of foul play. No blood or any wounds, at least none that were visible.

Perhaps he'd frozen to death or succumbed to sickness. Maybe he just died of old age. Indeed, was that a slight smile on his face? Maybe he'd met his maker with peace in his heart. Lucy hoped so, turning away.

She was about to leave when the stacks of printed materials caught her eye. Unlike at Master Aubrey's shop, these tracts and ballads were not tied in carefully organized bags hung from pegs. Rather, they seemed loose and unorganized. Many were covered with stains or mildew or were stuck together, carelessly preserved. She wondered if perhaps Master Blackwell had begun to be too ill to keep them in order, and she felt a sudden pang.

A closer examination, however, revealed that the printer did seem to have followed a rudimentary method of categorizing the different tracts, sorting them by type. Religious tracts. Petitions to the king. Monstrous births—there seemed to be quite a few of them. Witches. Merriments. And finally, a stack of murder ballads and tracts. She began to rifle through them, feeling uncomfortable, knowing that Master Blackwell was lying dead behind her. She set each one aside after glancing it quickly. Some she was familiar with, others she'd never seen before. *A Terrible Tale of a Most Barbaric Murder. An Unnatural Mother Kills Her Children. A True and Strange Tale of a Murder in Leicester.* And one she knew very well. *From the Charred Remains, a Body.*

As Lucy neared the end of the stack, one jumped out at her. *The True and Most Unfortunate Tale of a Player's Last Play, Having Been Beset by Thieves, on the Duke's Own Stage.*

She was about to put it in her pack when a thought struck her. "If I take this one tract, am I looting?" she wondered out loud. She looked guiltily toward Master Blackwell's still form. "Perhaps if I simply replace it with another?"

So she pulled out another tract and laid it carefully on the pile, not wanting either earthly or divine authorities passing judgment upon her.

"Rest in peace," she whispered to Master Blackwell's corpse before carefully shutting the door behind her.

Doubling back, she informed the Fletchers. As she imagined, they were deeply shocked and saddened by their long-term neighbor's death. It had been a hard winter on them all, and the bonds of community had yet to be reforged. Lucy left then, knowing that they would do right—belatedly—by their old friend.

·18·

The next morning, as the light of dawn filled the room, Lucy rolled over in her bed and pulled out *The Player's Last Play* from under her pillow. After she had returned from Smithfield last night, Master Aubrey had her doing all manner of chores. She had nearly embraced the printer when she saw him, hoping that he would never come to such a sorrowful and lonely end as Master Blackwell. Lach gleefully piled on as well, so that it had been quite late by the time she had stumbled in exhaustion to her chamber. She had sat down at the table, only to realize that Will must have used the last of the candle stubs she kept in a wood box by their small hearth. Too tired to sneak back into the shop, she had simply fallen into bed, immediately succumbing to a heavy dreamless sleep.

Since Will had not yet arisen, Lucy thought she would take a few minutes to read the tract. Only a few pages in length, it described how Basil Townsend had been set upon and murdered on the stage of the Lincoln's Inn Fields Theater. The rest was taken up by an account of a "*Strange Celestial Experience that had Beset the Evening Sky.*" Master Aubrey sometimes did the same, adding a bit here and there to stretch out a tract that was shorter than originally intended.

Just as Herbert Bligh had told them, the assault had seemed to occur well after the final performance had concluded for the evening. Few people had witnessed the attack, and those that had been around were vague in describing the characteristics of Townsend's assailant. One of the female players, Deborah Evans, called him a monster of a man, while Gerald Markham and another female player, Grace Little, called him a smallish sort of fellow. They both claimed that it might well have been a man named Abel Coxswain, whose wife might have sinned with Townsend.

They all agreed on one point, however—that the attack had occurred swiftly and the assailant had fled, after plunging his knife into Townsend's chest. Herbert Bligh said that Townsend, a bit of a rover, was not one to respect the sanctity of marriage, and had recently taken up with another man's wife. So Coxswain, it seemed, had been the primary suspect.

Nowhere did the account say, though, whether Coxswain had been brought to trial. Instead, the piece ended with a few words from Herbert Bligh, reminding the gracious reader that "the stage is just a poor substitute for the drama of the reality of every man's life." That sounded like the pompous player she had met.

Lucy went downstairs and began to prepare the morning

meal and start their business for the day. A strange fog seemed to have settled over her thoughts, due in part to poor Master Blackwell's sad demise. Still, the cloud over her thoughts could not keep her from thinking altogether. Could Esther Whitby have been responsible for the deaths of the family with whom she had lived?

When Master Aubrey was down in the cellar and Lach was out by the woodpile, Lucy stole the opportunity to ponder the tract again. Why had the searcher thought it important to provide Julia Whitby with information about Basil Townsend's death? *"This is the dandy I was telling you about,"* Lucy mused, recalling the line under the searcher's sketch. She read the tract again, looking for any detail that would help make the connection clear.

Then she held the piece closer to her eyes. A few words jumped out at her again, and suddenly something that had been hidden was clear.

"Master Aubrey!" she called down to the cellar. "It is vital that I speak with Master Hargrave at once." Without heeding his reply she began to run out of the shop, only to find Lach barring the way.

"Where are you off to now?" he asked suspiciously. "Leaving all the work to me again?"

"No! This is no jest. I think that the magistrate's daughter is in real danger. I am afraid for her life, I am. I know that I could lose my apprenticeship, but I must speak to Master Hargrave first, and then I must warn her. Please, I beg you. Let me by."

To her surprise, Lach stepped aside and let her through without another word.

Lucy rushed out the door and began to run, grateful that for once she did not have the heavy pack pulling painfully on her shoulder and bumping against her back.

When she arrived at the Hargraves' ten minutes later, Lucy breathlessly tried to convey to Annie her urgency in seeing the magistrate.

"He's not here, Lucy," Annie said, a scared look in her eyes. "Shall I fetch him? I know that he went to see Dr. Larimer for an early-morning meeting."

"Yes, no, I don't know," Lucy said. Now Cook and John were looking at her with deep concern.

"Lucy?" Adam appeared then, entering the kitchen. "What is it? I heard your voice and I could tell something is wrong. Why do you need to speak to my father? Is Will all right?"

"Oh, Adam!" she cried out, her voice breaking.

He drew her out of the kitchen then and into his father's study, shutting the door behind them, not caring about propriety. Holding out his arms, he embraced her tightly.

Then, taking her hand, Adam pulled her to the low embroidered bench under the window, one that she had frequently cleaned when she had served as his father's chambermaid, so that she was sitting close beside him.

"Now tell me," he commanded, turning her face toward him. "What is wrong?"

Lucy hardly knew where to start. In fits and starts, she told him what the Fletchers had said about Esther Grace, as well as seeing Master Blackwell's body. Although she expected his customary scolding not to undertake such investigations, instead he pressed her to him again. "Sweetheart," he murmured against her hair. "These are all terrible things."

"There's more," she said, extracting herself gently. She pulled out the tract describing the murder at the theater, and pointed to the name of one of the witnesses.

"Grace Little?" he read, frowning. "I don't understand. Who is she?"

"I think she is Esther Grace. Jacob Whitby's widow. And this one, Deborah Evans, I think she's Deborah, that other Quaker. She never seemed like the others, not a Quaker at all." She knew she was babbling and it was difficult to stop. "Maybe they are both impostors."

He took her hand then. "Lucy, you've had a bit of a shock and—"

"No, please, listen to me." She explained. "Your father is convinced that he had seen Esther Grace before. She came before him on the bench."

"Yes, he told me. He also told me that he looked through his trial notes, and he did not see her name. There are probably many women named Grace."

"That's true." She paused, trying to steady her jumbled thoughts. "All right, then. Let's set this murder aside. Consider what the Fletchers told me about Esther Whitby, or as they knew her, Esther Grace. They think that Mr. Beetner met her at a brothel on Leather Lane." In a small voice she added, "Are you familiar with that place?"

"Oh, let me think. Is that the one near the coaching inn? Or is it the one above the smithy's shop?" When she stared at him, he nudged her with a little laugh. "Lucy, I hope you do not think that I have intimate knowledge of all the brothels in the city." He sounded amused, although a little wary, too. "No, to answer your question. I am not familiar with that brothel."

Lucy flushed. Continuing, she said, "It's just that the brothel is not too far from Thiery's Inn. Isn't that where you lived, when you were finishing your legal studies?"

She spoke in a rush. She had seen Adam embrace another woman once, and that was painful enough to remember. She looked down, staring at a dark knot in the wooden floor.

"Lucy," he said gently, putting his hands on her shoulders. "Look at me." When she did, he continued. "I'm not a saint. I've never claimed to be. I can tell you this, I have never paid for a whore." He cocked his head, his grin returning. She could tell he was trying to dispel her conflicted mood. "I must say, I like seeing your jealous side. It makes me think I'm in your thoughts sometimes, when you're not finding dead bodies or hunting down murderers."

Seeing her exasperated sigh, he chuckled. "Ah, that is more like it. I am still not sure where you are going with this."

Lucy was still stumbling over her words. "That brothel is also very close to the Lincoln's Inn Fields Theater, and per-haps—"

A quick knock on the door caused them to move apart just as Master Hargrave entered the study, a serious look on his face.

He looked at Lucy, who had risen to her feet. "Sit, child," he said. "You look like you have had a fright." He then gave his son an expectant look.

In a clear and coherent manner, Adam summarized everything Lucy had just told him. He concluded, "She was just trying to connect Esther Grace with a brothel on Leather Lane, as well as to the murder of Basil Townsend, one of the Duke's Players. There are definitely some strange connections here, although I am not yet certain how—or if—it all fits together."

Lucy held out the tract describing Basil Townsend's murder.

"Oh, I remember that case," Master Hargrave said, a dawning look on his face. He turned toward the chest where he kept all his trial notes. They waited as he looked through the carefully stacked papers until he found the one he was looking for. "Ah, here it is. Yes, Abel Coxswain was accused and stood trial." He read through his notes.

"What was the verdict?" Adam asked.

"We had to let Coxswain go. There was no formal evidence against him, nor could we determine any motive."

"Sir, why had Mr. Coxswain been accused?" Lucy asked. "Do you know?"

The magistrate consulted his notes. "There was some indication that the murdered man and Coxswain had several altercations in the past. Fisticuffs. Spats. That sort of thing. There was also some evidence that Townsend had been involved with Coxswain's wife. Also, Markham claimed that he had seen Coxswain running away from the body. Another witness—a Deborah Evans—had accused Markham of the murder, except"—he skimmed the tightly written pages—"she appears to have recanted on the stand."

"What about Grace Little?" Lucy asked eagerly. "Did she appear on the stand?"

Again the magistrate consulted his notes. "No, she did not.

She never took the stand. I remember sending out a constable to bring her in, although the address she had provided was false. She had disappeared."

"Oh," Lucy said, disappointed.

"However," the magistrate said slowly, then stopped. He gazed at one of the dark beams that ran the length of the white ceiling. "I remember now. She was there. The woman we know as Esther Whitby. She was staring at the witnesses from a front-row bench. That's why I remember her piercing purple eyes, so harsh and so cold. She *was* in my courtroom, although I did not know who she was. Lucy," he said, looking back at her, "I believe you are right. She *was* connected with that trial. Whether she was connected with the murder, of course, I cannot say."

"Can we prove any of this?" Adam demanded. "Is there any proof that Grace Little and Esther Grace are the same woman? That she was present at the trial?"

Lucy thought about this. "Mrs. Fletcher said that Mr. Beetner seemed to have known Esther Grace straightaway. Called her by name, he did. So that would mean she was already Esther Grace when she became employed with the Beetners before the plague, but after this trial." Her voice trailed off. "What is it?"

Master Hargrave coughed again, looking away, and Adam looked embarrassed. Still, he answered her question. "From what you said, Esther Grace seems to have appeared on Mr. Beetner's doorstep, having known him, it seems, from the brothel. When he saw her, he called her by the only name she likely went by. Grace."

"Oh, I see," Lucy said, catching on, trying to ignore the flush that flooded her cheeks. "Since his wife was likely there, to cover up his indiscretion, he called her 'Miss Grace,' making her first name into her last name. To make her more reputable. Because he should not have known her in a more intimate way."

"She might then have created 'Esther Grace' on the spot," Adam said slowly. "Leaving in the midst of the trial. Finding her way to the Beetners."

"The timing is about right," Lucy said, then added, "Mrs. Fletcher suggested that Mrs. Beetner never saw a letter of reference. I don't imagine there was one anyway."

They were all silent as Master Hargrave read his trial notes again and Adam perused the tract. They were briefly interrupted when Annie came in with some steaming mugs. Giving them a quick frightened look, she set the tray down on the table and left the room. Only the magistrate reached for one, raising it to his lips, continuing to ponder the long-ago trial.

Lucy had begun to anxiously pace the floor, her thoughts still too unsettled for her to sit down.

"Lucy," Adam said suddenly, breaking the silence, "why did you think the Quaker Deborah was an impostor?"

Lucy stopped then and looked at him. "Why, I don't know exactly." She frowned, trying to think. "I suppose it's because she admired my boots."

Adam and his father exchanged a glance. Hearing how foolish she sounded, she hurriedly tried to explain. "I mean," she said, "she was not like Miss Sarah. Humble. Devoted to God." She glanced at the magistrate. "Forgive me, sir."

"That is all right, Lucy," the magistrate said. "Pray, continue."

"She seemed," she said more slowly, "as if she were playing at being a Quaker. That she had not truly been called to the Lord at all. Certainly, not as the others had. And—" Her mind suddenly summoned an image of Deborah holding the lacy handkerchief.

"What is it, Lucy?" Adam asked.

"She was holding a handkerchief. I remember admiring the stitching. Esther Whitby commented on it being too frivolous for the Quakers and bid her to put it away."

"And did she?" Adam asked her.

"No, not right away." Lucy hesitated. "It's just that I remember thinking that Deborah was sort of *taunting* Esther, in front of the others. It makes me wonder what was going on between them."

Something was still nagging at her. "Oh, and there was a verse inscribed there." She sang the tune. *"She clasped a little posy, a posy full of grace . . ."* She looked at Adam and the magistrate, saying the line more slowly, emphasizing certain words this time. "She clasped a *little* posy, a posy full of *grace*. Little and Grace. Grace Little! Maybe that handkerchief did not belong to Deborah at all!" She looked at them triumphantly.

Both Adam and the magistrate seemed to be weighing her words carefully.

"That would be quite a coincidence," Adam said slowly.

"And would she use another woman's handkerchief? A rather intimate object, wouldn't you say?" Master Hargrave added.

She felt her sense of triumph vanishing. "Maybe I got carried away," she said.

"Perhaps you did, Lucy," Adam said carefully. "Or not."

"Well, there's no time to waste," the magistrate said, setting aside his mug and standing up. "There is definitely something suspicious about *both* of those women. I intend to remove my daughter from their reach."

·19·

Panting heavily, the three arrived at Jacob Whitby's house about twenty minutes later. Master Hargrave had given John instructions to hire a hackney coach and meet them at the home of Jacob Whitby's widow without delay. Lucy wondered whether the magistrate was planning to forcibly remove his daughter from the home, and she hoped it would not come to that.

At the Whitbys' door, Lucy raised her fist and struck forcibly at the oak panel. She expected resistance, but instead, to her surprise, the door swung open. Startled, Lucy stepped back, looking behind her at Adam, who was heavily supporting his father on his arm. "How odd," she said.

Then she found herself pricking up her ears, having caught a strange sound from deep within the interior of the house. It sounded like a terrible weeping, an inarticulate lament that sent shivers up her spine.

"That cannot be praying," Lucy said, cocking her head. There was no exultant quality to the voice—someone sounded in genuine distress. "Something is wrong."

Scarcely stopping to think, Lucy went inside. She half expected the magistrate to reprimand her for her bold entry; instead, she found that Adam and the magistrate were directly behind her.

"Let us pray that it is not Sarah," she heard Master Hargrave mutter to his son.

They moved in cautiously, peering around and seeing no one.

"Upstairs," Lucy said, moving down the corridor to the stairs.

"Lucy!" Adam said, grabbing her arm. "Let me go first. Please. We do not know what we will find."

Lucy pressed against the wall so that Adam could ascend the stairs before her. Still, she stayed directly behind him, shuddering a bit as the weeping grew louder.

When they reached the top of the steps, they paused. Lucy pointed to the second door on the right, which was ajar. "That was Jacob Whitby's chamber," she whispered. "I think the crying is coming from in there.

Moving swiftly, Adam moved to the chamber door and knocked sharply. The crying abruptly stopped.

Squaring his shoulders, Adam pushed open the door. "What in the world—?"

The magistrate and Lucy moved in then, flanking him on either side. As Adam had done, Lucy could only stare, trying to understand the strange tableau before them.

Ahivah was kneeling on the floor beside Jacob Whitby's bed, cradling Deborah in her arms. The old Quaker's white clothes were stained with red, and it was clear from her heavy panting and tear-stained cheeks that she had been the woman they had heard crying.

"Is she dead?" Lucy asked, regaining her senses.

Ahivah just looked at her, a distant expression on her face, clearly in shock.

Lucy knelt beside Deborah and listened to her chest. "She lives," Lucy said to the others, relieved.

She began to look at the still woman more carefully, trying to determine the source of the blood on Ahivah's dress. "What is wrong with her?" Lucy asked Ahivah.

The mute woman pointed a shaking finger at a heavy iron candlestick that looked to be covered with blood, which was lying overturned on the floor. "Was she struck with that?" Lucy asked, gently removing Deborah's cap. "On the head? Who did this to her?"

Ahivah threw up her hands, a moan her only response.

"Let us see if anyone else is here," she heard Adam say in a low voice to his father.

The two men left the bedchamber, and she could hear them cautiously checking the nearby rooms.

Lucy ran her fingers lightly through Deborah's hair, exploring a red matted clump on the back of her head. "This seems to be the wound," she said, looking at her reddened fingers. Without waiting for an answer, she took a small cloth from atop the small table by the bed and pressed it against the woman's head. She was grateful that she had not needed to tear a strip from her own petticoats; she had ruined several underskirts that way. Indeed, the flow of blood was already subsiding.

"Let us lay her down," she said gently, taking a pillow from the bed and placing it gently under Deborah's head.

As she did so, she heard a scuffling in the hallway and several shouts. The next instant, Adam and the magistrate hauled an old woman into the room, each holding her tightly under one arm. Lucy recognized her immediately.

"The searcher!" she cried. "Sadie Burroughs! The one who told Julia Whitby about the murder at the theater! The one who sketches the murder victims!"

"Indeed," the magistrate said grimly. "Do you know what happened here?"

Mrs. Burroughs tried to break free, but Adam still held her tightly by her forearm.

The magistrate drew himself up. "Did you have something to do with this assault?" he asked sternly. "I demand that you answer me. At once!"

The searcher gave him a surly gaze. "I did not," she replied. "I can guess who did, though. That woman you call Esther Whitby."

"Where is she now? Where is my daughter, Sarah? Do you know?" the magistrate asked, trying to keep his calm.

The sound of people running heavily up the stairs kept the searcher from responding. The next instant, Theodora and Sam Leighton appeared breathlessly in the doorway. Seeing the magistrate, they both stopped short, identical looks of shock appearing on their faces.

"W-what—?" Theodora sputtered. "What art thou doing here? I hope thou dost not presume to cease our sister Sarah's mission on behalf of the Lord." Evidently her view of Ahivah and her bloodied niece was obstructed by the men standing before her. Jutting out her chin, she continued. "I demand that thou dost leave this home at once. Thou art trespassing, and I shall see thee in jail for this."

"Madam, I can quite assure you," the magistrate said, "that whilst I did come here seeking my daughter, I only entered your home at the greatest provocation. We heard a great crying from within, and I was deeply afeared for my daughter's life."

He moved aside so that Theodora and her husband could see Deborah lying on the floor and the others huddling around her. The couple stared in shock, their expressions probably much like Lucy's own had been just minutes before.

"What is going on here?" Theodora said weakly, sagging a bit against her husband. "Pray, what has befallen Deborah?"

"That is what we are trying to determine. She appears to have been struck over the head. By whom, we have yet to ascertain," the magistrate stated civilly.

"Maybe it was him!" Lucy said, pointing a shaking finger at Sam.

"What?" the Quaker replied, his face taking on such a look of honest confused surprise that Lucy almost felt deterred for a moment. "Why on earth would I strike that woman?" Beside him, Theodora drew herself up like a great bear, growling in anger at Lucy.

"I heard you!" Lucy cried. "The other night, when you were speaking to Gervase, outside this very house. You said that you hoped I would not tell the magistrate. What was it you were concerned about?"

Sam looked more relieved, though still a bit angry. He glanced at the magistrate and then looked away.

The magistrate spoke in his dry fashion. "Were you concerned that Lucy would inform me of conventicles that were transpiring in this home?"

Sam nodded.

"But then Gervase said you had dealt with the searcher. That her evil tongue would be stopped. What did you do to her?" Lucy persisted, rubbing her hand down the front of her face. Something was not making sense in her mind. Certainly Mrs. Burroughs had not been silenced, which she had taken as the meaning underlying Sam's words to Gervase.

Again Sam looked surprised. "I simply spoke to the old searcher. Thou canst see that she has come to no harm. I told her that she was scaring Esther, and in the name of the Lord, I prayed that she would see fit to leave our sister Esther alone. Gervase was there. He knows that I did not touch that woman, I just bid her to hold her evil tongue." He looked at the searcher, who, to Lucy's surprise, nodded, seeming to confirm Sam's tale. He nodded in return before continuing. "She did stay away then, at least for a while."

"Why did you purchase those tracts from Master Wilson?" Lucy asked, still feeling desperate.

"The tracts?"

"The ones that you sent to Julia Whitby?" At Sam's bewildered look, Lucy rattled off their titles.

Sam's brow cleared. "Oh, I purchased them because they feature Ahivah. I thought she might like them. Perhaps someone took them from her." His hand began to twitch before he tucked it into his pocket.

At the sight of this tremor, another memory flashed into Lucy's mind. "Your hand!" she said triumphantly. "Mr. Redicker said that a man with a tremor in his hand had come to see him. To pay him off! You were that man, were you not?"

At last Sam bowed his head. "To this last action, I do admit guilt, and shame as well. I paid that clothier money, mainly to help him regain his trade. One look at the man, I could see that the guilt of the accident was weighing upon him heavily." He sighed and sat down on a wooden bench. "I thought it best for his sake that he put the accident behind him. I thought the searcher might have even fed him the thought that our Jacob had been murdered, for the vicious woman hounded poor Esther mercilessly."

"Poor Esther?" The searcher spat, the spittle nearly landing on Adam's shoe. "Poor bitch, is more like it!"

Lucy looked at Sam. "Except Jacob *was* murdered. He *was* pushed. He told me so himself before he passed."

"Who did it?" Theodora asked sharply.

"I am thinking now it was Esther Whitby," Lucy said, with a quick look toward Adam.

Theodora shook her head. "That cannot be so," she declared. "Esther was with us when we received word of Jacob's accident."

The magistrate cleared his throat. "We hope to determine that soon. There are more pressing concerns at the moment. In the meantime, Mr. Leighton," he said to Sam, who was now looking at them all with a dazed expression on his face. "Pray, I would beg you to be so good as to fetch the constable here, and tell him that we need a physician to attend an injured woman."

"Right, sir," Sam replied, unconsciously deferring to the magistrate's authority. He took off. They heard the front door bang behind him when he left.

The searcher, who had been released by Adam during the last exchange, slowly edged along the wall, as if about to flee. Seeing this, Lucy nudged Adam's leg.

He stood up and effectively barred the door. "Sit down, if you would," he said firmly to the searcher. Although his tone was polite, there was an iron quality to his request. "You too, if you would, Mrs. Leighton."

Instead of taking a chair, Theodora knelt down next to Lucy and took Deborah's hand. Ahivah had resumed crying, although her moaned lament was nothing like the loud tears that had been pouring forth when they first entered the house.

"First," the magistrate demanded, "tell me where my daughter is."

Theodora licked her lips. "Truth be told, I expected them to still be here when we returned from market. Sam and I went to buy some victuals for the long journey of our dear friends. I cannot tell thee what happened in the last hour that brought all this about. Thy daughter, it seems, has been called to the wilderness of the New World. Do not despair," she said. "Sarah is an instrument of the Lord. As such, he will guide and protect her during their travels." She glanced down at Deborah, a puzzled look on her face.

"Why did you not go with them?" Adam asked, taking a step closer to her.

Theodora visibly paled, although she kept her chin steady and her back straight. Clearly this was not the first time she had stood tall in the face of authority. "As Sam and I did not receive the calling ourselves, we elected to remain behind. Esther told us that we could keep this house for the Quakers, and in exchange we gave her all the funds we had raised." Her gaze shifted back to Ahivah and Deborah.

"Where did they go?" the magistrate asked, clearly straining to stay calm. "Please. We must know their plans. I fear my daughter is not safe with Esther Whitby and the others."

Hearing this, Theodora's eyes widened. "They went to Bristol," she replied. "There is a ship departing for the New World at the end of the week."

Lucy's heart sank. Bristol was a very great distance away. At least a two-day journey by horse, even longer if the roads were in poor condition.

"Are you certain of this?" the magistrate asked. "We have reason to believe that Esther Whitby is prone to mistruths and lies, perhaps even murder."

"Before we left, I overhead Esther telling Gervase to hire a hackney cab, and that they could switch horses at a coaching inn. She did not know I was there, so it must be the truth."

Considering this, Adam seemed to agree. He looked at his father. "Perhaps we can overtake them. They might not have gotten very far. We've had some snow and rain. I imagine, then, that they would take the high road. They might have only a few miles' head start on us," Adam said.

The magistrate glanced at Deborah, who was still lying against Ahivah, unmoving. "Who struck her?"

The mute woman shook her head violently, tears dripping down her face. She had begun to make that horrible guttural sound again.

"We must revive her before we set out after Sarah," the magistrate declared, a note of quiet despair in his voice. "She may know something important. Let us hope the physician arrives soon."

Lucy frowned, thinking about what she had read in Nicholas Culpeper's book of remedies. "I have an idea," she said.

Ignoring their mystified expressions, Lucy walked out of the room and entered Esther's chamber. With a grimace she pulled a nearly full ceramic pot from under the bed and peered inside. At least the dratted woman had left something useful behind.

She returned to the room, carrying the pot expertly so that the contents would not slosh about and soil her clothes. She could not bring herself to look at Adam. When she had served as a chambermaid, she had tried not to carry such offensive items in the presence of family members. Personal bodily functions were rarely remarked upon by anyone except servants, except, of course, in jests and merriments. "I beg your pardon, sir," she said to the magistrate, "I thought this might help."

Kneeling down by Deborah, Lucy opened the lid of the chamber pot. A noxious odor filled the room, and everyone except Ahivah turned away, pinching their noses and gagging. Deborah's eyes remained closed, although Lucy could see her eyes starting to roll back and forth beneath her closed lids.

"She's stirring," Lucy whispered.

They all watched the woman. Miraculously, Deborah's eyes

fluttered open. She clutched at her head. "Oh, I have been killed!" she exclaimed.

Closing the offending chamber pot, Lucy set it aside and tried to soothe the woman. "No, no! You are all right," she said. "Help is on the way. Please, can you tell us what happened?"

Deborah looked around the room then, taking in the intent gazes of everyone around. With one hand still on her head, she spoke in a very dramatic fashion. "Pray, do not think me dead," she murmured. "Pray, do not bury me. I do still live."

"Deborah, please. We know you are alive. We know, too, that you will be all right," Lucy said again, trying to keep the irritation from her voice. "Could you tell us what happened to you?"

"'Twas your warning that did it," Deborah said, staring resentfully at Lucy.

"What?" Lucy exclaimed as everyone's attention swiveled toward her. "I never sent a warning."

"The warning came from your printer's apprentice," Deborah said more curtly now, as she struggled to sit up. "Said the warning was from you."

Recalling her desperate conversation with Lach before she raced away from the printer's shop, Lucy slapped her head. What a time for Lach to develop a conscience. "Oh, he must have thought they were all in danger, when really it was Sarah in danger of them. Oh, no!"

The magistrate asked Deborah to proceed with her explanation, which she did, all the while rubbing her head. "The carriage arrived. Four horses they had hired! I could scarcely believe it. Joan, of course, said she would rather walk to Bristol, that the Lord had not given her two feet to sit in such a thing. So she just started walking on her own."

Theodora nodded. "That makes sense. We believe that the Lord will provide shelter and sustenance to all who act in his name. We need nothing other than the clothes on our back and the Inner Light to guide us."

Deborah laughed scornfully. "Esther does not hold by that notion, I am afraid. She said that the Lord did not want her to miss boarding the ship. She seemed glad when Joan set off on foot, and it was not long before I discovered why." She paused. "She had several large trunks, no doubt full of valuables."

Theodora frowned. "'Tis not the Quaker way."

A smile still tugged at Deborah's lips. She seemed to be about to say something. Instead, she just shrugged. "I heard her tell Gervase that there would not be room for us all, so it was better that Joan had set off on her own. It was then that Esther sent me back into the house, to retrieve a mirror from Jacob's table, she said. I could not find it. While I was still turned to the table, I heard a step behind me. Then I felt a terrible blow against the back of my head." She frowned. "That is the last thing I remember before you thrust that disgusting pot under my nose."

"You did not see your assailant?" Lucy asked, disappointed. "You cannot say for certain whether it was Esther, or maybe Gervase?"

"No, I cannot."

Lucy looked at her closely. The woman seemed to be telling the truth.

"What about Sarah?" the magistrate broke in. "Where was she when this happened? Do you know if she was injured as well?"

"As far as I know, she is in fine health," Deborah replied. "When I last saw her, she was in the carriage. She seemed intent on staying near Esther, for some reason. Although——" She broke off, her eyes taking on a distant look. She appeared to be remembering something.

"What is it?" Lucy asked.

"I remember now Gervase whispering something to Esther. I do not know what he said exactly. I did hear her reply, though. 'We may need her, at least for a while.' That is what she said."

"We may need her?" the magistrate repeated, his jaw tightening. "At least for a while?" He looked at his son. "I am afraid that they may have taken Sarah, thinking that her presence would lessen suspicion, thus ensuring themselves safe passage. The question is, does she even know she is in danger yet?"

He turned back to the searcher, who had been watching the proceedings silently from a corner of the room. "I would still like to know what you were doing in this house."

"Perhaps she is the one who struck Deborah!" Adam said.

"Bah!" the searcher said, her eyes narrowing. "Now why would I do such a thing? No, I heard that woman you call Esther Grace bid this simpleton here to go inside. The man, he was tending the horses, and the younger woman—your daughter, I suppose," she said to the magistrate, "was in the carriage. I saw Esther Grace follow this one inside"—motioning to Deborah—"and then come out alone a few minutes later. Heard her tell the others that Deborah had changed her mind, and would not be accompanying them on their journey. I was . . . curious. What has that murderous impostor done now, I wondered." She chuckled.

Theodora looked up sharply. "Murderous impostor?" she repeated.

"I am afraid that Esther Grace was not truly a Quaker," Lucy explained. "Nor Gervase, nor Deborah." She turned and stared at Deborah. "Impostors all. They have fooled you."

"Even if she fooled us," Theodora said, reaching out for Deborah's arm, "she did not fool the Lord." With Ahivah's help, they brought Deborah to her feet and led her to Jacob Whitby's bed. "Who are they?"

"Players." Lucy pulled *The Player's Last Play* from her pocket and waved the murder ballad in the air. "It's all here!"

They all looked at Deborah expectantly. Her mouth tightened, although she said nothing. Lucy could see the fear that had filled her eyes. To their surprise, Ahivah reached over and pinched her niece's arm.

"Ow! 'Tis true!" Deborah said. "Grace and I were players, not Quakers. Gervase, too. He had joined the company a short time before. She and I were not regulars, though, just when they needed us to prance and trot about." She tossed her head. "We had," she said with a smirk, "*lived* at a house nearby."

"A brothel?" Lucy asked, darting a quick glance at Adam. "On Leather Lane?"

Deborah looked surprised. Still, she nodded her head. "Yes. We were quite favored by the players. And those swells from the Inns of Court, too," she said, batting her eyes at Adam, who looked away.

Now Deborah seemed more eager to talk. "Grace was the one who wanted to perform on the stage. So when Basil Townsend and Gervase started *calling* on us," she said with a wink, "Grace got them so heated for her that she could get them to do any-thing she wanted them to do. Still has Gervase wrapped around her finger."

"So you began to perform on the stage?" the magistrate asked.

Deborah shrugged. "Sometimes we just did little songs or dances before the show or after. I did not really care for it, ex-cept it brought in easier money than the way I usually made it. More patrons, too. I was glad enough to just sell oranges. Grace, though, she loved performing. Said she was born to play the stage. I believe it, too."

"So do I, verily," the magistrate said grimly. "Tell us more about the actor Basil Townsend. What is the truth of his mur-der? Do not be coy now. This is the time for truth."

Deborah's mouth tightened, but she did not speak.

"You saw it happen, did you not?" Adam asked.

"Yes, I saw it happen," Deborah said in a resigned way. Sigh-ing, she continued. "Gervase was the one who killed Basil Townsend. I know that it was at Esther's bidding. Stabbed Basil through and through, he did. Right there on the stage, ten feet from where I was changing out of my costume."

"Why did he do it?" Adam demanded.

"Was he jealous?" Lucy chimed in.

Deborah shook her head. "I am sure Gervase *was* jealous. The way Esther tempted and taunted Basil—it could have driven any man mad with jealousy. And Esther knew it, too. It was not Gervase's choice to kill his fellow player, but Esther had a way of getting under a man's skin. That is why she was so angry at Basil when she could not get him to do as she asked."

"Which was—?" Adam asked.

"Near as I can figure out, Basil had refused to speak to the duke—you know it was his company—about giving Esther real parts to play. She wanted to play Desdemona, Juliet—all those leading roles. And he would not make it happen."

"So she had Gervase kill him," Adam concluded.

"Yes! I was so angry about this! Basil had always paid me well, treated me well enough," Deborah said, the remembered fury causing a flush to rise in her cheeks.

"Why, then, did you lie whilst on the stand?" Master Hargrave asked, his tone steady—and still a bit menacing.

"They paid me a tidy sum to put the blame on Abel Coxswain. I told Grace that I would play along, so long as it helped me."

"You changed your testimony in the midst of the trial. Put the blame on someone else, who—praise the Lord—was not hanged for your perjury," the magistrate continued to scold her.

"I was already punished for changing my testimony!" Deborah cried, struggling to sit up. "I have the stripes on my back to prove it!"

Hearing this, the magistrate softened his tone. "Yes, I remember. I agree, you have paid for your lie."

"What about thy other lie! The lie in which thou didst claim the Inner Light?

Theodora broke in. She had been listening to the exchange with astonishment and now seemed on the brink of tears. "Why ever for? Why wouldst thou seek to betray us in such a way? What did we ever do to thee?"

Deborah put her hand to the wound on her head, wincing as

her fingers touched the bump. "After Basil was murdered, there was no place for any of us in the company. Not long after, the plague hit and the king closed all the theaters. We all had to flee elsewhere. I did not set out to be a Quaker. However, I found it became quite convenient to hide out among the Quakers." Without looking at her aunt, Deborah muttered. "'Twas easy enough, to be certain. Ahivah had come to the plays several times, so that I would understand that the Lord had a plan for me."

"And Esther Grace?" the magistrate asked. "What happened to her?"

"Esther disappeared—to live with that tailor, I know now," Deborah said. "She knew that I had gone to live with my aunt. It was me she was visiting when she met Jacob Whitby. He was entranced by her, as men usually were. The next thing I knew, the Beetners had died and she was wedded to Jacob."

"And then she killed Jacob!" Lucy cried.

Deborah raised her eyebrow. "That I do not know."

From the window, they heard a carriage pull up along the street below. "We must go," the magistrate said to his son. "We must go after Sarah. She is in danger." He looked back at Deborah. "We will have the constable deal with *her*." He took the searcher by the arm. "I would like for you to accompany us. There are still some questions I need you to answer."

To their surprise, Sadie Burroughs did not resist and allowed the magistrate to lead her out of the room. Lucy and Theodora followed suit, with Ahivah remaining behind with her niece.

Once they were outside, Theodora touched the magistrate on his arm. "We shall let you know, should Esther or Gervase ever return to London. It may well be too late. However, if we see them again, we will detain them."

"And then—what?" Adam raised his eyebrow. "Turn them over to the authorities?"

"Certainly," the Quaker said in an equally cool voice. "Gervase and Esther are not Friends. They do not deserve our protection." She smiled slightly. "We do what we do for thy daughter. We care about her, and we do not want her to be hurt."

"I thank you." The magistrate touched his hand gently to his hat, and the Quaker nodded. Nothing else needed to be said.

As they approached, John hopped down from the carriage he had hired at the livery. To their surprise, another horse, this one saddled, was tied behind the carriage. "Saw Sam Leighton," John explained in his typical clipped fashion. "Told me what happened. Thought you might also need a faster horse if you are trying to overtake them."

Indeed, the carriage looked durable, and the horses looked well rested and hearty. Adam clapped his father's servant on the back. "Good man, John. Excellent thinking." He began to untether the saddled horse from the carriage.

Hearing a shout then, they saw the constable and Hank running down the lane toward them. Sam was not with him, no doubt fetching the physician to tend to Deborah.

In quick, terse words, Adam apprised the constable of what had transpired within Jacob Whitby's home. He turned to his father. "I will ride ahead, Father, on the road to Bristol. If you follow me in the carriage, we will have a means to bring Sarah home. I will then double back to the carriage when I find them.

With any luck, this will be well before they reach Chippen-
ham."

"I will accompany you," the constable said, stepping forward.
"You cannot go alone. They could be dangerous."

John spoke up then. "No other horses at the near livery. Stable-
man said they had all been hired."

"No time to go to another livery," Adam said. "Constable,
you must ride in the carriage with my father." He frowned at
the searcher. "I know that you know more than what you are
saying, but I have not the time to deal with you now."

"I can attend to her," Hank said.

"No, we will bring her with us," the constable said. "I would
like to hear what she has to say as well."

The searcher grinned, showing her gaping smile. "It would
do my heart good to see Esther Grace arrested. Better still when
she is hanged."

"That is well enough," Adam said. "Father, if you would board
the carriage. We must make haste."

As Adam helped his father into the carriage, Lucy knew she
could not let them go without her. She stepped forward, putting her hand on the side of the carriage. "Please, sir," she said
to the magistrate. "Please let me join you. Sarah might need me."

She held her breath, knowing that adding one more body to
the carriage would keep the horses from moving as fast as they
might otherwise travel. They could only hope that Esther Whitby
was traveling slower still, with all the belongings they seemed
to have stuffed inside the cart.

Although she could see that Adam looked to deny her, the

magistrate leaned down and extended his hand. "Come, my child. Make haste."

With that, it was decided that Lucy would accompany them on this madcap race against time.

·20·

Lucy sank back into the cushioned seat of the carriage, too anxious to enjoy the unfamiliar luxury. They were moving now at a brisk pace. The city dwellings had already begun to give way to fields and pastures as they moved west. She hoped that their horses would not tire before they reached a coaching inn. Adam had mounted his horse, sitting straight and tall in the saddle, and ridden off ahead of them in an effort to catch sight of Esther's cart before she and the others got too far.

The carriage was not overly large, and the four of them were seated fairly close together, the magistrate and Lucy on one side, facing the searcher and Constable Duncan on the other. Certainly they were an odd group. Master Hargrave seemed to be deep in thought, and the searcher was watchful. The constable, like Lucy, seemed unwilling to break a silence that had been set by the magistrate.

Though she could not keep her fingers from twiddling in her lap, the steady clip-clopping of the horses began to reassure her somewhat. The forward movement suggested progress.

Still, it was hard to keep desperate thoughts away. *What if we never see Sarah again?* There was no way of knowing what Esther and Gervase might have decided to do with their extra passenger. She thrust the thought away. Right now they could only hope for the best.

Idly, Lucy touched the gleaming polished wood of the carriage door. When she had dreamed of riding in a fine carriage, it was most certainly not for a reason such as this. She glanced at the constable, who, to her surprise, had been watching her.

Duncan grinned wryly. "Today, it is better to ride, I should think," he said, referring to their recent conversation about the ability to hire a hack when one pleased. Lucy smiled slightly but did not reply.

The magistrate rubbed his hands. "All right, then. Shall we get started?" He leaned forward so that he could look the searcher in her eyes. "I believe, Mrs. Burroughs, that you have something to tell us?"

The searcher grinned at them, revealing the great gaps in her yellow teeth. "I have much to tell. But I am a poor woman, with little to keep me nourished in this world. Day in, day out, I ring this bell, calling for the dead, making only a mean wage from the parish priests."

"You will tell us what you know," the constable demanded. "Don't try your beggarly ways upon us."

Lucy thought for sure that the magistrate would echo the constable's sentiment, but instead he pulled out a coin and held it before the woman. Her eyes widened, watching it glitter in the sunshine. She reached out her hand to take it, but Hargrave pulled it up and away from her reach.

"Your testimony had best be truthful, or I shall have you arrested for telling falsehoods to an instrument of the Crown."

The searcher took the gold coin and placed it in a pocket hanging below her dirty cloak. Before speaking, she first leaned over and spat outside the window.

"The woman you call Esther Grace is my late son's daughter," Mrs. Burroughs said. "My son was Edgar Little, the product of my first marriage."

"She's your granddaughter?" Lucy exclaimed.

Mrs. Burroughs sniffed. "Perhaps. Years ago, her mother, a lying whore, told my son that the babe was his. So Edgar raised that brat Esther as if she were his own child. Maybe she's blood-related, but only God knows the truth of it."

"Esther Whitby said her mother had been a seamstress. That she did piecework," Lucy recalled, looking at Mrs. Burroughs for confirmation. "And her father—your son?—had worked for a mill, delivering cut linens and wools to seamstresses like her mother."

The searcher snorted. "Only thing he delivered was dung and piss," she said with great contempt. Lucy could not tell, though, whether the contempt was directed toward her son, Esther Grace, or even Lucy herself.

"Explain yourself," the constable growled.

The smile dropped from the searcher's lips. "My son was a raker."

Lucy tried in vain to hide the little shiver of disgust that passed through her. Like the searcher, the raker dealt every day with the great filth of the city, living in it, carting all that was disgusting and malevolent away.

"Edgar, though, he loved that little brat. Called her his little flower. Posy, he called her," the searcher said. "A breath of fresh air she was for him."

Lucy nodded. Did Lucy herself not carry a posy of dried flowers with her when she peddled, to keep away the disgusting smells of the city? She thought again of the verse on the handkerchief that Deborah had carried, humming the line under her breath. *"She clasped a little posy, a posy full of grace . . ."*

"Yes," the searcher said, having heard her. "She dropped the 'Posy' later, though. Began calling herself Grace, even though she whored herself out." She leaned sideways, toward Lucy. The woman's hands clenched. "She killed my son, she did, and never one lick of remorse from her either." Pursing her lips, she turned away from the others.

"What? She killed her own father?" Lucy asked. "Why ever would she do such a thing?"

"Though beautiful on the outside, there is a black venom that runs through her veins," the searcher replied with a disdainful shrug.

"So you do not know why she did it?" the magistrate asked drily.

"I am saying that you will have to ask the bitch yourself," the searcher said. "I for one would very much like to know why she did it."

Something was still bothering Lucy. "Mrs. Burroughs, you told me before that Julia Whitby had sought you out, to ask you about Basil Townsend's murder," she said. "How did she know that you—of all people—would know anything about it?"

"Never said such a thing," the searcher said smugly.

"You did!" Lucy said hotly. "I know you told me so. You admitted that you were the one who had sent her the sketch of Mr. Townsend's murdered corpse. Please"—she looked at Duncan—"I know she is lying."

"I am not lying!" the searcher said. "That is not how it happened."

"All right," the magistrate said, putting up his hand. "Tell us, then. How did you come to meet Julia Whitby?"

"Miss Whitby had called on the Quackers. I saw her go in," the searcher said. "I like to keep an eye on Esther's comings and goings."

"They said you were always watching them," Lucy remembered. Under her skirts she could feel Duncan's knees pressing against her own. When she looked up, he gave her a warning look. *Let her keep speaking,* he seemed to be saying.

Lucy gulped, hoping that she had not ended the woman's speech. Fortunately, the searcher continued. "When Miss Whitby came out, I could see she was very troubled, the way she was wringing her hands. She did not even see me—I know because most people cross the street when they see me coming." Mrs. Burroughs chuckled again. "When she passed me, I could hear her saying the same thing over and over."

"What was she saying?" Lucy whispered.

"She was saying, 'I know them, I know them. How do I know them?' I knew then that this could be Esther's downfall. So when she sat down on a nearby log, I sat down beside her.

She was so stricken, and I, as you know, am the kindly grandmother sort." The smile she gave Lucy then was so friendly and beautiful, and quite unlike her usual mocking grimace, that Lucy sat back, stunned. In that odd moment, the searcher looked just like an older version of Esther, even if she did not have the same brilliant amethyst eyes. There could be no doubt at all that the women were indeed related, despite the seeker's suggestion otherwise.

Satisfied by Lucy's reaction, the searcher continued, regaining her usual surly demeanor. "I just let Miss Whitby share her concerns, promising, of course, the secrecy of a stranger. So she opened up, pouring it all out. Her worry about her brother, her despair that he had been cut off from the family, and now this terrible concern about his wife and her companions. At first she could not place them, but she just knew that she had known them with different names. Naturally, I helped her fill in the gaps."

"She had seen them perform!" Lucy realized. "She must have gone to the play, perhaps even with her brother. She recognized them from the stage!"

The searcher again gave her a slightly amused look of approval. "Indeed. That is when I saw my chance. I could finally get even with *Posy*. I could finally ruin her, a fair revenge for killing my son. So I told Julia Whitby that she was correct. That her brother had married an impostor. Moreover, that she had murdered several people." She pushed back a stray hair from her face. "She demanded proof, which I was glad enough to supply."

"That is when you gave her the sketch of Basil Townsend," Lucy said. *"This is the dandy I told you about. Set upon and killed."*

"How did Julia Whitby end up murdered?" the constable asked.

The searcher shrugged. "Miss Whitby did not understand the nature of Esther's grip on her brother. I told her that she must be careful when she told him, but she was foolish. 'Tis no wonder she ended up with the scold's mask upon her. Those who deal in secrets should always know better."

Unexpectedly, her eyes met Lucy's, and Lucy felt a dark chill run over her.

The carriage turned then, lurching uncomfortably. From this new angle Lucy could just make out the last pinnacles of the London churches that had survived the Great Fire.

"Looks like we are on the road to Bristol," the constable said, peering out the window. "Thankfully, the roads look fair enough."

Lucy nodded, trying to take comfort from his words, trying to keep her fears from looming. She knew they were maintaining a quick pace, but how long could they sustain it? How long before the horses got hopelessly fatigued? What if they could not overtake the carriage? The image of Deborah's head wound was hard to set aside. What if something terrible were to befall Sarah as well?

John rapped sharply then on the top of the carriage. The constable stuck his head all the way out the window so that he could speak with John.

"Mr. Hargrave has returned," Duncan said. "He is approaching."

Sure enough, Adam had pulled up his horse beside the carriage and looked in the window. "Their carriage is just up ahead. Not more than a mile. If we pick up the pace, we can catch them." He looked at his father. "I caught a glimpse of Sarah, praise the Lord. She looked unharmed. She is sitting next to Esther Whitby in the cart. They are moving at a middling pace. There are just three in the cart, but I can see they are loaded with provisions." He called up to John. "Let us press on!"

His father raised his hand. "They will likely stop at the coaching inn. I know it is just a few miles now," the magistrate said. "Would it not be better to overtake them then?"

"The horses are getting tired," Adam said, after giving the steeds pulling the carriage with a critical eye. "If we can push hard for a few more minutes, we can overtake them. It may be easier to confront them on the open road than in an inn where there are more places to hide."

"I do not think we have long to wait," Duncan said. "We had best be prepared. When we approach, Lucy, you must stay here. You as well, sir," he said to the magistrate. "Until we can better see the nature of the threat ahead."

The magistrate drew himself up, looking rather like the king himself. "Constable, just so that we are clear," he said, looking more grim than Lucy had ever seen him. "I am going to do whatever I need to do to protect my daughter. Pray, do not try to stop me."

·21·

The next ten minutes passed anxiously. Adam had ridden ahead a few paces, disappearing on the dusty road ahead of them. After his taut words, Master Hargrave had fallen silent, uncharacteristically drumming the door of the carriage with his knuckles. The searcher had begun to hum in a tuneless tone that quickly grated on Lucy's nerves. She glanced at Duncan, who was still peering out the window. For a moment, she wondered if he would have preferred that he be out on the horse, scouting out the Quakers, instead of seeing the magistrate's son do it instead.

Finally the constable gave a low whistle. "I see your son, sir," he said to the magistrate.

A moment later, Adam had pulled up alongside their carriage, riding easily at the same pace. "They are just ahead," he said. "I suggest that we now proceed together."

"Keep left flank," Duncan replied. "In case they should look back, we do not want them to see you. Though John might be looking to be driving overly fast, they are unlikely to be warned of our presence."

Tensely they all clung to the carriage handles as they jostled back and forth. Twice Duncan stepped on Lucy's feet, apologizing greatly after each time. Another time she was nearly flung against him, but the magistrate grabbed her arm, steadying her at the last second. The same nearly happened to the magistrate as well, but he managed to catch himself.

Although she knew it was not at all appropriate, Lucy felt her lips twitch as she thought about what would have happened if the stately magistrate had fallen into the searcher's lap. When she caught Duncan's eye, he seemed slightly amused as well, as though he knew what she had been thinking. Abruptly, they both looked away.

"It is time," Adam said. "Be ready!" With that, he spurred his horse on, racing forward until he pulled directly in front of Esther's cart, forcing it to stop.

"Adam!" Lucy heard Sarah shout. "Whatever has brought you here?"

Meanwhile, John edged the carriage forward. The magistrate, looking twenty years younger, leapt from the moving carriage, calling Sarah's name.

The constable jumped out as well, issuing a stern warning to both Lucy and the searcher. "Stay here," he said.

Gervase was still seated at the reins, while Sarah and Esther were looking out anxiously from the cart.

Now seeing her father, Sarah grew more bewildered. "Father? What is going on? What art thou doing here? I know that I should have told thee that I was leaving, and I promise I was going to mail thee a letter once I reached Bristol and—"

"Daughter!" the magistrate exclaimed, cutting her off. "Come here at once! I need you away from these people immediately!"

"Father! You know that I was chosen by the Lord to be his handmaiden. We are going to the New World to—"

"To what?" the magistrate interrupted. "To live among criminals?"

"They are not criminals!" Sarah cried. "The laws that bind them are unfair!"

"I'm not speaking of their conventicles!" her father replied, shaking his hands in fury. Lucy could tell he was trying to regain his calm. "Please," he said more mildly, "I need you to climb down from that cart immediately."

"Father, I cannot do that!" Sarah said, looking meaningfully at Lucy. "I believe it is my calling to travel with Esther. To see her safely to the New World. Pray, do not try to stop me. I am quite determined."

Esther stood up then, putting her arms around Sarah as if shielding her from an unexpected blow. "My child," she said. "I am so sorry that thy father is so misguided, so possessive. That he will not let thee follow the will of God—"

The gross unfairness of her words made Lucy quiver. "No!" she shouted, stumbling out of the carriage. "Sarah, do not believe her! She is performing for you! She has been as a player on the stage—and more than that! She is a murderer! You are not safe!"

"Lucy, what are these words?" Sarah was looking more and

more confused. "Thou sayst that Esther Whitby, whom I know to be a good Quaker and a steadfast handmaiden of the Lord, is a murderer? Thou art greatly mistaken!"

From her angle, Lucy saw an odd look cross Esther Whitby's face. Though she seemed outwardly indignant, there was a speculation there, too.

The magistrate tried to regain his calm demeanor, although Lucy could tell he was struggling. "Daughter, that woman— you know her as Esther Whitby, née Grace. But that is not the truth. She is an impostor."

"F-Father?" Sarah asked. "I do not understand—?"

Esther clutched at Sarah's hand. "Sarah, dearest handmaiden of the Lord! I do not understand what thy father is proclaiming. Thou dost know me! I was born Esther Grace, and I married thy friend, my dearest husband, Jacob Whitby. Although earthly courts may not recognize our marriage, being that it was done in the Quaker way, thou knowest that I was his wife. As such, I am Esther Grace Whitby, handmaiden of the Lord." Her face was impassioned, exultant, and for a moment they were all stopped by the fierce goodness that seemed to emanate from her very soul.

From behind Lucy, Adam began to clap. "A very fine performance indeed."

The magistrate looked up at Sarah. "Daughter, believe me. We have evidence that this woman, whom you know as Esther Grace Whitby, has killed several people, and not even two hours ago struck another woman down, leaving her for dead."

Hearing his daughter's shocked gasp, he continued. "Would

you like to tell my daughter what happened to Deborah?" he asked Esther.

Esther Whitby put her hands to her mouth. "Did something happen to my dear companion?" she asked, the tiniest quaver in her voice. "Before we left I begged Deborah to come with us. She told us that she had been bidden by the Lord to stay." Her eyes were wide, and she began to tremble. Once again Lucy found herself watching her, unable to look away. Indeed, the woman's performance was remarkable. "Tell me, did something happen to her?"

Sarah reached over and patted her arm. She looked at her father. "I do not understand, Father! Deborah decided not to come," she said, looking anxiously at the faces of her family. "Ahivah stayed behind with her niece. They changed their minds. Or, like Sam and Theodora, not everyone is called. Perhaps they came to that realization as we were leaving."

"No, that is not it. She didn't come because Mrs. Whitby had struck her over the head and left her for dead!" Lucy exclaimed, unable to contain herself. "Isn't that so?"

"What?" Sarah exclaimed, looking at Esther. "That cannot be true."

"Did she tell thee that?" Esther Whitby asked Lucy, while casually putting her hand on Sarah's forearm. The gesture seemed to be simultaneously protective and possessive.

"Well, no," Lucy admitted. "She did not see who had struck her, although Ahivah—"

"Did Ahivah see something?" Esther interrupted with a smile. "Did she *say* something? Oh—forgive me. She does not speak. Cannot speak, can she?"

Seeing the uncertainty that continued to riddle Sarah's face, Lucy spoke more earnestly. "Sarah! Please! This woman is a murderer! She has killed several people, including her husband. You must not go anywhere with her!"

Esther climbed into the front of the cart and took up the reins. "Now, that is a fine thing to say," she said, looking back at Sarah. "We who have taken care of thee. Surely thou cannot believe such a thing. I can assure thee—there is no evidence that I have committed the crimes of which I have been accused." She shook the reins, causing her horses to sniff at the others. "If thou canst believe such terrible things of us, then we must part ways now. I leave thee in good faith, and a blessing upon thee."

Adam's horse began to move out of the way as the cart pressed forward.

"I do not know what to believe," Sarah said miserably to Lucy and her father. "I cannot believe what you say of my own dear companion is true."

"You cannot outrun us," the constable called to Mrs. Whitby. "I can arrest you now."

The magistrate glanced at him but did not say anything. Lucy guessed what he was thinking. Since they were well outside the city boundaries, the constable had no authority to arrest anyone. She had learned that a year before when they were in pursuit of a murderer in Oxford. Since neither Gervase nor Esther looked alarmed, they might have been aware that his threat was empty.

"Mrs. Whitby," the magistrate called. "If you do indeed have nothing to hide from my daughter, I ask you to stay and answer a few harmless questions. Let my daughter be the judge. If you answer our questions in a manner that satisfies my daughter, I will allow you to pass. No authorities will pursue you, and I will leave you to proceed in peace, never to trespass upon you again."

Esther flicked her eyes toward Gervase, who responded with a nearly imperceptible nod. She reined in the horses. "If my dear sister Sarah believes my testimony—and indeed, why would she not, given that I speak with the truth of a handmaiden of the Lord—then thou wilt allow us to proceed, unmolested?"

The magistrate bowed his head. "I do declare that to be true."

Adam and the constable both shuffled their feet, clearly unhappy with the magistrate's words. Neither would speak against him, though.

Perhaps sensing this, Esther turned to them. "Do you also agree to this?" she asked them.

They both nodded, reluctantly, after the magistrate gave them a meaningful look.

"All right, then," the magistrate said. "Please join us down here, so that we may proceed."

Carefully Esther climbed down from the cart, and after a moment, Gervase followed her down, still holding the reins. Sarah climbed down as well, taking a step away from the other two.

Briskly, as if he were presiding over a real trial in a courtroom instead of in a muddy field along the road to Bristol, the magistrate began. "We are called here to present testimony to my daughter, Sarah Hargrave, so that she may better understand the monstrous nature of the individuals she once called her friends."

"Sarah," Esther interrupted, turning with imploring eyes

toward the magistrate's daughter, "I implore thee to remember our heartfelt talks and our solace in the Lord. To recall how steady in our friendship I have been, how I have been a true friend to thee, first in honor of my husband, and then out of the love I have felt for thee, bursting from my own bosom."

Sarah's eyes were now glistening as she listened to Esther's impassioned words. "Thou hast been a good companion," she whispered.

"I took thee in when thy own father cast thee out," Esther continued.

To Lucy's dismay, Sarah nodded. "That is so."

The magistrate coughed loudly, bringing his daughter's attention back to him. "First, the evidence of this woman's identity. We allege her to have been born Posy Little, although she came to call herself Grace Little, and later, Esther Grace. She changed her name yet a third time after marrying Jacob Whitby, so that she now alleges herself to be Esther Whitby."

Sarah looked confused. "Changing one's name is no crime," she said.

The magistrate looked up intently at Sarah. "Daughter, this woman appeared at my bench before the plague. I remember her well."

"That is a lie!" Esther said, her manner still calm. "I never gave testimony before this judge."

"That is because you left the courtroom before you provided your testimony. But I remember you, sitting by the bench."

Moving alongside the cart, Lucy produced *The Player's Last Play* and showed it to Sarah. "This is the trial of which your father speaks."

"A play?" Sarah said, glancing at the title. "I do not understand. We Quakers do not attend plays."

Lucy shook the penny piece at her. "It mentions a woman, Grace Little, who witnessed this murder. We believe this woman—this *actress*—is the woman standing next to you. She has been lying about who she is ever since."

"Thou cannot prove that person was me," Esther said, a bit smugly now. "Besides, being a witness is a far stretch from being a murderer."

Lucy wiped her hands against her skirts. This interrogation was not going well. She handed *The Player's Last Play* to Sarah to read for herself.

"Look, Sarah, read the name of this witness. Deborah Evans. You know her! Ahivah's niece."

"A common enough name, I should say," Esther said conversationally to Sarah, who nodded.

More desperately now, Lucy said, "See, read this part. Miss Evans had first claimed the murder had been committed by another man, before changing her testimony. I think that man she saw commit the murder was Gervase."

"It does not say Gervase, now does it?" Esther chuckled. She seemed to be enjoying herself now. "If thou lookst closely, thou wilt see the name is Gerald Markham, not Gervase. Regardless, it is clear that another man did the deed."

"Why are you so familiar with this penny piece?" Adam asked. "You know the circumstances of this murder very well."

Esther shrugged. "I enjoy a good murder as well as anyone else. *That* is not a crime," she said pointedly to Adam and his magistrate. "If it were, well, thou wouldst need to arrest *her* as well," she said with a meaningful look toward Lucy. "I say as I did before. Thou cannot prove that woman was me, nor any of the other accusations thou hast lodged my way."

"*I* know it was you." The searcher had come out of the carriage. "Posy. Little." she said, spitting after she said each name.

Esther's eyes widened, and she took a step back. For the first time, there seemed to be the tiniest crack in her composure.

"You!" she exclaimed, dropping her Quaker speech. Turning to the constable she said, "Constable, this woman has long been harassing me. Following me, making threats against me. Anyone can tell you that this so!"

"'Tis true, Lucy," Sarah said. "This woman has been pursuing Esther, in the most disturbing way. I have seen this myself."

"This woman is Esther Grace's grandmother," Lucy said. "Her name is Sadie Burroughs."

Esther Whitby scoffed. "My grandmother? I should say not! If she told you that, then I can assure you that she is lying! I had never even laid eyes on this miserable creature until she started stalking me a bit back. She is a madwoman!" she said, growing excited. "Look at that bell she carries! Searching for the dead has driven her mad! There can be no truth to her words!"

Adam stepped forward then. "Fortunately, we have evidence that Gervase—or do we mean 'Gerald Markham'—committed this murder. An eyewitness, as a matter of fact." He looked at his father. "Since he never stood trial for this murder, he can certainly stand trial now."

The magistrate nodded. "Indeed, that is so. Constable?" He beckoned to Duncan. "Please arrest this man. We will bring him back to stand trial. He should be swinging by the next sessions, to be sure."

Gervase began to shift his feet back and forth, looking uncomfortable. "Wait!" he said, trying to shrug off the constable's hand on his arm. Unasked, John had moved beside him as well, although he did not touch the man. "She made me do it!"

"Gervase!" Esther said, a taut warning in her voice. "*There was no witness.* They cannot prove what they are saying."

"No?" Adam said, taking a step closer to Gervase, who was starting to sweat. "I believe you were about to tell us something?"

Gervase crossed his arms, trying to look confident, but Lucy could see beads of sweat forming on his forehead. He kept his lips clamped tightly shut.

The constable tightened his grip on his arm. No one spoke. Lucy looked around. They seemed to be at an impasse.

Making a funny choking sound in the back of her throat, Mrs. Burroughs stepped forward. "I have seen him kill before," she snarled. They all turned toward her, stunned. "I was there when he killed Julia Whitby. I saw him do it." Though Lucy was fairly certain the searcher was lying, her accusation clearly rattled Gervase.

"No! That cannot be true!" Gervase shouted. "No one was there! We checked everywhere! That building was empty when I brought that bitch inside! Grace was the only one who was there!"

"Fool!" Esther Whitby cried, at last losing her composure. "Rutting fool! Keep silent!"

Now, under the threat of arrest, Gervase would not be silenced.

"She is the one who did it!" he shouted, pointing at Esther. "I did not kill Julia Whitby! She did it! She also made me kill Basil Townsend—a fellow player! And she made me push Jacob Whitby in front of that cart! She is a devil, she is!"

"Listen to the idiot speak! He has just admitted to murdering two people!" Esther Whitby screamed.

"I heard him admit to murdering two people, that is true," the magistrate said. "I also heard him say that *you* were the one who murdered Julia Whitby."

"Made her put on that scold's mask, and then ran a blade through her, she did," Gervase said.

"Posy, Posy, Posy, what a very naughty girl you've been," the searcher began to sing, a malicious smile on her face. "Oh, the things that I have seen!"

"Do not call me Posy!" Esther Grace cried, putting her fingers in her ears.

"Posy, Posy, Posy," the searcher continued to chant in a taunting way. "What would your father say? Well, he cannot speak now, can he? Seeing as how you put him in the ground yourself."

"Father got what he deserved!" Esther shouted, an ugliness overtaking her features, her earlier mocking calm completely shattered. "After my mother died, he passed me among his friends to pay off his debts. He made me into a whore!"

Lucy shivered. Briefly, she felt sorry for the woman standing before her.

The moment passed, though, as Esther Whitby continued, her voice cold. "He had taken everything away from me, and left me with *nothing. Nothing!* So I killed him."

Sarah was staring at her in horror, having not moved since the accusations began.

"That's right!" Esther cried, completely undone now with emotion. "I slit that damn bastard's throat when he was sleeping! Then I carted him off to Houndsditch in his own cart! I dumped him there, among the vermin and the rats and all manner of foul things." She spat at the searcher. "*That,* dear Granny, is why I stopped calling myself Posy and became Grace Little. And I turned to the only thing I knew how to do. Selling my body for a few coins." She angrily brushed away a tear and faced them all defiantly.

"So the truth finally comes forth," the searcher said, a deep chill to her voice. She seemed unmoved by the circumstances that brought about her son's murder. "I always knew you had killed my dear Edgar."

"*How* did you know?" Esther asked, sounding almost petulant. "I thought of everything!"

"I had come by to see him when I saw you put his body in the cart. From then, I began to watch you, follow you. I could not let you out of my sight." She sniffed. "Saw you take up with that cathouse, too. I know that's where you met *him.*" She pointed at Gervase. "Posy had you wrapped up in her finger from the day you met her."

"Don't call me Posy!" Esther Whitby shouted again.

"Oh, it is true. Anything you bid this man to do, he did. Isn't that so?"

"I knew she wanted to try her hand at being an actress, so I was the one who brought Basil Townsend to her. She is everything to me," Gervase admitted, looking at Esther with adoring eyes. To Lucy's disgust, the false Quaker smiled back at him, with the air of a princess bestowing a favor on a witless suitor. Clearly she was still trying to use his adoration to her advantage.

"She would see you swing!" Lucy burst out, unable to stomach the man's obvious devotion to the murderess.

Esther ignored her and turned to Sarah. Her earlier pretense long dropped, her countenance was now sneering. "That's where I met Jacob, you know," Esther said. "At the brothel. Although he came to me so full of spirits—and not that tiresome Spirit he spoke of later, either. He did not even remember me when we met again at the plays."

"That is how Julia Whitby recognized you," Lucy said, watching Sarah sink further against the carriage. "She had seen all three of you before."

"I suppose," Esther sniffed.

"After Basil Townsend was murdered, and you found your way to the Beetners," Lucy said, slowly sorting it out. "That is when you became Esther Grace."

"The Beetners were certainly helpful in that regard," she said snidely. "Mrs. Beetner had it in for me, so I knew it was a matter of time."

"So you slit all their throats and claimed that they had been killed in the plague," Adam said.

"And then you took up with Jacob Whitby," Lucy concluded, feeling a pang as Sarah's face blanched again.

Esther snapped her fingers. "He had been so besotted with me when he met me as Esther Grace. I knew I would have no trouble convincing him to marry me." She laughed, a surprisingly musical sound. "I knew he had become a Quaker. So I sought out Deborah, since I knew that her aunt—the famous mute Ahivah—had made her take up that dratted conviction, too."

Sarah, who had long been silent, wailed, "Why marry Jacob? Thou couldst not have loved him?"

Esther made a contemptuous sound. "As if I'd ever be tied to a Quaker. Oh, he'd been amusing enough before he gave up his 'lustful ways,' as he said. That marriage was not even legal. Just a bunch of nonsensical declarations. That's not to say we did not live as husband and wife." Here she looked spitefully at Sarah again.

Sarah flushed and looked away.

"Then he went and gave away his family's fortune. Gervase and I had expected to get something for our troubles. I was so angry when the Whitbys cast him off."

"So you were cuckolding him?" the magistrate asked sternly.

Esther shrugged. "He was the foolish one."

"Why?" Sarah wailed again. "Jacob loved thee so very much! He was trying to protect thee! He made me promise to protect thee, too!"

"Jacob was in the way," Esther said, standing up. "I did not need him. I did like being with the Quakers, though. Only Deborah and Gervase knew of my past, and the Quakers shielded and protected us in a way that no one else could have done."

"Pray, tell us, *why* did you kill Julia Whitby?" Lucy whispered. "She was no harm to you."

"She was a threat. I could see my *husband's* sister was going to ruin everything," Esther said matter-of-factly. "Tell Jacob about my . . . er, indiscretion at the theater with Basil Townsend. My dear granny told me she planned to tell Julia Whitby everything, but we were not sure if she truly did so." Here she glared at the searcher. "If she would have just kept her own mouth shut, we would not have had to kill my husband's only sister." She threw up her hands. "I tried to warn Julia. I assumed she would understand the warnings!"

"You sent her *A Lamentable Warning* and *The Vision for London*," Lucy said slowly. "And wrote the word 'Behold!' on the top."

"Obvious if you think about it," Esther said, sounding cross. "How could we have been more clear? We thought she would keep her mouth shut about what that wretched woman had told her. However, Jacob told me then about his sister's letter." She heaved a deep mournful sigh.

Lucy was simultaneously fascinated and repulsed. Did Esther Whitby truly believe that she was without blame? That it was the searcher who had brought Julia's end upon her?

Esther went on. "Jacob told me what his sister had written. That someone near him was an impostor. Thankfully, the stupid chit did not think to tell him who that impostor was! He said he would go to her right then and there, because he was more worried for me—for my life!—than he was for his own." She took a deep breath. "So I told Gervase what to do, and he did it."

"He did it," Sarah repeated, looking gray. She was starting to tremble, and she had sunk to the ground. "He pushed dear Jacob in front of that cart!"

Lucy went over and knelt beside Sarah. She looked up at Esther. "Then you had Gervase grab Julia Whitby before she could flee to her friend's house."

Esther snorted. "Yes, I sent her *The Quakers' Final Warning.* I ask you, how could it be more clear? I just knew that she would understand the message and flee the house. It was a gamble, that is true." She chuckled. "That simple girl. So easily led. So predictable! She was as a sheep to the slaughter. We had to find out the extent of her knowledge, you see, and what she planned to do with it." Then she turned to Gervase, sounding, of all things, indignant. "I told Gervase to scare her. Leave her in the scold's mask for a while, so she would learn her lesson about speaking of things that did not concern her. Thought it would shut her up for good."

"She kept trying to scream. She begged me not to put it on her face, not to kill her," Gervase muttered. "I was not going to kill her."

"When I arrived, Gervase called out my name," Esther said, sounding disgusted. "She knew exactly who I was and what I had done. I could not have that. So I ran her through with a knife."

"I see," the magistrate said. By his calm and quiet demeanor, they could have been talking about the weather. "Tell me," he said, "why did you let Sarah come along with you?"

Esther shrugged. "I did not expect her to. I thought she would go along with that nonsense that Joan was spewing, about the good Lord's admonition that we *walk* to Bristol. When Sarah decided to accompany us, I must say I was surprised."

"She did so out of loyalty and a sense of duty to you!" Lucy cried. "She believed it was her obligation to protect you."

"Yes, well, I see that now," Esther said almost gaily. She climbed back into the cart. "Rest assured, we had not decided what to do with her. We thought about getting some ransom from her—the magistrate seems rich enough, and besides, that would allow us to fulfill our promise to the Lord." The last was said with great sarcasm. "Or else we thought we could just pitch her overboard during the crossing, and start anew as husband and wife in the New World." She laughed and flicked the reins. The cart began to move forward. At the same time, Gervase stepped aside.

"We cannot let her get away!" Lucy cried. "She is a murderer!"

Without thinking, Lucy scrambled up on the cart, not heeding the dismayed shouts of the others, and began to try to forcibly wrest the reins from Esther's hands. Esther pushed back, and the cart lurched forward.

The momentum caused Lucy to fall sideways against Esther. In a sickening tangle of arms and legs, they both fell over the side of the cart. With Esther underneath, they hit the ground hard. Lucy gasped at the great burst of pain from her knee.

For an instant, both women lay stunned. The breath seemed to have been knocked out of Esther, for she was not moving.

From her strange view from the ground, she saw Gervase break past and catch hold of Adam's horse and swing himself upon the saddle. John began to chase him, Adam at his heels a second later. A strange whistle pierced her ears, although she did not know the source of the sound.

"Lucy!" she heard Duncan cry out, his voice strangled as he raced toward her. "Watch the cart! The wheels!"

Dimly, Lucy saw that the horses were anxiously pulling the cart forward. Just in time she managed to pull her legs out of the way, although Esther was not so lucky. Lucy heard the sickening crunch as the back wheels of the cart passed over the woman's legs, likely breaking at least one bone, perhaps more. Esther's eyes fluttered for a moment, and a small animal-like shriek burst from her lips before she passed out again.

Duncan had reached Lucy and dropped on the ground beside her. "Lucy, are you all right?" he asked. "You were not injured by the cart, were you?"

She swore under her breath, still tightly grasping her kneecap. "Hit my knee when we fell," she gasped, the pain still coming at her in waves.

To her surprise, Duncan pushed aside her woolen cloak, gently feeling her knee beneath her skirts. "Can you move it?" he asked.

Gingerly, she straightened her leg back and forth. Pain shot through her knee, but she knew it was not broken.

"I will be all right," she said, looking straight into his anxious eyes. "Thank you."

"That was a very foolish thing to do," Duncan said, his hand still on her knee. "Did you truly believe that Esther could have outrun us in that cart, loaded down as it was with all those provisions?"

Seeing him chuckle, Lucy smiled ruefully back at him. "I suppose you are right," she said. "I do not always think before I act."

"That may be so. But you are brave." He pulled her cloak gently into place and stood up.

The sound of a galloping horse made them both look around. "Gervase! He is getting away!" Lucy struggled to get up, but the pain in her knee caused her to sit back to the ground abruptly.

"No, look!" Duncan said, squinting. "The horse has returned without him!" He took a step away from Lucy. "Master Hargrave and his son appear to have taken care of that scoundrel."

Sure enough, Adam was holding Gervase while the magistrate tied the false Quaker's hands tightly in front of him. John had captured the horse and was now stroking her nose.

"I am all right," Lucy called to the others. "What happened?"

Adam approached them. "Gervase did not count on John being able to call back the horse. At that whistle, the horse bucked him off." He looked at Duncan. "Constable, he is all yours."

Duncan nodded stiffly and moved to help John tie Gervase inside the cart.

They looked doubtfully at Esther, who was lying still, her body twisted awkwardly on the ground. 'Twas no small mercy that the woman had passed out from the pain, for surely when she awoke, she would be in agony.

Nearby, Sarah was softly crying. Lucy wanted to go to her, but her knee was still throbbing painfully. The magistrate knelt beside his daughter.

"Father, I was a fool," Sarah said, tucking her hand in her father's, as if she were still a little girl. "Trusting them in such a way."

"Dearest child," Master Hargrave said. "The devil took possession of their hearts, filling them with murderous intentions. Esther Whitby created her own masque—a performance that was truly inspired by all that is base. Lust, greed, and all of the other evils." He pulled his daughter closer to him. "She was a brilliant performer. No one can blame you for believing the best of others. She manipulated you and made you another player in her masque."

Sarah looked back at the woman, still unmoving on the ground. "The Lord's will be done," she whispered, and Lucy could not help but agree.

The magistrate's voice grew a bit husky. "Sarah, pray, come home. I swear, I shall never ask you to go against your conscience."

"Father, I cannot ask thee to harbor a Quaker in thy own household," Sarah replied, her tears lessening. "Nay, do not be concerned. I shall stay with the Leightons, even as I follow the will of the Lord. I promise thee that I will always be thy own true daughter." They sat together, right in the middle of the dusty road, shoulder to shoulder.

"Let us tie Esther inside the cart," the constable said grimly. "This will be a bad ride home, to be sure."

Before they moved her, John brought over several strong sticks that were intended to brace Esther's legs.

While the others put the unconscious woman on a make-shift sling, Adam knelt down beside Lucy. "I must say I did not expect to be doing the constable's duty, Lucy," he said quietly. His tone was lighthearted, but he seemed to be watching her intently.

"Do not let Lach know, or else he will write a merriment about you. He likes to tease the constable, you know," Lucy said, smiling. When he did not smile in return, she tried to dispel his worry. "My knee will be fine, Adam," she said. "Do not distress yourself."

"I am glad of that," he said. "Let me help you to the carriage."

He pulled her up and put his arm around her waist. "Let us proceed slowly. Yes, that is it," he said as they began to walk toward the waiting carriage. Wincing, she was able to take one careful step after another. Out of the corner of her eye, she noticed Duncan watching them before turning away.

After a few steps, Adam spoke. "Lucy," he said, "I think I understand something now that I did not understand before."

"What is it?" she panted. "What do you understand now?"

"I understand why you do not wear my bracelet."

"What? Oh, Adam, it's a beautiful bracelet and—"

"I have something different for you." He opened the carriage door and helped her inside. He settled himself across from her. Reaching into his coat pocket, he pulled out what looked like a silver stick. "I have been carrying this around for a while. It is a pen—different from those quills you usually use. See how there is ink inside there?" He opened it up.

"Oh, Adam, how lovely!" she exclaimed. "But—"

"No buts," he interrupted her with a short laugh. "Father told me how his friend Sam Pepys had such a tool. I thought, *I know a young woman who might like such a thing, too.* You can keep it hidden," he said, for the first time sounding a bit anxious, "so you do not need to fear it being stolen or broken. I know that was what concerned you about the bracelet. I hope you will still wear it from time to time. I hope, too, great things come from that pen."

"Thank you, Adam," she said, laying her hand over his. "Truly, I will treasure it."

He took her hand. "Lucy, there is so much about you that I admire, from these ink-stained fingers"—he smiled down at her—"to your great capacity for love," he said. "I think, though, you have known something all along that I have not understood. Something that perhaps I have not allowed myself to see."

"What is it? What do I understand that you do not?"

"I do not mean to speak in riddles. But I would not want to take you away from what you love."

"I do not think you are trying to keep me from working for Master Aubrey," Lucy replied. "Indeed, this pen could offer no greater proof."

When he remained silent, she rushed on, trying to dispel his odd mood. "I just never wanted you to resent me," she whispered. "People will always remember that I was a chambermaid in your father's household, even if I am a printer's apprentice now."

"I would never resent you." Adam swallowed. "But that is not what I am referring to now."

"What, then?"

Now Adam's smile no longer reached his eyes. "When you knocked into Esther and you both fell over the side of the cart, I saw Duncan's face. Like he was fearful of losing the most precious thing in his life."

Lucy could feel her heart starting to pound, and she began to tremble. She knew there was a truth to what he was saying, but she had no words.

Adam continued. "Then he ran to you. He saw the distress you were in even before I did. It was as if he simply had to be by your side." He swallowed again. "It was not just the constable's face I saw, Lucy. You looked at him, too, in a way that showed me you were not displeased by his attention."

"Adam, I——" she began, but then stopped. "I do not know what to say."

"You do not need to say anything right now." He pressed her hand. "Lucy, I am not angry at you. How could I be? I have told you before that I am willing to wait, because you are worth waiting for. But if your heart beats for someone else—well, I would want to know that, too."

Taking her hand, he turned it over and kissed it. Then he stepped out of the carriage and paused by the window. "I just ask, Lucy, that you think about this new world that has arisen since the Fire, and know that how it once was may not be how it will be tomorrow. Promise me that, at least."

"I promise, Adam," she said. "I will."

"Then farewell, for now."

As he began to walk toward his horse, which was grazing on the side of the road, she was suddenly afraid that he was walking out of her life. "Always have to have the last word, do you not?" Lucy called after him, her voice a bit shaky.

He looked back at her and grinned in his old way. "This time, yes."

From the window, she saw Duncan approaching the carriage, a thick blanket under one arm. "Mr. Hargrave," he said to Adam, "thank you for your assistance in apprehending these murderers."

"No, Constable," Adam said. "It is I who should thank you. You traveled all this way to save my sister, a fact I will never forget"—he paused, glancing back at the carriage—"no matter what the future may hold." He held out his hand. "Thank you, Constable."

The two men looked at each other, something unspoken passing between them. Then Duncan grasped Adam's proffered hand, and the two men shook hands vigorously before going their separate directions.

Walking toward her, Duncan called, "I thought you might want to prop your leg on this blanket. I took it from the other cart." He passed the wool blanket through the window, a shock passing between them when their fingers touched.

"Thank you," she murmured, the memory of Adam's words bringing a flush to her cheeks.

He looked at her curiously. "You will be all right?" he asked. "I will drive the other cart back, to keep watch over our felons until we can get them safely locked away." He took a step and then touched the window near where her hand was still holding the frame. "Perhaps I will see you soon? Perhaps at a time when there is no murderer lurking about?" There was a question in his eyes.

"And when would that be?" Lucy asked lightly. "Sometimes I think there are murderers everywhere." She drew back slightly, knowing she was not addressing the question he was asking. Truly, she needed to ponder what Adam had said to her, and her thoughts were so disquieted from all that had happened, she scarcely knew what to think.

She expected him to leave then, but instead he traced his fingers along the carriage door. "You know what I was wondering?" he asked. "Why did Esther Grace not simply kill Mrs. Burroughs?

Would that not have been easier than hoping that her secrets would not come out? After all, Esther killed Julia Whitby for the knowledge the poor girl held. I do not think, given her record, she was too concerned about killing family members!"

Lucy had been thinking about this, too. "I think Esther knew that no one would take the searcher seriously. But more than that, I think she needed an audience," she said slowly. "Like the magistrate said, Esther had created a masque around her. Gervase and Deborah would not do, for they were players, too. They were focused on their own roles. She needed someone who would appreciate how her character had changed between acts. Someone who would appreciate the intricate nature of the masque that she had authored."

Duncan nodded. "You have a good sense for this," he said.

She did not catch his next words, for an image of a printed ballad floated in her mind. Not *The Scold's Last Scold,* as Master Aubrey had requested, but something altogether different.

"The Masque of a Murderer," she said, nodding her head. "Yes. That is what we will call it." She pulled out her new pen and smiled brightly at the constable. "Now, Duncan. How about finding me a piece of paper so I can get this tale told?"

HISTORICAL NOTE

Readers sometimes ask me why I selected 1660s London to form the backdrop of my novels. Naturally I reply, "Plague and Fire! What's not to love?"

But the reality is, I came to appreciate this time period when I was a graduate student in history, primarily because I was entranced with the notion of a society in intense flux and unprecedented social mobility. Following the plague of 1664–1665 and the Great Fire of London in 1666, social and communal ties were greatly disrupted after thousands died or fled London altogether. People were no longer around to affirm or deny the identity of their neighbors. Even more tangibly, many records—wills, marriage and death certificates, baptismal records, property deeds, titles, and the like—were destroyed in the Fire. So essentially, many people could—for a short time—forge their own identities. And even if they did not commit identity theft outright, many honest people like my Lucy also could—for a brief period—take advantage of the diminished labor force and explore new opportunities for employment.

This is why I thought it reasonable that Lucy could become a printer's apprentice. While it may not have been common, examples abound of women becoming apprentices in a range of trades and professions, and even owning their own businesses. Indeed, there were a number of women working in the book-selling and printing trades (which for ease of understanding, I collapsed into a single trade in my novel).

Also, while some of the tracts described here, like those by Smith and Calvert, were real, most were made up by me.

While I did take some license with Constable Duncan's duties, as well as Adam Hargrave's legal responsibilities in the Fire Court, some of the stranger details in my novel were faithful to the historic record. For example, the medieval scold's bridle was still being used to shame and punish women, although by the seventeenth century, the bridle was more an object of jest. Quaker women like Ahivah did speak out against the king and Parliament, in written tracts as well as in fervent public laments. While the real Ahivah did not have her tongue cut out, there were laws in New England that listed "tongue-boring" as the punishment for a third-time offender.

Last, the winter of 1666–1667 was quite harsh, with the Thames freezing over more than once. Even in March, the diarist Samuel Pepys had noted that "the weather, too, being become most bitter cold, the King saying to-day that 'it was the coldest day he ever knew in England.'" Amazingly, despite the chill, the Fire did still smolder for months afterward, a surprising fact at which Pepys and other Londoners marveled.